# The Big Light

Michael Wisbach

Grosvenor House
Publishing Limited

This book is published by
Grosvenor House Publishing Ltd
Link House
140 The Broadway, Tolworth, Surrey, KT6 7HT.
www.grosvenorhousepublishing.co.uk

This book is a work of fiction. Any resemblance to
people or events, past or present, is purely coincidental.

A CIP record for this book
is available from the British Library

ISBN 978-1-83615-300-9

For Bob, Rosie, my wife. And to you,
dear reader, for making this journey worthwhile.

# Pyjamas in the daytime.

Through cupped hands and a squint, Ben is staring through the dirty glass of the Pink Moon pawn shop.

His vision is fixed upon the shelf above the counter where a stern brown case with tartan inner lining sits. Inside it, his concrete grey Lettera 22 typewriter.

He bangs again on the door. Nothing. Only the shake of precarious glass in the thin wooden frames and rumbles at his feet, disturbing the floor lamp and the crude old portrait of some snooty, pompous fat cat from a different time.

"God damn, this is jive man."

No one cares. Everyone just keeps walking.

Ben flicks his collar and lifts his pace as he is already running late for his appointment.

\*

The face of the suit now shines with a dirty smile. As does his name badge that is glimmering in artificial light. The name 'Chris Walker' stamped on it. Ben feels he looks more like Ken or a Stuart though.

"You're not going to like this. Says here you must attend a welfare and employment course." Chris says with a duping lip.

"Another one?" Ben says with surprise.

Phones are chiming, and there is a constant tap of keyboards, which is frustrating for Ben.

"I've just been on one."

"Yes, that's true, but you didn't complete the whole nine days you see." Chris says with a grin.

"When does it begin?" Ben asks.

"Next week. Unless…?"

Chris is looking around the vast and noisy room before leaning into the desk.

"You into cars?"

"Nope."

"Well, I only ask, as there's a great opportunity for you. Great little earner with scope to rise in the ranks, as they say. Plus, it will get you out of the nine-day course." Chris says.

Ben does not have any interest in cars and his distaste for the ask was clear to Chris.

"Think it over, Ben. I do strongly suggest taking the opportunity offered here. It's in your best interest." Chris says sternly.

He slides some paperwork across the table and Ben signs for his welfare cheque.

*

There is a rumble of distaste as the university library trolley screeches over the harsh red carpet. The students all look the same, both in costume and in eager posture. A parent's pleasing piece of paper awaiting their palm.

But only if that darn trolley stops churning. The last screech echoes as the young, newly graduated gentleman presses on the rubber brakes and heads behind the counter.

An attractive freckled lady is tapping her nails. Watching the paper shudder from the printer before the trolley pusher scrapes it along the perforated line with the glow of satisfaction for the clean tear.

The freckled lady playfully snatches it from his claw.

"Good to see you're putting your new qualification to good use, Sam."

A sarcastic tone suits this guy.

"I take it this is for your own amusement. And is legal?" he asks.

She ignores the question, too busy looking over her printout. Scanning it to the bottom. She shakes herself away from it.

"You got any files or archives on crime patterns or stats from the last…"

She taps a finger on her chin.

"Three years, actually, no, the last decade?"

The young man is staring in confusion. The freckled lady was one hell of a looker, but her thought process and general outlook scared him.

He points toward the Microfilm and filing system. His creased forehead turning smooth again.

"What you up to?" he asks.

Again, she ignores the question. Having one herself.

"You seen Keith lately? Been by his office, but he wasn't there."

"I've seen him around. He's doing freelance work now. You must have burned him out with your excessive need for learning."

Sam is looking at the printout. As she is walking to the Microfilm, the young man again is keen to know what the over educated freckled lady is doing.

"Well? You going to make me guess?" he asks.

"Haven't you got some wheels to oil?"

Sam giggles into her hand.

*

On the library table, piles of printouts and newspaper clippings. A 15-year-old headline interests Sam. Dated 1973.

It reads:

'TEEN KILLS BROTHER IN CRASH.'

Running her finger down a list, she bangs the table with a delightful smile, as she has found something of even more interest. A document for various businesses. She scribbles a few notes down on a pad before tidying her mess and leaving.

*

Bee Arden, a well-educated 23-year-old, is sitting in the small office of the psychiatry unit at the city hospital of Dalton West. Anxious and uncertain about the visit, but with it, a sense of control over the matter.

The clock ticks loudly as she itches under her bandage wrapped around her left wrist. Only stopping when the door creaks open. The assigned croaker steps into the room. She is wearing an expensive looking black dress and a well-rehearsed professional smile that is cracking from her over made-up face. Bee needs to avert her vision from the lipstick, so she looks towards the sink.

"Beatrice. My apologies for being late."

She is now expecting her visitor to accept or acknowledge the apology.

"Er, sorry. It's Bee. Not Beatrice. If you don't mind."

"I see. Well, Bee. My name's Dr Moran. I will be your health professional for the time being. You've been told already what these three sessions entail?"

"Yeah, it was in the letter sent out to me." Bee says.

Again, she has a slight twist in her lips as the doctor's lipstick once again is averting any rational thought. It is bright red and shiny, and Bee is wondering why the doc dresses like that. Was she attending a fashion or awards show? It was a possibility. Got ready so she can leave straight from work.

Bee looks down at her choice of attire. Jeans she has worn daily for the past week, and a faded denim jacket recently bought from a flea market. She felt comfortable.

Dr Moran looks at the clipboard.

"Different address?"

Bee takes her sight once again from the questionable lip colour. This time staring toward a BMI chart pinned on the wall.

"I've moved. House share, west of the city."

"Very nice. So?"

The doctor has the clipboard on her lap. Locking her fingers together. A look of 'shall we begin?'

Bee has pursed lips. Raised eyebrows. The ticking clock makes the awkward silence a little more bearable. She knows the croaker wants her to talk first but is uncertain how. And more importantly, why?

There's movement outside the room. Bee shuffles in her chair and itches under her bandage. Witnessed by Dr. Moran.

"Why don't we start with how you came to be here? How's the arm?"

"Well, it's still attached."

Bee expels a genuine laugh that has not gone unnoticed by the experienced professional, who is now responding with her own genuine smile. Yet eager to explore a little further.

The uncertainty Bee was feeling prior to the appointment was now pushing forward in her head. She taps her chin. The action picked up by Dr Moran.

"What are we thinking?"

A sneaky open question from the well-dressed enigma.

With curled lips and a heavy sunken brow, Bee catches herself again, staring at the shiny lips. A quick tap on the door rings out, then followed by a thin tall man entering with his white coat tails wafting around his legs. He whispers in Moran's ear. This does not faze Bee. In fact, she welcomes interruption.

"Will you excuse me for a moment?"

Dr. Moran puts the clipboard on the desk as she moves towards the door.

The two leave Bee to sit and stare at charts or at her boots. She taps her worn knees a few times and exhales a long-drawn-out breath.

5

"Screw this." With no second thought, Bee heads for the exit.

*

Neon drenched streets drown the arriving night-time as Ben is watching feet pass the telephone booth. The new receptionist, Barbara Maddox, of the Hazy Jane publication office, picks up the call.

"Hi. Bob Rosiemon please."

"I'm afraid he's left for the day, my dear."

"Oh, I see. Well, when's he back?"

"Try tomorrow morning. He should be in the office first thing. Or leave a message if you like?"

Ben is now rummaging with urgency, looking for change, but there is no rattle from the struggling writer's pocket as the beeps arrive. A warning of disconnection. The call then cuts out. He lights a cigarette.

Leaving the booth, he stumbles slightly and bumps shoulders with a middle-aged man with a dipped head. Ben apologizes, as people do. The bowed head looks at him and does the same. Ben is unaware that the bowed head now heading into the Hopper's jazz bar is none other than Bob Rosiemon.

*

Mac the plaque, named purely on account of his poor oral hygiene, gestures Ben into the house. He is quick to notice the industrial sized toilet roll under his arm. Intrigue has him but is yet to ask. They head into the kitchen where the water on the stove is ready to pour. Mac is fishing around the drawers looking for assorted items. A small-scale set, more specifically. Some cling film as well. On the table is a copy of the independent magazine 'Subhuman.' A short piece written by Ben on how parents constantly lie to their children is on page 12. He hopes to not have to converse about any of it, though, and starts making two coffees.

Mac slams ¼ of cheap resin on the table. Money exchanged, stuffed into a denim pocket. Ben places the block of hash into his tobacco pouch.

"So, what's with the T. P Ben Bam?"

"Let's just say if I were a believer in heaven and hell, I'll be needing sunscreen."

Mac lights a joint.

"I'm afraid you're gonna have to explain it to me like I'm a five-year-old." he says.

Ben finds what he is looking for, however, not the expected silver spoon but a package of fifty disposable ones stuffed in the drawer. There is no milk, though.

*

The smell of the tinned vegetable curry will linger for days and add to the trapped cycle between the thick walls and a high ceiling. Smoke swirls in apparent malice. The tapping on the door is faint, over the Simon & Garfunkel 'Bookends' record. Ben turns the volume down. Wafting away weed smoke and tinned processed necessities.

"Who is it?" he asks in a stern tone.

Through the heavy dirty gloss door mumbles a reply. Ben barely hears the noise as Tony from the bedsit upstairs continues to state his business.

Ben opens the door. A wide stare from the skinny man. His jumper tucked into his jeans. Hair receding. The kid is only in his mid-twenties, but appearance and posture age him. He has come down to spin some jive about needing to collect the coins from the electric meter. At the request of the landlord.

"What's that smell?"

Tony is sniffing the air like a dog sensing a faraway meal.

"Tinned curry. Listen, this is the first I've heard anything about collecting money."

Tony is still chancing it.

"Yeah, asks me first thing this morning."

"Yeah, well, you'll have a hard time collecting from here. There's nothing in it."

"Sure. No problem. Hard times for us all, my friend. Hey, you're welcome to our room sometime. Have you met Lisa?"

"In passing. Listen Tony, not to be rude, but I'm kinda busy now."

"Say no more."

Tony holds his hands up as a way of accepting the dismissal as Ben closes the door.

Tinned curry splashed on the wall. He serves it up and has a slice of bread to dip.

The note pad waiting on a page already inked. It reads:

*'A whippet in a trench coat smokes a long thin cigarette as he stands on the corner. He has been patient for some time and although his hind legs are strong, they are tired. Nevertheless, he will keep waiting for the cat to arrive or wait until told otherwise.'*

\*

A modest kitchen with a stern table with a half-eaten bowl of home-made stew on it. Bob Rosiemon is sitting with a cigarette and half open mail.

"I smell moo moo stew." The voice floats from the hallway.

As she enters the kitchen, Sam fluffs her hair with her fingers to rinse the drops of the rain off. She kisses Bob on the cheek and heads for the fridge for two beers.

There's mail for her. Bob takes it from the pile and places it in front of her.

"I'll heat some moo moo for you." Bob says.

She hears him, but the mail has her attention.

Bob sips the beer, and Sam drops the letter on the table.

"An employment and welfare course." he says.

"I only applied for welfare a few weeks ago. Thought they would give me a little time to look for work." Sam says.

The stew is bubbling gently in the pan and Sam scoops a healthy portion into a bowl.

Bob remembers about the hairball gel for cats he bought. He finds it in his jacket pocket, hanging on the chair as Sam is looking through the cupboards.

"Any bread?" she asks.

"Where it always is."

The bread bag is under a tea towel, however, and not in the bread bin.

Bob holds up the hairball gel. Sam takes it.

"For Simone. Figured that might help." Bob says.

"Thanks pa."

"That little fluff ball still trying to find her way back here?" Bob asks.

Sam places the hairball tube down.

"Yeah. Found her at the back of a pawn shop a few days ago." Sam says.

She takes a big spoonful of stew from her bowl.

"She's a plodder." Bob says.

The two are now sharing a comfortable and familiar silence only broken with clinks of spoons and sips of beer.

*

The two cops are sitting in their patrol car watching the young man, only 17 years old, walk towards the park entrance. A call had come in from the pharmacy manager expressing concern for someone sleeping rough in the doorway. Known in the law game as a 'Valentine' due to still being relevantly clean and not suspected of any narcotic use. A fresh runaway. The rookie is about to call it in. Inform them of their actions and put a notification into the services.

Instead, his senior takes the radio from him and puts it back in its cradle.

The rookie will make a mental note instead. Time of call out and a description of the rough sleeper. He may even check the files for any fresh missing kids. But as of now, he is learning to keep holes shut. Get branded a 'jobs' worth' early in his career for doing the job of a cop.

Right now, he is trying to stop reality clashing with personal conflict. Right now, he's trying real hard to not lose his job by breaking the nose of his senior officer, who is now scoping the betting pages.

\*

The feline's bell chimes as her paw beans patter in a state of partial confusion and opportunity as Swan, the owner of Queen Z's bed and mattress store and his associate Henry Bullman, are awkwardly gripping the new mattress halfway up the flight of stairs. Once on the landing, they slide it across the floor and lean it on the side of the bed in Sam's room. Swan is scribbling on the invoice and drops it on the desk with a business card attached while Henry and Sam pull the plastic covering off the mattress.

"Thanks so much for the quick delivery gentlemen." Sam says.

Back towards the lounge where Simone the cat is cautious of the thuds heading her way. As she finds space on the sofa, she coughs. The two men look at her, then at each other.

"Hairball I think." Sam says in a passive tone.

"Well, thanks for going with Queen Z's."

Swan flicks his index and middle finger from his head and watches Simone as the two men head for the door before Swan turns sharply back towards Sam.

"Almost forgot."

He reaches into his inside pocket and hands her a pink, fluffy sleep mask.

"A complimentary gift."

"Thanks." Sam says.

She walks them to the door and closes herself back into a quiet, still, and unfamiliar room. She has done her research on the two other tenants. She couldn't help herself. Her studies and level of education twinned with the interest in crime from an early age was second nature. Nothing concerned her about the findings, but she was questioning a few things.

*

The TV is on but mute as the stereo is humming out Bob Dylan's John Wesley Harding record.

The room becoming dusty with smoke as two joints are burning. Mac is flicking through the subhuman magazine. The one with Ben's writing in. Two multi-pack spark plug boxes sit near the ashtray on the polluted coffee table.

"What did you think of my article?" Ben asks.

"Does that stuff pay well?"

"Nope. Pennies. But I'm hoping for some good news on my near complete novel. Chasing ghosts with getting it out there though. Tristessa up in the pawn shop too."

"Who's Tristessa?" Mac asks.

"My typewriter. The goddamn pawn shops' been closed for some time now. I'm losing the will. What's with the boxes anyway?"

He is now pointing to the two boxes of spark plugs.

"I need ya to hold for me. Just for a short while. Ten days tops." Mac says.

"Nope."

Ben is holding his hands up and shaking his head.

"No way." Ben says.

"Hear me out. The two boxes have a jury in. Hold it for me for just a short while and you keep two ounces. Sound good?"

Ben has gone from a stern definite no to a more accepted manner with the ask. He hits the joint with a face in thought.

He will do the ask but wants to keep Mac guessing for a while, so he stares at the TV. Just to be awkward. The silent anchor woman's red lips look like she is chewing. Flashing up on the screen is a picture of the young valentine boy from the Pharmacy doorway. Found dead in the park by a dog walker.

"So, we good?" Mac asks.

"Yeah, we good. But there's no way I'm carrying twelve ounces home. You'll need to drop it off."

The weather on the news says there is a low chance of rain as drops smeared the window. The vinyl popping and fizzing out static.

*

Rummaging through the kitchen drawers, Sam is not finding the documents she needs for the employment course. Only instruction manuals for various appliances and old receipts. On the table sits mail. A red letter from a collection agency which she folds and puts in her pocket. And an invitation to the Annual writer's & publicist award ceremony. She taps the pile before heading upstairs.

Her bedroom has not changed for some time. She has always been into The Smiths and has walls dominated by posters that she has framed. The single mattress was no match for her new king-size one. She finds the documents tucked under some old magazines in the wardrobe's bottom before laying on her belly to scoop under the bed to retrieve a small bundle of cash, clumped together with an elastic band. She stands up and looks over the room. Placing the cash in another pocket before straightening her Gary the gorilla stuffed toy near her pillows.

On the wall in the hallway, framed certificates proudly announce themselves and welcome all visitors. Even if they were not to cross the threshold, a first in Criminal psychology with a level 5 in Profiling & Human behaviour shines out the door.

Sam taps each one with an index finger before flicking the light off and leaning into the breeze and rain.

*

The old croaker's slender, almost transparent hand scribbles on a pad. He rolls the pen free from his fingers and leans back in his chair. His bushy eyebrows appearing to shadow his vision. The office is untidy, with files in piles and research books stacked on shelves.

Swan is fishing for cigarettes in his pocket with pursed lips. Watching the rain and wondering if the doc can see OK with all that fluff above his eyes. He lights his smoke to only quickly take it from his lips. The doc understands his expression and holds his hands up to let his client know he has no issue with him smoking, then pointing to the ashtray sat on the edge of the desk. A fire hazard with the filing system of papers of confidential print and invoices. The croaker knows why the man opposite him is there. A nod of appreciation to the strength it takes for this seemly hard-headed heavy-set man to not only know he needs therapy but to attend such an arrangement has him admire the works of the human condition. Plus, the man, simply known as Swan, is paying him well for the private, confidential appointments. Though after two sessions, the doc is yet to successfully prompt his client to talk.

"Tell me a time you last felt at ease." The doc asks.

"Every day is like Sunday." Swan replies.

"You mean bike rides through meadows and family time?"

"Not as such."

Swan smiles as he leans forward to allow room to lift his wallet from his back pocket, taking out four crisp notes and chucking them onto the top of a drug reference book.

"I'm guessing you haven't adhered to the suggestion I made. About writing a few things down? Like we spoke of.

You can keep it safe somewhere, remember. Or rip it up." The doctor says.

He is waiting for an answer, but his patient is quiet.

"I'm afraid I won't be available for the next couple of weeks. Green slip season, you see."

"What's that?" Swan asks.

Crushing his cigarette into the tray.

"All those involved in medicine and psychiatry must surrender paperwork to prove ethnical and certified to practice, for medical law, as well as filing our finances correctly and not self-medicating."

Swan is smiling at the irony and gets up to leave. He has some items to pick up and was reminded more than once this morning, to pick up a pack of plastic spoons.

"I'll see you around doc. Good luck with your slips or whatever."

"You still have forty minutes left on the clock. You sure you have nothing to speak about?" The doc asks.

"Maybe next time."

Swan is now sharply leaving the dusty office but quietly closing the badly stenciled door. It rattles as the doc spins his chair to look out at the smeared glass with a bushy vision.

*

Marie Clarke is running late but still walks into an empty room. She has with her a bag of clothes to donate to the people attending the sessions. The table in the corner has steel flasks with hot water in. Plastic tubs with sugars, tea bags and dusty coffee granules. She dumps the clothes in the corner and takes the list of attendees from her purse. She cracks the window to smoke a cigarette as the door slowly creaks open. It is Ben.

"Morning. I'm Marie. I'll be running the sessions for the next few weeks. And you are?"

"Hi. Ben. Turrell. You mind?"

He points to the coffee.

"Help yourself." Marie says.

She ticks next to his name on the list.

Ben is looking for spoons. Instead, he tips the coffee dust into a cup and uses his pen to stir. Sucking the remaining drips of free caffeine from the pen as he can feel eyes on him.

"No spoons." Ben says.

"Apologies. My fiancée was supposed to pick some up. Seems he forgot."

"Not to worry." Ben says.

A skinny, tame man with thinning greasy hair has since crept in. He pays no attention to the pair and now is bee-lining for the coffee.

"Ah, Donald. Nice to see you again."

Marie ticks next to Donald's name.

Ben could not stop watching the new man in the corner. A face bearing marks of a constant downturn and self-pity. Ben thinks he was not born that way. No one is. Donald may not have ever grown a backbone. Or it has since shrunk, hence the slouch.

The door again creaks open, this time with a bout of confidence. Sam enters and turns swiftly to keep the door open. A wide pleasurable smile appears on her freckled face as a heavy-set man in a well-worn grey suit shuffles into the room. It is Wesley Banks. A quiet and once a successful businessman who now lives with aching bones, a change of name, ulcers, and with demons on his shoulders. A bearing weight held by those very demons that keep him stirring at night. A man not deserving of such torment.

He bows a little towards Sam before turning to the room.

"Thank you, my dear." Wesley says to Sam.

He is short of breath but is controlling it well. A method with which he is comfortable.

"Morning. I'm Marie. I'm running the sessions for the time being. And you are?"

Marie holds her palm out towards the grey suit.

"Morning, young lady. I'm Wesley Banks."

The grey suit is now heading to the chairs that are spread in a circle centre of the room. A generic government funded shell. Benefit fraud posters and the smell of stale humans and unemptied bins.

"I'm Sam."

She waves a little and heads to the coffee table.

Two more ticks for Marie's paper.

*

A large sign is hanging from the entrance of the park, asking for information on the dead valentine. Mac ignores it as he is more concerned with the scarred cheek and scraping knuckles on the main street. With eyes heavily pinned on him, Mac is now certain he is being followed. His shadow is Gary Thompson. A shady character, but not the worst. Yes, in the eyes of the law, he is a gangster. To his mother, he is her little chicken. The streets get quieter. Mac jogs. That is all he can muster, on account of an unhealthy diet and lungs with holes the size of golf balls. Only a few minutes from Ben's block. Though he wishes it were sooner. The bag around his body feeling heavier with every step, bouncing off his thigh. One short glance behind him as he reaches Ben's door. The buzzer screeches and the door clicks open.

*

Although heavy in footing and with broad swagger, Gary has perfected the art of floating lightly. He has his ear to Ben's door. Inside, unaware of their listener, Mac looks over the room, remembering it to be much bigger on his last visit.

Ben tips the 12 ounces from the spark plug boxes. The scent of cannabis still does not overpower the scent of tinned curry.

"Ten days, yeah?" Ben asks.

He wants a firm verbal response. Instead, Mac is holding ten fingers up and nodding as he heads for the door. He is cautious but has done well to conceal it from Ben, who would no less flap at the extra inconvenience. Mac quickly swings the door open to an empty corridor. Dipping his head out and sharply scoping it before turning back into the room. The random act witnessed but is not to be questioned as the action is just an add on to other bizarre events by Mac. Ben remembers Mac had once begun counting to seven while undertaking mediocre tasks such as filling a pan of water or washing his hands, but he stopped doing it after about three days. The consensus, amongst a few, is OCD. Mac, however, disagrees.

"Ten days, yeah?" Ben asks with a stern tone.

"Ten days my friend. I'll see you before then, though. Stay breezy." Mac says.

Now flicking his index finger off his temple.

Ben gets to work by taking his cut from the pile of bags. He takes a handful from one of them and sticks the remaining dope under the sink. Just behind the bowl and in between the pipes with sticky tape and stuffing the remaining ten ounces back into the boxes before sticking them to the base of his unmade single bed.

*

The church mezzanine appears forgotten with dusty chairs and Christmas ornaments with faded appeal. Only a thin flight of wooden steps separates the quiet of the downstairs from Ben, who has been spending the last week tucked away in the corner. A quiet scribble above those praying and those seeking shelter.

*The whippet don't run like a whippet should. Those long legs gain ground but the pace slow. His thin smoke still hanging. He's blaming the trench coat. Heavy. The cat was curious, cautious, and cunning.'*

Below, tapping echoes, disrupting Ben's flow. As he leans over his God like shelf, he catches the old man who tends to the church, slotting back a thin wood panel into the front step of the stage. Ben quietly buries himself back in his gap and leans into his work before again, being stirred to the outside world, this time by heavy footing. Another lean forward has him watching a curvy blonde walking to the corner section. It is Bee, who is now tapping her pockets and scanning the red cloth on the table for a pen. The candles on there are currently unlit, with an empty charity and suggestion box.

As Ben finds his mojo shaken and with the possibility of it not returning soon, he heads for the exit with sharp steps approaching him. As he opens the thick heavy door, he turns, surprised to see the blonde so close to him. Bee is holding up her hands as a way of apology. Her bandage was showing, but she was paying no mind to it.

"I wonder if you may have a pen?" Bee asks.

She is pointing towards the table.

"Perhaps I suggest that this place needs more pens."

Bee catches herself being awkward, however, she continues to speak, more a justification of what she has just said.

"Because of the suggestion box. You need pens to write, so..."

Bee grips her bandage to soothe herself. scratching under it with a dipped smile. Embarrassed.

The smile on Ben's face is not helping either. He was finding the encounter to be charming, however.

"Here."

Bee's hand is soft and warm as she takes it.

"I'll return it in just a moment. Thanks."

Bee turns quickly, back towards the suggestion box.

"No need. Please, keep it." Ben says.

He watches the blonde a few moments before heading to the main street.

*

At the lights, Ben is blinking in time to neon flashes. Breathing through his mouth to avoid the stench of the street and trying to remember his thoughts over the noise.

His sleeve tugged. He swings around in defense, sees Bee. A big smile and a pen in hand.

Ben takes it and thanks her.

The lights change and they walk, apparently in rehearsed steps, as jazz music is spilling from Hopper's bar. Bee holds an index finger in the air to the sound.

"My housemate plays that kinda music. He's in a band too, I think."

Now pointing at the entrance, she quickly grabs Ben's wrist and pulls him into the bar.

*

Applause for the band. Who cling to the small stage with dug in heels.

Ben is sipping and smoking in the booth as Bee is walking back from the bar.

More concerned with the atmosphere rather than keeping the fluid in the glasses. A wide eye and general lost demeanor to her.

Ben shouts over the crowd.

"I'm sorry, but I can't return the favour."

He is pointing to the near spilt drink while stubbing his cigarette out with his other hand.

The erratic and fast pace of the band has the place excited.

Bee's eyes now following a small crowd, their neon drenched faces and bodies throbbing in time to the melody. The environment is a new experience for the more well-to-do young lady. A butterfly at a wasp convention. Her flutter no concern of sting though. Dark corners hide her bandage and shadow, lying still and accepted by the occupants.

Ben wonders what suggestion she had made at the church, though he will not ask. None of his business.

*

As Wesley takes a second look at the clock, he wonders where the rest of the attendees for the employment course are. His side is giving him hell, blaming the mattress for the sharp bursts of pain and the ulcer. A condition diagnosed by his doctor from stress which the old man has no intention of needing a second opinion on. He knows exactly why his coffee intake is minimal and the nights awake, not just from protruding springs from thin material, but from the sheer torment of the past.

Marie is smoking at the window. She checks her watch and looks towards the door in wait for the remaining attendees.

*

Meanwhile, on the sofa of Bee's lounge lies an awake Ben. The humming of Dylan's 'All along the watchtower' is creeping from the corner and he assumes the radio has been on all night. His head is pounding and has a fluffy creature confused and cautious of his breath and shoes on the floor. He rubs his index and middle finger together and makes the generic wisp tone to attract the cat to him. The feline has no interest, instead just potters away. Satisfied that the stranger is neither of no threat nor of any gain. As he checks his left shoe for money, keys, and tobacco, he spots a note on the coffee table.

*Ben, help yourself to coffee. Make sure the cat doesn't run off when you leave. I'm sure my housemates will be OK with you being here too. It was nice meeting you. Bee. X*

Uncomfortable with the absence of his inviter, he now hurriedly pulls his shoes on and flings his coat around himself. As he is heading for the door, he recognizes the lady who has appeared at the foot of the stairs. Her splashed freckles blending, along with a friendly, unfazed smile.

Sam points to the radio.

"Gotta say, the Hendrix version is far better." she says.

"I agree. One hundred percent." Ben says.

He is feeling awkward and is hungover.

"I tell ya one tune that has never had a better version. 'Love don't live here anymore.' Rose Royce. Hands down." Ben says.

Ensuring again that he has all his belongings and moves slowly to the front door.

"Though now it comes down to best cover of the song." he says.

"Let me guess. Madonna and Jimmy Nail, right?" Sam asks.

She waves to follow her into the kitchen where she can make coffee and offer some breakfast to the guest.

"I've got a soft spot for both versions. I'm just not a Madonna fan." Ben says.

His throat is dry and vision still blurry.

"The emotion of Rose Royce is hard to beat. She's a fine singer. You can really feel her words. Powerful stuff my friend." Sam says.

"Jimmy Nail has more of a working-class relation to his, I think. It fits nicely." Ben says.

Sam has now dipped her head into the fridge where she is tapping the door and is in thought. She lifts herself upright again, only bringing with her to the counter a 1/2 pint of milk.

The sight of which turns Ben's gut.

Sam fills a glass of cold water and hands it to him.

Ben nods and smiles before gulping hard as Sam is now slotting bread into the toaster.

"Bee can't half drink." Ben says.

He gulps the rest of the water and wipes his lips dry.

"You want some breakfast? We have corn flakes. How about coffee?"

Ben is holding his arms up as a way of being thankful for the offer but feels he has overstayed his welcome.

"You going to the course." Ben asks.

"Nah. I'll give it a miss." Sam replies.

He is unsure if he is going to attend the course himself. Bad guts from too many drinks, courtesy of Bee's apparent bottomless purse.

Simone the cat has no reaction to the front door being opened as she is indulged with licking her paw and scraping it over her pointy ear and cheek.

The radio now playing Ralph McTell's 'Streets of London.'

Ben nods towards the radio as a way of letting Sam know he thinks it is a fine tune.

"See you round Sam."

Simone has now stopped cleaning her fluff for a second before coughing in short one-off bursts as she watches daylight shadows shivering on the wall through the gap in the curtain. Sam watches her twirling her hips and tail in a circle before promptly dumping herself into a small dip created by her.

Sam heads for the phone and dials. On the small table sits the papers and research she has been working on since her library visit, with around twenty more pages added. The click of the receiver chimes where Sam assures Henry Bullman that the mattress is perfect, and would like to speak with Swan. She's asked to hold the line, and starts picking at the fleck of wallpaper escaping the wall, humming as she does so.

"Man, Madonna's version is great though." she says.

*

Richard Wright, a close associate of Swan is still unsure of the plan as he is stirring sugar into his coffee using a plastic spoon from the bag of 100s. Of course, he does not know who Sam is, but what he has heard from Swan appears to be one smart cookie that scares him. She has clearly done her homework, but what is also disturbing is Swan, having no reluctance for her request.

"Don't worry about it. I've done my research on her; a freelance adviser says he used to teach this Sam." Swan says.

His eyebrows raised, and both arms were up in the air.

"Yep, she's a clever one, but I figure we give what she wants and that'll be the end. We just need to stick to the plan."

Swan's words fall short as Richard still has a concerned look as he turns to face the TV screen. The news anchor is speaking of the dead valentine found in the park with a group of people protesting the police and the treatment of humans.

Their banners painted brightly with the words:

'NOT ECONOMICALLY VIABLE' & 'HOMELESS NOT HOPELESS.'

"The pawn shop still closed?" Swan asks.

Without taking sight off the TV screen, Richard nods before sipping the coffee. The Commercials have his attention. New chocolate finger buns at Bunty Cakehorn's bakery.

*

Grabbing toilet paper and his copy of Burroughs' Junky', Ben forgets to lock his door as he hurries to the communal bathroom. The beer guts will have him sitting in there for a while, unaware of the faint taps on his unlocked room door. Tony chances it and enters quietly into the tinned curry scented bedsit. He heads straight for the electric meter to empty the coins as a tap on the door rings out. This panics him.

Another tap on the door. Tony is now pacing the small rectangle room.

Answer the door and play host or hustle by with an excuse. A voice is now calling from the hallway.

"Hello sir, madame, fire service, just need to check a few things."

Tony takes this opportunity to leave, hoping to explain it is not his room.

Two heavy set men greet the wide-eyed, thin man and have no trouble ushering him back into the room, which results in Tony falling to the floor. Gary Thompson stands over the weak man as his associate Jimmy pulls out drawers and dishes through them. The heavy also explored the cupboard under the sink, but with the two ounces hid well and not seen.

"Where is it?" Jimmy asks as he too is now standing over the mistaken identity.

"Listen, fellers, you got this all wrong. I don't live here."

Tony edges to the door using one hand, scraping his cheap denim across the bearing carpet. The other hand is in the air to show no threat. Not that he was of any. The two seekers were twice the size and twice as mean. He could only keep squirming to freedom without further engagement with the two gangsters. Gary is sniffing the air.

"Well, if it's all the same guys. I'll be leaving now." Tony says.

"Whistle to anyone about this and I'm coming for your tongue." Gary says sternly.

His face then crinkles.

"What's that smell?" he asks.

Tony is now in the hallway. His voice heard as the heavy door slams behind him.

"Tinned curry." he shouts.

The two gangsters again start looking for the missing weed. A drop to the stomach and a small peek under the bed has Jimmy grabbing for something. The two men now leave satisfied.

Meanwhile, unaware of the events that had occurred minutes ago, Ben is grateful for toilet paper and is reminding himself to take it back to his room as he reads Junky for the fourth time.

*

Bee is resting her head on the steering wheel. Looking like a kitten at a puppy convention in her second-hand car with a two-tone paint job. A red shell with the two front doors white. There is a tap on the window. The tall athletic blonde with dimples and cats' eyes blows a bubble with thick pink gum. Peering through the dirty glass. Bee slowly winds down the window with effort. This was not the time to have her sister Sally on her case. Not with this hangover.
Bee wonders how she made it all the way across town in the state she is in.

Sally walks up the street.

"Your headlight is broken by the way." she says over a shoulder.

Bee is winding the window back up with some hesitation in entering the family home that she voluntarily left only a few weeks ago. She checks her hair and make-up in the rear-view mirror, sighing and wondering about her reluctance and the reason for her visit in the first place? She scratches her wrist under a fresh bandage.

*

First enters Swan. Hit with an overpowering scent of clean and fresh clothes being churned in the oversized dryers with neat piles on top of them. The coin slots rattling in time with one another as washing machines swirl dirt from the owner.

Before Swan can say his first line, Sam is shaking a rounder's bat loose from her sleeve. Once wriggled out, she holds it in the air. Her confidence is apparent and is growing rapidly as she places the bat over her shoulder and begins pacing around the launderette.

The two gentlemen throw faces at one another. A shared confusion amongst the associates.

"That wasn't the plan, little league." Swan says to Sam with a grin.

Sam heads to a pile of clothes and swipes them. Fresh scent expels as they fall and scatter. She points the bat at Richard.

"Right bubbles, you know what we're here for, so hand it over."

"Bubbles?"

Richard is confused and is upset by being regarded a 'normie' by an actual 'normie' acting like a thug. He heads for the office to get what the freckled lady is there for. A box of money. 500 notes of Swan's own money who is taking the time to compose himself while Sam still behaves like a summer wasp. Unpredictable as she is buzzing around the small confines. In her own world and enjoying herself.

Richard arrives back and throws the box onto the floor.

Sam tucks the bat back into her jacket and picks it up. She is now walking to the exit with a swagger, tapping a box of Calgon soap powder as she passes the machine. Barely sparing any sprinkle. The door squeaks closed after her.

"Bubbles?" Richard expels loudly.

Swan can only laugh as he is leaving the warm air and fresh meadow scent within the launderette.

*

Marie is sorting the clothes Wesley has chosen from the donation bag, while the old man is looking over the employment room, wondering how he wound up in a place like this. The trouble of the past creeping at his feet today and his ulcer is throbbing. Marie placed the clothes on the chair next to him where he notices her engagement ring. As a jewellery shop owner at one time, he knows that the stone and colour of the ring is not a cheap one and hits in the mid-range of £2000. He does not allow himself to make talk of her item, however, a symbol of love or possession of oneself. Talking fondly and with the certainty of such things will only remind him of bad investments, bad apples and wolves howling at his rented door as he has been paying off law firms and creditors for the last 15 years for mistakes made by others. Even after selling his business and most of its contents, he is still double-checking locks on doors and ensuring there is money for the knock on his bedsit door. The constant torment of this would be easier to deal with, having it not be the fact that his prize possession, an item to be passed down from generation to generation, currently sits in the pawn shop with no clue when he can retrieve it. Or indeed how.

*

Mac assumes the whole jury is missing as he stands with his hand on his chin before pacing the small room.

Ben is wiggling a finger in the air. A look of certainty and relief on his lips as his assumption leads to Tony being the one who stole the drugs. A wild guess, but it must be somewhere. He heads for the door and gestures for Mac to follow him upstairs.

The two are now standing outside room 10 and, after tapping sternly on the fading gloss door, they are sure there is someone at home.

Mac is licking and smacking his lips together. A craving for chocolate.

"What's running fourteen miles gotta do with chocolate? Marathon bars I mean."

"Nothing, considering a Marathon is twenty-six miles." Ben says.

Mac taps on the door again.

"They should change the name." Mac says.

"Well, if it ain't broke." Ben says as he is turning to leave. Suddenly, a female voice hits from inside the room.

"If yer looking for Tony, then get in line. He ain't here." Lisa says.

"It's Ben from room 6. Just need to ask yer boy a few questions, that's all."

"Like I've told the others, I don't know about any meter coin collections. Sorry." Lisa shouts.

Ben nudges Mac before walking off. As they do, the door to room 10 creaks open.

There in a robe, hair tied back and with an artist's paintbrush held like a long dripping cigarette, stands Lisa. Behind her, a wide stare like a bunny on a battlefield. Lisa is now doing her own nudging. Jabbing the ribs of Tony.

"Tell them what you'd just told me."

Lisa is now escorting Tony closer to the threshold where the two gentlemen await some explanation.

*

While Barbra Maddox is using the last bit of toilet paper to sob and scrape away her running make-up, Bob is sitting with uncertainty on the edge of his desk. Uncertain what to do for the best.

Because of financial difficulties and a lack of writers signed up to him, he was now at fault for the blubbering, freshly unemployed receptionist.

A few options come to mind. He has opted for reassuring her physically with a pat on the shoulder and a verbal one, stating that when things pick up, she'll be the first person he calls. Her response is a dab of the eye with a pouting lip and nod, before a tight scrunch of skin, expelling tears once again.

A pat on the shoulder did nothing. Verbal contract not received.

Bob clicks his fingers. He has the invitation to the writer's ceremony. It was the least he could do but have Barbra as his guest as she had spoken of how exciting it must all be. Maybe lunch now too, as he was getting hungry. He could tell her about the awards show over an egg cress baguette and free refill coffee.

*

Bee is watching the steam bellowing from the kettle while she sits at the island in the big and bright kitchen. Expensive, unused appliances line the counters, as do tea and sugar containers.

"You here to apologize to your mother? You really were not nice to her before you left to go live God knows where."

"I'm sure she'll live." Bee says.

She needs to burp, but she is fearful of being sick. She scrapes her hair back and lets out a sigh.

"I assume she is more concerned about this silly awards ceremony than her own family. But that's our mother." Bee says.

Sally hands her sister a cup.

Bee slurps at it. She knows it is a cheap shot and would make Sally upset. And make Bee feel better, if only for a dirty second.

"She's worried about you." Sally says.

Wanting eye contact, instead, must resort to watching her sister scratch under her bandage.

"Worried for her reputation, more like." Bee says.

Her words have silenced them both. Only cut by them being irritated at each other's sipping habits.

Sally goes to a drawer and produces an envelope. Dropping it in front of Bee as she walks to the door.

"What's this?" Bee asks.

Sally shouts from the hallway.

"I don't know. Try opening it. And you stink of booze, by the way."

Bee tears the envelope. Inside is a cheque for the sum of £1000 and a note:

*'Just in case,' Elaine.*

Bee slides the note and cheque into the ripped slot. A disappointing shake of the head and pursed lips for how her mother has signed the note.

\*

With a gloved hand, wood and metal are being manipulated. After a few jolts, the springs flick out and the Pink Moon's pawn shop door flicks nicely open. The dim night and quiet streets were a good thing. It is their matching tracksuits that would raise suspicion. Purchased on separate occasions, but from the same fallen crate.

Marty Davidson is the first to enter. Followed by his associate, Henry Bullman.

Marty holds a small piece of paper in the air to catch it in the streetlamp's light. Behind the counter, they both begin looking through drawers and small wooden box containers. Marty picks out a small rectangular box. The numbers on the tag match the ones on his list, but on closer inspection sees there are only nine small gems instead of the expected ten. He scans around the area as Henry checks the numbers on the tag of a heavy gold wristwatch. He is admiring it for a second before noticing a small engraving on the back but does not have the sight nor the time to read it. Suddenly, a sharp car headlight shines from the street and hits the store front. The two men duck behind the counter until it passes.

They agree to leave now, with a familiar, shared glance.

Henry slides out and wastes no time heading down the street. Marty is taking his time though and is clicking the door shut before jogging to catch up with his associate.

Seconds later, Gary Thompson is now arriving at the pawn shop. Surprised and now cautious as the door is unlocked and inviting. Slowly he slides sideways into the dark and the uncertain.

Tipping out drawers and taking no care, it's clear the items he wants aren't to be found. He stands still as a car passes before heading back onto the street.

*

Ben wonders how Chris Walker can afford a good-looking, well-fitted suit on a civil servant wage. Not that he had any knowledge of this attire, but it certainly looked made to order with a crisp sleeve as he was shuffling papers for Ben to sign, agreeing to work at the garage, more specifically in a customer-based position. Handling and supplying parts for cars and vans. Maybe delivering and dropping parcels off, too. Ben had no care or any sort of knowledge about such things, but with the threat of his welfare being cut, he has no choice, so he signs.

Chris taps the papers.

"There's opportunity here son, much more of it too, if you stick it out, which I suggest you do."

His tone is heavy as he is sliding a sheet of paper over the desk. The name and address of the parts shop, who to report to and start date.

"Don't mess this up." Chris warns.

*

The razor bling of the ringing phone shakes Swan from his thoughts. He rests it on his ear and takes a pencil from the stationery holder.

"Queen Z's. How can I... Oh, hi sweet pea. Everything OK?"

He drops the pencil down and lights a cigarette.

"A delivery? OK..."

He is shuffling some papers around.

"Cash on delivery or... what?... for free?... how is that good for business? Giving away profit does not sound like good business to me, especially with your big day coming up."

He corrects himself sharply.

"Our day. I mean."

The office door then creaks open. In walks Sam.

Swan gives a gesture to sit and holds an index finger up to signal that he will not be too much longer.

She clicks the TV on and helps herself to coffee. Plastic spoons sitting on the table.

"OK, OK. What's the name and address?" Swan asks down the phone.

He scribbles on a pad. A sharp glance towards Sam takes his attention before swiveling his chair to have his back to her.

He quietly speaks down the phone.

"Yeah sure. Chicken sounds good, kid. See ya."

He swivels back to face the redhead. Dropping the phone down.

Sam wants to poke fun at him, knowing that it is his soon-to-be wife that wears the pants in that setup. However, she lets it slide and without taking her sight off the TV, she asks if there's some more jobs she can tag along on.

Swan figured she could help with delivering the mattress his fiancée wants him to donate. He did not know who it was to be donated to, and didn't really care. But he had established early in his relationship that he would do anything for his future wife, Marie.

Swan wonders about the freckled enigma sitting in his office. Growing fond of her strange and undisputed approach to the less ordinary.

He stubs the cigarette and is heading for the door.

"Wait here. And don't touch anything." he says.

As the door closes, Neil Diamond's, 'Girl, you'll be a woman soon' echoes from the store front until the door traps the noise.

Sam flicks through the channels. She halts at the new advertisement for Bunty Cakehorn's new chocolate finger buns.

"Ooh, chocolate."

*

Dope smoke fills the room. Creeping and swirling in sequence to Led Zeppelin 'Tea for one' on the record player. A look of malice as it sweeps the ceiling. Looking for an exit.

Another letter of rejection lies on the bed. The explanation for it, that, currently, no short stories are being accepted.

Ben scrunches the paper and throws it in the corner. The second letter has his heart skip.

Hoping the logo of 'Arden Publications' brings with it some good news but, on reading further, finds it is another rejection letter with the wish of good luck in future writings. A kick in the gut. He scrunches the paper up and throws that too, into the corner.

The third letter's logo is for the 'Lane dental company.' It reads:

> 'Mr. Turrell, please stop sending your stories to our address. We are a dental company who have occupied this office for quite some time now. And, although your stories are good, we can't help your cause. We do, however, wish you luck in future writings.' Dr Lane,

Ben smiles. A bittersweet.

*

Meanwhile, the soft shine from the sky is bouncing off the roof of Queen Z's van as it is stuck in traffic. Swan is smoking and Sam chews on gum, which is quickly losing flavour.

Neither were sure what to talk about. Of course, Swan needed answers, although if this strange, freckled lady wanted to involve herself in other people's business, it might be wise of him to play along, as he was still uncertain of aim or motive. She may have something more damaging and detrimental up her sleeve, rather than just a bat.

The traffic is now moving as the young protesters obstructing the streets, now spread away to the sides. An ambulance is asserting authority as it edges closer to each bumper as the crawling cars ahead begin to part way. The urgency of the shouting vehicle now clipping Swan's wing mirror as it pushes by. Leaving a crack of plastic and glass. Swan is inspecting the damage with distaste as Sam is looking for something to spit her gum and finds an old invoice for the 'Trucking Good' car parts shop. As she spits the flavourless gum into the paper, she too is inspecting the damage as they're being hurried by drivers behind.

"Head left at the next turning. I'll grab my cat, Simone, then we can drop the mattress off after the vets." Sam says.

"What? I never agreed to this."

"Pretty sure we spoke of it back at your office. Did we not? Oh yeah. Bunty Cakehorn's too. They've got these new chocolate bun things. Think they come in a six-pack."

"What's wrong with it again?" Swan asks.

"Her, and hairballs. I think."

They fall silent for the rest of the short journey.

*

Creaking floorboards beneath Paul Briggs' feet as he is descending the stairs. He is unwell. Pale with sweat beads rolling closer to his red eyes. No Sam, Bee, or Simone. The ashtray was empty, and the still air was messing with his head. He finds the business card for Pink Moon's pawn shop on the table near the phone and dials. Answering machine. He slams the phone down and heads back up the creaking stairs, quickening his step as Bee is wrestling with shopping bags as she opens the front door. She is hoping Simone is in slumber, instead, no feline or human.

*

Bee is dividing the toilet paper. She calls out for Sam and Paul from the middle of the hallway. After a short gap, she concludes she is the only one home and goes to make some food.

Paul, meanwhile, sits in his room. Quiet and still. A phone cord wrapped around his bicep, his gear drying on the spoon as the needle slowly slides from out of his vein and lands on the floor as he nods.

*

The reception desk is long, spanning the length of the lobby. Behind it are rows of mailboxes for each room and a door leading to a small office. The caged lift has an 'OUT-OF-ORDER' sign on it. The stairs to the side are narrow. It will not be easy getting a mattress up them. No matter how much they pivot and squeeze.

Swan rings the bell on the counter. An old man with a walking stick barely makes it through the door as it aims an attack on his backside as it is springing closed. He has a blend of suspicion and discontent, like the two visitors disturbed him from doing whatever he was doing behind the heavy door.

"Hi, got a delivery for er…" Swan takes the slip of paper. "Room 27." he says.

The old man looks the pair up and down.

"What exactly are you delivering?" he asks.

"A mattress sir. Is the resident in?" Sam asks with a pleasant smile.

"How would I know if they're in? Second floor, second on left. Why don't you go find out yourself?"

The old man is shuffling back to his closed door.

*

The door is ajar. Sam taps gently. They can hear quiet moans coming from inside. Swan pushes the door, but something is stopping it from opening. The force, however, has given Sam enough space to put her head into the room. She instantly recognizes Wesley, who is lying on the floor, clutching his arm and is pale and sweating. Tears filling his eyes as blurred vision looks up at Sam. She backs out into the corridor.

"I think he's having a heart attack." Sams shouts.

Swan pushes the door again. This time, enough for him to stick his head in but quickly retract back into the hallway.

"Holy shit." Swan says.

He quickly heads back down the narrow stairs.

"I'll call an ambulance."

Sam listens out for movement before calling out to Wesley through the gap. Reminding him they had met once before, and an ambulance was on its way.

*

The doctor was kind enough to tell Sam a little more than he should, as Sam was not family. Swan had excused himself from standing around the hospital ward to go make a call, so had not heard it was lucky the two arrived when they did. The doc also advised that Wesley was now sedated and is being regulated. Expected to make full recovery, although he will have to follow a strict diet and have other health problems attended to while admitted. Sam wants to stay around for a while. She was somewhat fearless, but waking up alone in a hospital bed scared her and did not want Wesley to experience this for himself. However, there was Simone needing picked up from the vets.

She ponders a while and begins thinking of her father. Lucky to have him.

Outside, Swan stands at the driver's door smoking a cigarette. Wide-eyed and in deep thought as he is inspecting the damage of his mirror.

Sam approaches. She is wondering why it was so difficult for one human to ask another for a favour. Granted, she was not a close associate, and she also did not want Swan to feel the ask was to take any liberty, like she can say 'well, if you don't do it, there'll be consequence.' This was not the intention. She was also questioning what course or qualification she may gain to understand more of this common behaviour in humans.

"I think I should stay." Sam shouts.

Still a few feet away from the van.

"Doc told me we were lucky we found him when we did." Sam says.

She knows something has spooked the man who is named after a bird. Her mind now churning with curiosity and theory. But now is now, and arrangements need to be met.

"Hate to wake up alone. Wouldn't you?" she asks.

"It's your life, little league."

Sam is now pouting and dipping her chin, gazing at her brown boots before lifting her freckles from under puppy dog eyes. She is ashamed to sink low, but again, her fascination with humans is overruling.

"It's just, I need Simone picking up from the vets." she says.

"You're a pain in my gut." Swan says.

He knows exactly what she wants from him.

"Thank you. So, I trust you with this." she says.

Sam places a key into Swan's palm.

"Just drop her off at my home. Open the basket and run." Sam says.

Swan climbs into the van with Sam pushing the door shut. He nods and drives off with Sam wondering what was eating at her suddenly.

*

To the disappointment of Ben, the church is closed. He felt like shuffling in his hiding place and really getting into the zone today. He heads for the back of the church. There, the door is locked too, although, through the window, he could see movement. Ben peers in to see the old church worker and Gary Thompson placing jewellery, drugs, and envelopes into the small hole in the stage, where the panel of wood slots in place to conceal the goods. Ben quietly walks to the main street.

*

The senses are conflicting. The smell of clinical waste and wet dogs with constant stomps of anticipation and excitable yelps while panting with loose, dangling tongues. The only calm it seems is the tortoise in its size eight shoe box, chewing on a green leaf and Swan wonders how the owner knows there is something wrong with it. What signs does something like that show?

A shout from an open door is asking for Sam Rosiemon for Simone. The vet's tone is crackling and nervous, with his posture shrieking at the size of the man who is now heading towards him after manoeuvring around shoes and excitable animals' bee-lining toward Swan's crotch. He nods at the small vet as he enters the consultation room, and, although quieter, still has a stench. Simone sits in her basket on the table.

Swan points to it.

"We good to go?"

He takes the basket. Looking inside to see an undeniably cute cat.

The vet is holding up a finger and is attempting to make a sound. Instead, he just goes and retrieves a small envelope, the size the dentist would put your tooth in from a drawer. He slowly opens it and with a shake in his hand shows the contents of it to the room. Swan smiles, looking again into the basket and takes the envelope from the pale, sweaty palm and puts it into his inside pocket.

"Well, that is a stroke of good fortune. Ms. Rosiemon was looking for this. I'm sure she'll be most thankful. Happy her cat is good too."

Swan is now heading for the door, but the vet has finally cleared his throat enough to talk. Eyes adverted from the chest of Swan.

"It's just…well policy states that some items must. Er, anything that may appear…"

The vet stops talking as Swan sternly glares at him before smiling.

"How much do I owe you doc?"

Placing Simone down, Swan pulls out a nice wedge from his wallet, holding it up to the face of the small man with dog hairs on his scrubs and a confused look. The vet throws his hands up in a way of defeat and is now heading to the door.

"The bill needs to be settled at reception, sir."

Swan feels he has done a considerable amount of wondering today as he dips from a wet nose at the reception desk. He wonders why the vet did not keep the item. An easy slip into his pocket and then home time would not be long.

"How much!" Swan gasps at the bill.

He slides some money out of his wallet, shaking his head in disbelief, now wondering how he is stuck paying the bill.

"Well played little league. Well played."

Smiling a beaten smile, he leaves for fresh air. Simone unfazed and relieved too, to feel the air brushing her soft body through the gaps in her basket.

\*

Windows smashed and property defaced, including Pink Moon's pawn shop as protesters for the dead teenager are shouting and throwing batteries and rocks.

The first seven cops are 'horseshoeing', with the other seven cops stomping forward with aggression. Baton on shield technique. The aim is to push the protesters back in to the confines of the park. Away from the public and businesses. The plan is soon in motion where the crowd opposite descends like a herd in the direction the cops wanted them to go.

Paul Briggs has been watching this from behind the police. Sat on the pavement waiting for his opportunity, which has now arrived as no cars or footing are close. His shaking partly because of nerves but mostly due to needing a fix. Fumbling over a book basket, Paul is now in the pawn shop. Beads of sweat and second thoughts, along with low light as he is navigating blindly around the establishment. Having no regard for items. Not until he finds his friend, the one that sits proudly on the counter. Paul rushes over, ensuring there is still no soul outside, and clicks a beaten and worn case open, which houses a beautifully maintained bass trumpet.

Suddenly, a beam of light shoots over him. He ducks enough to be concealed but can see a cop car drifting up the street. He counts to five, locks the case and heads for the broken window.

"You stupid or something."

Paul turns to see a fat old blob of a cop. Baton in hand.

Feeling no threat, Paul spins around and starts walking.

"You head that way boy, you'll have fifteen cops on ya." The cop says.

Paul stops walking. Turns to face the red-faced civil servant.

"Come this way, I'll break yer arms."

The cop has a locked stare as he is reaching for his radio.

Paul rushes forward, swinging the trumpet case. The cop steps back before falling heavily onto the concrete and banging his head as he does so. Paul steps back too. Shocked at what he has done. The cop is attempting to get to his feet but collapses between two parked cars. Blood spurting from the open head wound and now struggling to retrieve his radio from its holder, only clicking a button as it lies at his side. The static echoes, but the cop can't talk. He is pale and falling unconscious.

Paul runs.

\*

Jimmy Hall is sticking notes on a few of the small cages that houses assorted items. Either to be picked up or to be delivered. The sound of the sticky tape being pulled off the roll makes Ben cringe and there is a stench of weed roaming the air. Ben was told that Jimmy won't be at the 'Trucking Good' parts shop much and had spent only five minutes explaining that a customer will probably have a slip of paper, which will correspond with the number in the cage and if it is prepaid.

The ringing phone breaks the silence.

"Trucking Good."

Jimmy rests the phone on his ear as he is writing on a pad.

"Yeah, I'll get it dropped off later today. Right, yeah... You want me to look for him? Sure thing, boss."

He hangs up and slips his jacket on as a customer enters.

An addict. Thin, unwell and on edge. He is unfolding a slip of paper as he is approaching the counter. Glancing with caution as Jimmy slides over the counter and towards the exit.

"All yours bud. I'll see ya later. And don't fuck up." Jimmy says to Ben.

The customer slides the slip of paper over the counter.

"Make it quick, will ya."

As Ben looks for the item in the cages, he notices the boxes of spark plugs taken from his bedsit. He finds the customer's item and hands it to him and with no thanks, the on-edge man leaves quickly with his goods. Ben waits until there is no one outside before heading back to the cage where he takes one box and carefully opens it. In there is the weed. He places it back. Confused and unsure of what to do.

\*

Bee feels six years old again. Looking through the glass in the door on her tiptoes. Like a child keen and eager to witness what taller folk are to witness. Her reluctance to attend the sessions, however, was justified and now confirmed as she is watching five of the attendees sitting in a broken circle, all with down-turned eyes toward their dirty shoes. A woman in a blue suit jacket and skirt is dominating the space with wide hips, pacing, posturing, and pouting with a look of disgust over them, ready to hiss from her cigarette shrunken lips. The woman has now clocked Bee's hair line and squinting eye. Bee lets out a high-pitched shriek and drops to flat feet, which drops her completely out of sight. She spins quickly and paces wide strides towards the stairs. Thinking of a book which reminds her of the awful woman behind her but cannot think of the title of it.

\*

Bob is hurrying out of the office toilet to catch the phone ringing. He stumbles over the chair as he is reaching for it. On the other end, Ben is in the booth tapping the phone with frustration and bitter acceptance of hard luck. That is until he hears an answer to his call.

"Hazy Jane's. Bob Rosiemon here."

"Hi, my names' Ben. Ben Turrell. My money isn't going to last, but I wonder if you have time to meet. To discuss my writings."

Bob sits and takes a pencil from the holder. He can hear beeping, but it is louder at Ben's end.

"Hopper's bar. After 6 o'clock. It's east of the..." The phone goes dead.

Ben slams it down.

"Hello?" Bob drops the phone down.
He writes on the pad:

*'Six o'clock Hopper's bar. Ben.'* He also writes: *Get toilet paper!*

\*

From the hospital bed, Wesley is stirring from his sleep. His vision blurred until he swiped his eyes. Only then can he see Swan lingering. Swan cannot just leave now, so thinks quickly of something to say.

"You changed your name." Swan says.

Instantly regretting what he said as they were to be the first words spoken to the old man for many years.

"You! Don't tell me that beautiful, caring girl associates herself with you?"

Wesley attempts to lift himself up a little.

Swan wants to help. Instead, steps further away.

"She assumed you don't have any family." Swan says.

"She assumed right."

Wesley turns his head to look out the window.

A soft tinkle of metal chimes from Swan's hand. He is holding the watch taken from Pink Moon's by his two tracksuit wearing associates. Swan turns the heavy and expensive watch over and looks at the engraving.

*'TIME PASSES THE HAND OF THE CLOCK 'AS THE CLOCK WILL PASS THROUGH HANDS.'*

Swan walks to the bedside table and places the watch gently down before turning to leave. All the while Wesley is paying no attention to his actions but will not let the visitor leave before he says what he needs to say.

"There's no forgiving you. Never." Wesley says.

Swan dips in posture. Deflated.

"Take care dad."

He hurries out of the room.

Wesley waits a few seconds before looking toward the door, then seeing flickers of artificial light bouncing off the expensive, well-crafted watch. A bittersweet.

*

The Trucking Good parts store was dusty, and smoke riddled. Jimmy is behind the counter on the phone. He wants the caller to ensure the information he's given is legit and fact, as he is scribbling on a pad. As he slams the phone down, Ben arrives. Stoned and deep in thought about his writing.

Jimmy throws his coat on and barks that Ben will need to drop items off around the city today.

Sharply, Jimmy leaves.

Ben sticks his middle finger up, only then quickly dropping it as he sees a punter peaking over a newspaper.

The Headline of it reads:

'Cop kill a revenge.'

Bee crumples the paper into her thighs. Her smile is familiar. As is the scent of perfume over the sweat and poor atmosphere.

"Hi Ben."

Bee points toward the garage.

"Mechanic says it won't be long."

"You need to pay?" Ben asks.

"Nope. All paid."

Bee is now folding the newspaper as she heads up to the counter and drops it down.

"They say it was protesters, you know; cop was killed in protest."

Not too sure how to respond, Ben just nods with pursed lips. His connection to the incident was minimal, but the consequence of said incident appears to have his Tristessa evermore further from her home.

"Sam tells me you had met before. At the employment course thing." Bee says.

Ben is not really focused on Bee's words, however, as he is now busy fighting with the machine coin slot as it has eaten his money but has not delivered his order of coffee.

Bee clears her throat.

"Those places are strange, right? The employment place? The lady running our sessions didn't seem very nice."

Bee is pulling a face like she is tasting mud.

She then raises her eyes to the sky along with an index finger, which drops sharply to her lip, which she is now tapping. A moment for herself to recall that darn book she has forgotten the title of.

Stirred from her thoughts by the door creaking open. A slob of a being with grease medals and shiny fingers is standing there. A cigarette hangs from his mouth as it calls out for Bee. Her car is done, and he will pull it up outside. Ben is back at the desk, shaking his head at the list of addresses he must deliver to. He flaps his arms in the air.

"They think I can drive. These addresses are for all over town." he says.

Outside, the greasy man beeps Bee's horn. She responds with two thumbs up.

"I can drive you." Bee says.

"I couldn't possibly put you out."

Bee holds her hands up.

"Really no problem. I'll meet you outside."

Ben has no time to respond as Bee is out the door. He watches her walk with purpose towards her car and wonders if that 'go lucky bounce' is rehearsed or that Bee was indeed a genuinely happy person. However, he wondered about the bandage on the left arm and who Bee was. He stuffs the packages for delivery into two bags, ensuring the numbers are the same as they are on the list. He takes a beat before also stuffing the two spark plug boxes into the bag, which fills the air momentarily with the scent of cannabis. A heavy, audible gulp keeps Ben still for another few seconds. Heads, or Tails. 'Screw it.' Ben keeps the extra parcels, locks up the store and climbs into the rusty car, which is rattling and shaking as he slams the door. Bee is clicking her fingers. That book is driving her insane. Ben rests the bags down and hopes there is a seatbelt.

*

Wesley is sitting on the bed, rolling up his sleeves. He is being discharged and is waiting for the doctor to arrive back with some meds and some literature to look over. Suddenly, the artificial light gets trapped as Jimmy is dividing the room with conflicting shadows and shapes.

"Well, I'm certainly popular." Wesley says sarcastically.

Taking the chance to gain ground from his visitor and putting the bed between them. Now keeping his balance on the windowsill.

"No visit from that cute TV weather girl, though. Oh well." Wesley says.

Jimmy walks into the room and picks the clipboard up from the end of the bed.

"Well, maybe if you owed her money too, she might have taken time to come visit ya. Instead of telling us it's still pissing with rain."

He's looking at the pages but not really taking anything in.

"The boss wants what's owed." Jimmy says.

Wesley is dabbing his forehead. His complexion is now pale, and with lungs contracting.

"The merchandise I took was over spill. Not part of the agreement. You've seen my life boy, I have nothing." Wesley says with some difficulty.

Jimmy replaces the clipboard.

"Well, that's not strictly true, is it?"

He places a firm eye on the gold watch which sparkles on the limp wrist of the old man.

Beads of sweat are now stinging Wesley's vision and down his cheeks. Wiped away with a tissue.

"Keep drooling pal. I have parted with this thing only twice in the last 27 years."

Wesley is gasping for sharp bouts of air.

"I ain't gonna lose it today to a two-bit thug."

Feeling like he was having another heart attack, Wesley is now heading for the door but staggers to the ground.

Jimmy catches him for a second before easing the frail, heavy body to the cold, sterile tiles. Stripping the ill man of his watch as he does so.

Wesley is now falling unconscious and as the doctor enters, he immediately sees the emergency. Beginning first aid and shouting for help. Jimmy steps back as others rush in. He turns and quickly leaves.

*

The car pulls up as Ben is checking the address on the box. He is grateful for Bee's kind nature to drive him around. Even if he felt like a mushroom at a carrot convention, sitting in a rust tin whilst surrounded by the clean air and big houses with iron gates and well-kept gardens.

"I used to live around the corner from here. Further up the hill." Bee says as she scratches her bandage.

"That so." Ben says.

The car and second-hand clothes could not conceal Bee's poshness. Quite endearing, in fact, Ben thought.

"So, 740 Morgan Avenue." Ben says.

Bee is pointing to the grand house on the corner.

Ben feels there is something not right and is wondering why a household with five bedrooms and a Mercedes on the drive wanted with a Volvo part? He was sure it was none of his concern and that we all had something to fill a void. However, knowing the weed wound up at the parts shop, he pondered whether to open this box. Bee catches her passenger in thought and wants him to share.

"Well. You going to drop it off or what?" she asks.

"Something doesn't feel right." Ben says.

"What do you mean? What, with the package?"

Bee is now looking around and through her mirrors.

"You should open it." Again, she takes a few glances around. "Go on."

Ben too looks around.

"You're a bad influence, kid." he says.

Yet opens the box without further prompting.

An urgency lifts in Bee's voice.

"Wait..." Pointing with her two index fingers towards the box.

"Wait a minute. What if it explodes? Or worse?" she says.

Ben has no concern that the box will explode, and there is enough of a gap to establish the contents is not for a Volvo, or for any car, for that matter.

"What could be worse than an explosion?" he asks.

"A severed finger, or toe. That'll be gross. I take it back. Don't open it."

He has no response. Instead, he has his attention on a heavy score of heroin staring back at him.

"Huh." Ben says.

"What is it?" Bee asks.

A bright smile matching confusion with a crinkled nose.

"Nothing. It's exactly what it says it is. I'll go drop it in the mailbox now."

Ben climbs from the car, slamming the door, which shakes Bee in her seat.

He takes no care in stuffing the package into the cast iron letter box attached to the grand six-foot gate and is back to slamming car doors in seconds.

Bee is sniffing the air as she turns the engine. They pull away toward the next address.

"Can you smell weed?" she asks.

*

Sam was feeling guilty to be waiting in Bunty Cakehorn's for her Chocolate finger buns just after visiting the hospital to be told Wesley has died. The notion that a dead man with no apparent family is now to be just a statistic. A number tag hanging from a toe. An addition to the tax bill that funds many ceremonies of strangers, never to be met. What surrounds her now are the exhausting and dooming sighs of the depraved sugar-addicts as she has taken the last six of the chocolate finger buns and now feels like a chicken at a wolf's convention. She pays and leaves, now wondering why she would have to feel guilty for having something that others wanted. This was out of her control. Not her fault the bakery can't supply more treats. She heads for the university library. Thinking about Wesley, her own family and how they get the chocolate into the buns.

*

Jimmy is admiring his new watch as he's on the phone to the left-hand man of their boss. The sight and weight of it takes the distraction from being sternly told that he was as useful as a vegetarian at a roast beef convention due to not finding what they are looking for from Wesley. Jimmy excuses himself as the Trucking Good door creaks open. Telling the caller, he'll speak with a few people and get back to him soon. The watch slipping down his arm as he swipes his hair back. A business grin towards the customer. It's Swan. He sees the watch but is playing it cool.

"What can I do you for my friend?" Jimmy asks.

Still with a grin on his shiny face.

"Wing mirror kit. For a Ford Transit."

Swan can't help but try to burn a hole in the thief with his hard stare.

Jimmy looks over Swan's shoulder to see the van. Before looking in the cages for the parts.

"Don't seem to have one to hand. Have to go check next door my guy. Won't be a tick."

Jimmy opens the door behind the counter, which is expelling loud talk and tools.

Swan is wondering if he should just lynch the scummy bastard. Give him a kicking and take the watch. It will take mere seconds. He decides against it. Counts on the man knowing and having more to offer than a dirty boot. The door creaks again, with Jimmy holding the item Swan needs. He rings it up while Swan flicks some money off a small roll.

"You own this place?" Swan asks.

"Nope. I just manage it." Jimmy says.

"I see. I only ask to be nosy. Only I couldn't help noticing your watch. Doesn't look cheap and so figured I was in the wrong business." Swan says.

He chucks the money on the counter. Parts in hand.

"Be seeing ya." Swan says.

"Hey. What sort of business you in any way?" Jimmy asks.

Now it was Swan's turn to put on a business smile. Answering with a passive, yet stern tone and a firm stare on the thin rat.

"I make sure people sleep well." Swan says.

He nods and exits.

Leaving Jimmy confused yet intrigued.

*

The air is ever denser with cannabis. Bee can't hold off saying something.

"There it is again."

"What?" Ben asks.

"The smell of weed. I thought it was one of the packages you were dropping off. But now..."

She leans into Ben and sniffs up twice.

"I think it's you."

"Or your top lip." Ben says with a slightly defensive tone.

She's taken aback by the response, then falls quickly into a laugh.

Ben smiles. He takes one of the spark plug boxes from the bag and opens it slightly.

Bee is looking with wide eyes.

"Ten ounces, give or take." Ben says.

"You mean to tell me; we've been driving around dropping off drugs?"

Ben is now worried and begins wrapping the bag around his wrist to leave where possible but met with an excited laugh and banging on the steering wheel.

Ben feels he should explain.

"You see, a friend of mine asks for me to hold it for him for a while, so I did. Only to have some heavies..."

"Heavies?" Bee interrupts.

"Yeah. Like criminals. Gangsters I suppose." Ben says.

"Sounds exciting. Sorry, go on."

Bee puts an index finger on her lip.

"The kid living upstairs was trying to rob me. Then he's caught up with two dudes wanting their stash. Thinking he was me. I started this gig at the parts shop and bang, there's the weed."

He looks at Bee to gage some reaction.

She is looking unfazed and doing the right thing by keeping her eye on the road. She pouts, wondering to tell the truth about only trying weed twice before, but feels the information is irrelevant. The feeling she was now experiencing seemed to be one of rebellion, one of something out of the mundane and exciting.

*

Simone is curled up like a hairy bun on the sofa. Dreaming of shiny possessions and downpours of tuna with no care of Ben, who is sitting next to her. He's stubbing out a half-smoked joint while Bee twists the dial on the radio for the jazz station. Coltrane is making her feel good and is embracing the new experience. She laughs, then stops abruptly as she realizes she had not felt this good in a long while. Her initial take on her guest never had her question or assume anything, but now she wonders if he thinks she is an oddball. The door creaks. Bee is now wide eyed as Sam is creeping in with caution for Simone who hasn't stirred. Still in slumber and content. Bee's eyes follow the Bunty Cakehorn's bag, which is placed on the coffee table next to some buds and mugs.

Sam takes a deep breath in, looking towards Bee. Then to Ben.

"We meet again." Sam says.

Heading to the phone.

Ben lifts his mug up and hopes there's no politics in all this, that Sam is cool with the weed and a stranger in her home. One that really wants a finger bun but will not ask for one. He had seen the commercial on TV but could never afford such desire and indulgence.

"Help yourself Bee." Sam says.

Bee reaches for the bag. Taking out a dusty chocolate bun and unwrapping it as she nods to the tune. Coltrane is still blowing through the smoke and dense heads of the room. And now Sam's, who is leaving a message with her ex-tutor Keith Slone, to call her back when he can. She pressed the button on the phone to end the call before calling Swan's number but again met with a machine with a human tone. She leaves another message, this time telling the tape she will visit Queen Z's mattress store later but for Swan to call her back if he gets this message. She hangs up, slips her coat off, and inspects the mess on the table.

"I should really find some jazz records sometime. I'm loving this." Bee says.

Now wiping chocolate from her lips with her sleeve.

"Think I'm gonna head off. Wanna see if the pawn shop is open." Ben says.

Scraping up the buds of weed and ensuring he has all his belongings.

"Pink Moon's?" Sam asks while heading to stroke a sleeping Simone.

Wondering if the fluffy soul was stoned.

"That place hasn't been open for a while now."

"Don't I know it. Got something in there I really need back." Ben says.

"I think Paul, our housemate, has his trumpet in there. Fairly sure that is the exact spot that cop was killed. Outside the pawn shop." Bee says as she licks her fingers free of chocolate.

Sam is now talking aloud.

"Unlikely premeditated. Could be. Self-defense? Victim of circumstance? No, momentary lapse of reasoning?" She clicks her fingers before raising the index one.

"Momentary psychosis? Maybe?"

She looks at Ben, then Bee.

Bee, deciding now, she wasn't acting strange, not compared to the freckled redhead, not after that little outburst.

"And the cop is dead?" Sam asks.

"Yep." Bee confirms this with a hard head shake.

Now rummaging through her purse, pulling out around 300 notes.

"Can I buy some of that?" Bee asks.

"What you got in mind? A Henry? A daughter? A full slice?" Ben asks.

"A who, who and what?"

Bee slaps the money down on the coffee table.

"I thought perhaps two of the big bags you've got there. I don't know, really."

Sam is stroking Simone again. Keeping her business to herself but wonders why Ben has so much weed and if Swan will return her call.

"I could get some heavy porridge doing a large one like that, my friend. Then again, I consider you right." Ben says.

"OK. I don't mind admitting, I do not know what any of that meant. Look, how much can I get for that?"

Bee points to the money.

Ben takes two bags of weed out and puts another half of a bag into one of them. He puts it on the coffee table and promptly pockets the cash. Checking for his notebook as he does so.

"Anyone asks or you decide to carry it around. You don't know me, agreed?" Ben says.

Bee is inspecting her purchase, quietly shocked at the amount she has. She answers Ben without taking her eye off the bag. Sniffing the potent stench of sticky buds.

"Agreed." Bee says.

"Well ladies. It was a pleasure. I'll be seeing ya."

Sam heads to the door with him, handing over the Bunty Cakehorn's bag.

"Keep your sugars up." Sam says.

He thanks her and leaves. Bee is still fondling the weed and digging the radio.

Sam takes her coat from the back of the sofa and kisses Simone on the head.

"I'll see you later, Bee."

Checking her pockets and leaving. As the door clicks, as do Bee's fingers. Holding her index finger in the air.

"One flew over the cuckoo's nest. I knew it would come to me."

She only then realizes that no one is in the room. She examines the weed again. The jazz is erratic and exciting to the listener.

Meanwhile, upstairs creaking from the floorboards, Paul is standing at his door inside his room. He has heard most of the conversation from below and feels the only thing to do right now is take another hit.

*

The van blends well with the other parked vans around the Trucking Good parts store. Swan monitors the back of his van through the newly fixed mirror while Henry is complaining about the lack of new chocolate finger buns at Bunty Cakehorn's.

"I mean, these companies pay fist in backside to advertise, then have the balls to not come good? Think about it?"

Richard lights a cigarette.

"Take it as a sign. Yeah. Like there was a reason you didn't get what you wanted. That's how the world turns, my friend. Every action and all that." Richard says.

Now turning to Swan.

"Ain't that right?"

Swan is still paying no attention. He's in his own world and thoughts.

Henry scratches his head in a confused way.

"So, you're saying, the turning of the world is the reason I didn't get what I expected? And I use the phrase expected, because in this instance, the consumer, me, expects a company, such as Bunty's, to have the goods they advertise." Henry expels with little breath.

"Well, no, because it's not Bunty Cakehorns' who's at fault here." Richard says.

Almost defending the bakery.

Henry leans into Swan.

"You getting any of this?"

"Nope. Sounds like gum flapping to me." Swan says.

Still monitoring the back of the van and rear exit of the Trucking Good shop.

Henry laughs as he lights a cigarette. While Richard stubs his, thinking over his words. Eventually talking with no conviction or strength.

"Wait no. If you'd gone somewhere else, then, as the world turns, the outcome or the reasoning would then shift. What I'm trying to say is there is always a reason for something. Which, at present, has you bun less and there's a reason for that. I think..., ah fuck it. Whatever."

Richard throws his arms up in defeat.

Henry takes an opportunity.

"You OK? I didn't mean to cause any bubble, eh, I mean trouble."

Swan and Henry laugh.

Richard waves his hand at Henry as if swatting away a fly.

"Fuck you." Richard mumbles.

The back doors of the van suddenly slam shut, followed by two stern taps to let Swan know to drive.

*

The invitation to the Annual Writers and Publicist Award ceremony is harder to ignore now that it is leaning on Bob's freshly opened beer. Sam was never subtle, he thought. A smile hitting his round face. As he sits, he wonders what Sam is doing back in her old house. Not that he was at all concerned about anything, in fact, he loved having his little girl with him. He misses her dearly and, although still unfamiliar why she moved out, he accepts she was now a young lady with her own life. How proud he was of the freckled face. What father would not be proud of a daughter taking life by the scruff and dragging it along? Her terms and her time. He hoped the bat he gave her was never to be used, and, in fact, had given it to Sam, more as a joke, rather than a weapon.

However, Bob did indeed attempt to educate his daughter and how, when, and where if she ever swung it at anyone. This, however, fell on deaf ears as a daughter, and was dismissed as a student because of her knowledge of the law in certain circumstances more than her loving and caring dad. Bob quickly moves the invitation from view and begins opening the other pieces of mail, piling up on the corner of the table. He sees a receipt for full payment of a debt he was having trouble with. He knows full well Sam has paid it. He figured she should not have bothered as business was slow, so in essence, the payment made for late rent with another four weeks' advance was just burning away space. Bob was more frequently regretting going solo and leaving the steady, well-paid gig, only quickly shaken from the thought as he reminded himself why he did. Money driven, no sense for art. Or 'hacks' as Sam has put it more than twice.

"Right. I'm hungry and you need shopping." Sam sips quickly as she rises from the chair.

"I'll go get freshened up and then I'm buying you lunch." she says.

Bob smiles with an accepted nod. Lucky to have her.

*

Swan pulls in next to another van as Henry is closing the shutters of Queen Z's warehouse.

The men climb out, each doing something. Lighting a cigarette or fixing their jacket. In the back of the van sits Marty. A little disheveled from the trip back. He stumbles out of the van with a Bunty's bag and brushes himself down.

Swan looks closely at an unconscious Ben, tied to a wooden frame attached to the side of the van. A pink fluffy sleep mask over his eyes.

"Who's that?" Swan asks.

Marty looks into the van, then at Swan.

"The mark. Isn't it?"

Swan paces, rubbing his hands sternly through his hair.

"Ladies, we've kidnapped a normie." Swan says.

"You might feel different when you see what he's got on him." Marty says.

pointing to the Bunty Cakehorn's bag.

"Three hundred cash in his pocket, a crop of green, a notebook and a stub for the hock shop." Marty says.

Henry's eyes are wide at the sight of the treat bag.

"Are they what I think they are?" he asks.

Now heading to the bag to discover not only drugs but chocolate finger buns.

"Well, I'll be. The world is turning bubbles."

"Put it back. Now." Swan says sternly.

Henry throws the bun back into the bag.

"Where's the notebook and stub?" Swan asks.

Marty hands both the pawn stub and notebook to his boss.

"I'm gonna make a few calls." Swan says.

He places the notebook into the Cakehorn's bag.

"What about him?" Marty asks.

"Marty, you make sure the kid does not swallow his tongue. When he wakes, be kind. Offer him a cup of tea or something. You two, take the other van and if the opportunity arises, grab the right man this time." Swan says as he is heading to the office.

Henry and Richard pull a quick rock, paper, scissors to determine the driver. Richard wins it with a rock.

Marty dips a look at the tied-up man before going to start the day's crossword puzzle.

*

Swan dials the number for Keith Slone. The answer machine clicks, and the caller asked to leave a message after the beep. He slams the phone down, lights a cigarette and leans back. Watching the busy life outside the window.

He then notices his answering machine has a message waiting to be heard. He clicks the button to hear Sam. He sighs. Not only at the insistence of the freckled redhead enigma but at the list of to do's prepared by his fiancée sat in front of him. He again leans back in his chair to absorb any quiet time he can get. His mind intertwined and knotted like a bowl of spaghetti.

\*

Ben is stirring awake. In a panic he shouts out, bending and scraping his wrists still tied to the slim wooden panel. This knocks Marty out of deep thought from the clue in the crossword puzzle and is now heading quietly to the van. Peeping around to see Ben attempting to stand.

"Hey buddy." Marty says with the softest tone he can muster.

This startles Ben as he's trying hard to see under the fluffy sleep mask and pushes himself deep into the corner.

"What the fuck's going on? Where am I? Look, if this is about the weed, I can explain. Please." Ben shouts.

"Bit of a boo hoo on our part, I'm afraid."

Marty is now climbing back into the van, which shakes it side to side, only adding to the strain on Ben's wrists and soul.

"Stay away, you monkey thug. I work out, man. Don't test me." Ben says with an unconvincing tone.

"Cool ya boots. I'm just gonna untie your hands, OK."

Marty flicks a 4-inch blade, grabs the weak wrists, and slits the plastic tie. He backs off a little.

Ben quickly lifts the mask from his eyes.

"Where's my stuff?"

Ben is looking around as he is rubbing his wrists, taking daring glances upon the heavy-set man.

"I can explain. About the weed. Please. I'm sorry. There are 300 notes somewhere. Have it."

Marty is giggling. Making his broad shoulders bounce under his heavy jacket. This is worrying Ben.

Marty points to the table.

"Over there. Let's take a seat." he says.

Ben feels he has no choice and just does what is being asked. As he's stepping out the van, he looks for exits or some form of escape.

"How about a nice cup of tea?" Marty asks.

"I don't drink tea." Ben says.

Marty is taken aback by the comment.

"What do you drink then?"

*

As the phone echoes through the house, Paul is shoving clothes and his works into a suitcase. His trumpet and jazz records sit next to it on the bed. Across the hall, Bee is taking a shower. Unable to hear anything except her humming and draining water. Eyes stinging with running shampoo.

Paul steps quickly but silently out of his bedroom. Suitcase, trumpet case and jazz records under arm. He also has a note between his lips and hopes the phone won't have Bee rushing down to answer it. However, the rings abruptly stopped. Leaving only a purr from the sofa and a beating water pipe. He leans the jazz records on the leg of the coffee table and places the note on the table.

'FOR BEE, SORRY...'

He then takes one of Bee's bags of weed and puts it in his suitcase.

He strokes Simone from head to toe as Bee is leaving the bathroom. Innocent stomping and the click of her bedroom door closing. Paul looks over the room before picking up his things and heading for the door. When he opens it, he'll make sure Simone does not escape, instead she is sniffing at the records and contemplating water. Quietly, Paul has gone.

*

Bob's office is nearly empty except for a diary and phone that he has just hung up after failing to get an answer. The man in overalls is looking over the room and then looks at his list, then flicks his index finger towards Bob as he disappears from the doorway.

"Take care buddy." he shouts.

Bob leans on the windowsill with a cigarette in his mouth. The still air and hushed city life were welcoming. The melon collie is a natural accepting habit. Not at all unpleasant for a man losing. He looks out to the rain, only to turn back again as a knock on the door hits out. It's overall man again.

"Sorry. Says here I need to take the phone too."

Bob holds it out for him.

"Don't forget the welcome mat too, yeah." Bob says sarcastically.

The tone has gone unnoticed.

The overall man instead is looking at his list.

"No. It's not on the list. I'll take it anyway. Just in case." he says.

Wrapping the phone wire around the disconnected phone.

"See you around."

Bob checks his watch, then turns to face out of the window again. The city now looks a little more tarnished with the damp sky being filled with human error but keeping with it a sense of romance and warmth. He hasn't noticed the well-to-do, elegant visitor now standing at the door. Her expensive scent, however, was the trigger for Bob. He keeps his back to the room as Elaine Arden looks over the space, paying some attention to the spines of light hitting the bare carpet.

"I know you're a simple man with simple needs Bob, but some things are necessary. Like a desk. Or chairs." Elaine says.

Bob hangs his head and sighs.

"Hilarious. I'd be quick if you have come to rub dog dirt into the carpet as a last insult. The man in overalls might want to claim it."

Truth is, Elaine knew Bob was having 'the spell'. She figured so early in his solo career; it was inevitable to have some hurdles. She didn't know it was this bad though.

However, her publication company didn't get to where it was with feeling pity or any kind of sympathy for other publications. Business was business, and Bob was fully aware he could have his old job back if he just asked.

"Well, there isn't much left to take unless you want my last match?" Bob says.

Elaine looks through her purse.

"Hold on a second. Just looking for my violin. Play you a sad tune."

She stops rummaging in her bag.

The overall man has now returned, and Bob retrieves his diary from the floor.

"Well, hello there." The overall man says with a flirty tone to Elaine.

"Yes, what is it now?" Bob asks sternly.

The overall man is finding it hard to take his eyes off Elaine, who's finding his actions amusing.

Bob clicks his fingers.

"Oi. Casanova. What do you want now?"

"What? Yeah right. No, there doesn't appear to be a welcome mat. Or any mat, for that matter."

The overall man still has an eye on the well-dressed and attractive scented lady.

Bob sighs and shakes his head in disbelief.

"I'm going home." Bob says.

He's followed out of the office by Elaine.

The overall man peers his head around the door, watching the backside of the leaver.

"Hope to see you around Ms." The overall man says.

"I've got four weeks left on this place." Bob says.

*

The noise of Marty eating visibly disgusts Ben. Chocolate on his lip, too.

The door clicks open, which now has Ben on edge.

Swan gestures for Marty to come over.

"We good? You get anything from him?"

"No boss. Just kept him calm and sweet. Didn't push."

"Fair play."

Swan looks over to the table.

"What, no tea?" he asks.

"He doesn't drink it, boss."

"Who doesn't drink tea?"

Suddenly, the buzzer for the main store entrance rings out.

"Go see who that is, will ya."

Swan moves aside so Marty can go and investigate.

"And wipe yer lips too."

"Sure boss. And kid…"

Marty points over to Ben with a sincere look.

"Sorry for choking you out and, you know, putting you in the back of a van and all that." Marty throws a thumbs up and leaves.

"These things happen." Ben says in a sarcastic tone.

"Well, this is a little out of the norm. Wouldn't you agree?" Swan asks.

He sits next to Ben, who's wiping chocolate off his lips. He's offered a smoke and takes it.

"I suppose you want an explanation. Mind you. I would appreciate one myself." Swan says. After lighting his own smoke, Swan throws his hands up.

"I'm sorry. Let me introduce myself. They call me Swan. And you are?"

"Ben."

They shake hands.

"Kid. We both got something on one another. Yeah. I'll be the first to admit. We fucked up. However, judging by the contents of your bag, I'm sure you don't want to pursue any complaint. So, I figure we sort this out quickly. In a way that suits both parties. What you say?"

Swan's glare has Ben on edge.

"Sounds reasonable."

Ben didn't convince himself of the words he had just spoken but wanted to get out of there. He looks through his Bunty Cakehorn's bag.

"Don't worry. It's all there." Swan says with conviction.

"The weed isn't mine." Ben says.

Putting the notebook and money into his pocket. He stubs the cigarette. Looking at Swan through the corner of his eye.

"Frankly, I have no interest in that side of things. I do, however, wanna know who you work for. What's the name of yer boss and associates? You do work at the parts shop, right?" Swan asks.

"I don't work for anyone there, really. Not directly. Forced into it off the dole. My employment guy got me the gig. No choice but to work there or my welfare gets stopped." Ben wondered why he was so forthcoming. He didn't particularly have concern for himself now, like his fear has dipped, known he'll be leaving soon.

"What about the stub? In the notebook?" Swan asks.

"It's a pawn stub." Ben says.

"Yes, I'm familiar with such an item, but what's it for?"

Marty is now at the door. Clicking for his boss's attention. Not that he needed to. It was clear the man was present. Broad and unavoidable.

"Er boss." Marty says.

He's pointing over his shoulder as Sam glides around him, now standing in front of Marty, who is towering above her.

"Hi Sam." Ben shouts over. Surprised to see her.

"Hi Ben." Sam responds with the same surprise to see Ben there.

Swan goes to the doorway and gestures for Sam to follow him to his office. Marty goes to sit back down at the table.

"Bye Ben." Sam says.

"Bye Sam."

Ben flicks his index finger from his forehead as Swan and Sam are leaving.

"The guy at the parts shops' going to be wondering where I've got to." Ben says.

"I wouldn't worry too much about him." Marty says with a duped lip.

"You like jokes?" Marty asks.

Then offering a cigarette. Ben lights it.

"Sure."

*

Swan is looking out the office window with his index finger to his lip. Sam is sitting watching him. Wondering why Ben was sitting in the warehouse. Her intrigue swarms her like a spiky blanket, but her teachings have her reserved on the matter for the time being. However, it was likely Swan would enquire about her association with him.

"You any more work?" Sam asks.

Swan is waving his hand in the air. Attempting to choose his words. He goes and slumps into his chair.

"Aren't you a little...?"

"A little what?"

"Smarter than all this? I mean, why in God's armpit do you wanna involve yourself in such things? Of course, I can't ignore the concerns of my associates either."

"Did we not already establish this?" Sam smiles.

Getting up from the seat to look out the window.

"Indulge me." Swan says.

Sam takes a beat before turning to face the large clean office.

"I get bored. Really bored. Thought I'd put some theory into practice is all."

Sam goes to sit back down.

Swan doesn't like the answer, but the information he got from Keith Salone about the freckled lady was enough for him to feel OK about keeping her at arm's length and playing the game for a while. Life was too short, and he was becoming somewhat fond of her, though unsure why.

"So how do you know that kid in my warehouse, then?" Swan asks.

"Met him at an employment course."

She half cups her hand around her mouth.

"Oh, and I know the launderette job was a fix, by the way." She whispers, then winks.

Swan can only chuckle as he is docking his smoke.

"You want a job kid?" he asks.

He looks through a drawer. Finding what he's looking for. A wrapped pink fluffy sleep mask and a 20% off coupon for the store.

"You think you can keep him sweet? He's aware of our complaint procedure. Though I'm pretty sure he's not prepared to go down that path. Just make sure he's on the same page. And here."

Swan hands the sleep mask and coupon to Sam. Along with her key.

"Why's he here?" Sam asks.

"Mistakes happen. What can I say?"

Sam smiles before heading to the door.

"That cat of yours? She ever go wandering around the streets. To the main strip or back alleys?" Swan asks.

Sam keeps straight. But she is intrigued.

"Yeah. I think she's looking to head back north. Back to her old house. Why?"

"Nothing. She's a sweet kitty. You should treat her to some tuna or something."

Again, Sam is heading for the door before stopping abruptly and tapping her head. She spins on her heel.

"Oh yeah. That man we were delivering the mattress to. Wesley? He died. The nurse told me when I went to visit. Shame really. Anyway."

She waits a second or two before pulling a sympathetic kind smile.

The door clicks shut behind her.

Swan grits his teeth and then swipes items viciously off the table. The picture of him and his younger brother as children crashes to the floor and smashes on impact and again, feels guilty that he has damaged something dear to him. He picks himself off the chair and begins pacing with deep throbbing breaths as he steps over the broken picture frame and paperwork.

Meanwhile, back in the warehouse, Marty is telling this joke, slowly, like he's trying to remember it.

"So, the politician puts the jar of coins under his arm and before leaving, turns to the whore and says…

"Hi Sam."

"Hi Ben."

"What are you doing here?" Ben asks.

"Trial period. You can go. The only thing that's asked is that you keep lips tight. They don't care about your stash or money. And here."

Sam holds out the sleep mask and coupon.

"Great, thanks." Ben says in a sarcastic tone.

Marty rises from the chair and holds his hand out for Ben to shake.

"Well, sorry for the trouble and for, you know, throwing you in a van and all that." Marty says.

"You know, for a gangster, thug heavy. I might consider you right."

Ben shakes the firm hand before grabbing the Bunty Cakehorn's bag and heads for the exit.

Sam is following him. Marty shouts over.

"I have no change. The politician says… I have no change. Do you get it?"

Marty has his eyebrows raised and hands held out at hip level.

"Yeah, I get it. Good one. Stay breezy." Ben pulls a polite smile.

Outside, Sam is looking Ben up and down, looking for injuries, but he doesn't appear to have any. She also finds it somewhat strange that he does not appear to have much concern about the past couple of hours.

"Well, that was quite an experience. Not everyone can say they've been kidnapped, right?" Ben says.

Tapping his pockets and checking the bag again to ensure he has all his belongings. He licks the cigarette paper and rolls the smoke.

"What are you doing hanging around people like that, anyway? You living a life of crime or something?"

"Or something. It's complicated. I feel awful about what happened to you. Is there anything I can do?"

Sam again looks him up and down.

"I'm gravy. Really, I am."

He stops walking. Hit with an idea. Not a good one, but an idea.

"Though if you're not shy of a little wrong doing then..." He walks ahead a little. "Nah, forget it."

"What is it?" Sam asks with a slip of intrigue.

Ben had been weighing up his options those past few hours and now, with a knot in his gut, he was about to ask someone to commit a crime with him.

"I need something back. It's of some urgency, in fact."

"Go on." Sam says.

Ben tells her about Tristessa and the hock shop. He talks about taking back what is his, only to leave cash for the owner. Sam was excited. Smiling wide, which has Ben on edge even more.

"So, you got a plan?" Sam asks.

"Nope. Was gonna wing it." Ben replies.

Sam paces up and down along the edge of the parking lot. She then stops and stands facing the traffic.

"Count me in." she says.

"Really?" Ben says in a surprised tone.

"Sure. So, first we ditch our possessions." Sam is holding her arms up like the plan is now set in stone.

"Drop your stuff at your place. Second, when we get there, look out for any obstacles. You know, coppers or creepers, stuff like that. Only then do we decide on an entry point. We only need to establish an escape route once in, and meeting point. We can do that later. Simple."

Ben is speechless, confused and, if he was to be honest, a little turned on. Who was this freckled enigma? His expression picked up instantly by Sam. Now wondering if she needs to explain herself.

"What? It was part of my studies at uni. It's a basic pattern. Right, no time like the present. Come on."

Sam is now talking more to the traffic than Ben, who is watching her walk with purpose. His smile slicing across each cheek.

*

The attractive blonde Anchor-woman is being instructed and directed by the cameraman. Waving his hand to gesture what direction and how many steps to take to have the perfect shot of the concerning environment surrounding her expensive smile.

Further up the street, Ben regrets the plan with every car and foot passing. Sam can see he is hesitant but will not let him bail. She nods towards the pawn shop door and walks to it with a quiet purpose.

"Here's the thing about people. We're only mostly concerned when there's something to be lost. Or gained." Sam points around the street.

"What I'm saying is, him or her don't care what you're doing. They're in their own self-obsessed world. You just think they care because you're conscious of your own actions right now. It's the spotlight effect Benny boy." she says.

Suddenly there's shouting intruding at the park entrance. Then a wave of blue uniforms being pushed by angry crusties towards the pair. Sam is scanning the streets while Ben sees in the distance another wave of cops approaching.

"Screw this kid. I'm leaving." Ben says.

He was already stepping across the street as he was talking, only then to turn on a heel to see the swarm of uniforms and waves of biotic material pipping Sam into the store entrance. Sirens are now ringing through the air, drowning out Ben's shouting for her as a fresh crop of cops rally out of a van. The crusty folk are now retreating as the piles of cops are picking themselves and others up from the dome shape. Ben quickly dips into the mass. Sam is lying unconscious with a cut to her head.

*

The ringing phone has no care about the public health officer, who is quickly chewing on his egg mayonnaise sandwich with a crunch of lettuce. He's figuring the phone will stop ringing so he can have another crunchy bite, but it's persistent, as is his boss who is sitting in his glass house with a frown that is aimed at him, so he has no choice but to answer the phone with a mouthful of early lunch.

"Public health declaration office..." he mumbles.

He can hear a muffled voice.

"Wesley Banks. You get payment for him?" The voice asks.

The officer swallows the last of his wholegrain crust and cannot stop thinking that he should have made two sandwiches and not one.

"I can check for you. Are you a relative?" The officer asks.

He hears nothing from the other end.

"Hello?" he says.

Still nothing but as his boss is still glaring over, the health officer just looks up the request, breaking many rules and procedures in doing so.

A few flicks of the papers on the shared clip board reveals full payment for the funeral and collection of artifacts.

"There's a Truman. A Wesley Truman. Previously known as Banks. Is that who you are referring to?" The officer is waiting for a response. Still nothing.

"Sir? Well, it's paid in full and there's a name to contact for after the ceremony. As requested by the payee."

The phone clicks so the officer hangs up, looking over at an empty manager's office, and, like a professional, slits the foil of his Kit-Kat.

*

Many people walk in these corridors. The unwell, the worried, uniforms with clipboards, the warmth seekers, white coats, paramedics. And now Ben. Being softly guided by a nurse as she asks what relation he is to the freckled lady, as well as seeking information that Ben advised he does not have. He can only supply a first name and an address for Sam, received with a warm smile from soft cheeks, a practiced and well-rehearsed action but carrying with it genuine care through those brown eyes. The nurse takes a pen from her breast pocket and a small pad from her side pocket. Ben writes in block capitals. He's told he is free to wait around, but he is uncertain what to do as the clock above the reception is reading 3.50pm. His appointment with Bob at Hopper's bar was approaching, and it was a fair distance from where he now stands. He heads back to the waiting room.

*

Bee is rubbing her hair hard with a towel after her shower as the phone rings. Her gut is telling her to not answer, but her brain already has the phone in hand. As soon as she heard smoke being blown out on the other end, she knew it was to be her mother Elaine Arden, most likely calling from the Arden publishing offices.

71

"Beatrice? It's your mother."

Elaine is assuming it's her daughter who has picked up the call.

"Hello mother." Bee rolls her eyes.

"I heard that eye roll, Beatrice."

Bee sees the vinyl leaning on the table leg. She stands on tiptoes, confused why they are there. A sleeping Simone on the chair. Peaceful, content and unfazed.

"I came by the house." Bee says.

Changing the already dense and awkward tone. Though very much used to it.

"Yes. Sally said you had. Said you looked well."

Bee's eyes roll again. The last time she saw her sister, Bee was hungover, unwashed and evermore lost.

Elaine lights another cigarette, which helps to fill the silence.

"You got the cheque, yes? You need more?" Elaine asks.

Bee does not want to continue the conversation. It's stirring emotions, but she is controlling them well.

"What can I do for you, mother?"

"The awards ceremony. It's approaching and Sally has kindly waived her guest seat." Elaine blows smoke down the phone. From her end, it bellows back up after bouncing off the receiver.

"I told you, mother. I have no desire to go."

Bee is again trying to see what vinyl is leaning on the coffee table leg.

"Yes. I don't need to be reminded of your dislike for all that. Your little outburst before leaving was quite a show. No, I was wondering if you still have that nice little blue dress anywhere? Louise, from next door, will take the guest seat. I offered her the dress. Which you have never worn, I might add."

Elaine sips some wine.

"Loose Louise is going? What the hell?" Bee says.

"Beatrice, be nice. You and your sister had no interest, so Lou Lou will now be attending. She's keen on the industry. Now, I expect to see you at church on Sunday. No excuse. Twelve thirty, and wear...."

"Long sleeves?" Bee interrupts.

"What?"

"Nothing, I got to go."

"I'm expecting you, Beatrice. We have guests coming, and your little mishap has not gone unnoticed by many. It is going to take some work for me to rectify that sort of behaviour."

"Bye Elaine." Bee slams the phone down.

Then, walking to the couch, she picks up the note from Paul and notices one bag of weed has gone.

*

Ben is sitting in the corner contemplating what to do. Opposite him, Bob sits, filling in with a rushed and uncaring manner the forms given to him by the nurse. They meet eyes and both smile and raise eyebrows. The typical interaction expected.

Bob checks his watch and lifts himself up as Ben does the same, now standing at the entrance to catch sight of the clock. Time is pushing on. As he turns back into the waiting area, his elbow meets the soft gut of Bob. Apologies are made, and Ben watches the stranger disappear around the corner before he sits again. Contemplating. Toss of a coin. Heads he will leave for his appointment, tails, he will stay. Sam is now being wheeled into an elevator by a porter. Catching sight of her dad, she waves him over and they enter the elevator together.

*

Heads' coin toss won, so now Ben is looking around the bar for Bob. Though he could be one of the many occupying the space.

The small group of musicians are at the piano, tuning up. The pool tables have crowds around them. Ben orders a pale ale and thinks his luck is in when seeing a vacant booth, only to find it has a broken lamp. There's also spilled drinks and broken glass on the seat. Careful not to cut himself, he uses his sleeve to brush it onto the floor.

The stub for the pawn shop falling on to the table as he is flicking to the page he had written on.

*'The lost souls with no sense of hope looked as if they were on a constant slouch. Bound to the bars and parks, never appearing to sit still, always around but with nowhere to go. Slouching over bowls and stools with a constant drip.*

He has a twisted lip and a frown, unhappy with the written words. He scans the room again, unable to establish whether those attending the bar are waiting for someone, just as he is waiting for someone himself. He flicks to another page.

*Although dominant from crawl, fall and step she's been there without judgement. Some days she will bite. Pausing a second for reaction... There's emotion there too. That some question. Misinformed of the yearning. A giver and a taker which some are exhausted and helpless by. Never discouraged, she'll stay close by until your mood turns where she'll be ready to fulfil your needs, lust and wonders like a passive innocence. without a loss. A loss somewhat expected.*

He is flicking the pages over again. Doubts entering his mind. What was he to show this Bob guy when he arrives, if he has not already arrived? Ben reminds himself that confidence is overrated, and the mind is to be no support most of the time. Like his own body and organs are against him. Perhaps the body was right. Was he ready to have another failed attempt? Was this to be a sign that he still sits alone with a tattered notebook with work known only to him? Never to be read in libraries or left on a train platform bench. He lights a cigarette, hoping the action helps forget and cloud the negativity, but continues to read from the notebook.

> 'She would never have suggestion, nor preference. She would go with the flow. She would care for nothing. Even for the euphoria she was willing to share.'

The jazz band plays. The man at the bar is a potential to be a Bob. He has a suit that fits better than the usual second hand or hand-me-downs that wave over the floors of the main street bars this side of town. Sitting on his own until greeted by another well-crafted suit.

Bob's associate, perhaps? Ben wonders if he should approach the men. Introduce himself and hope it was to be the owner of Hazy Jane's publication. Instead, he watches the two men leave as the crowds compete for volume over the band hugging in the corner. Ben gulps at the drink then heads for the exit himself.

*

Paying no attention to the passing feet and speech. Ben, instead, remembers what Sam had said about no one caring about him and his actions, only that he was conscious of his own. An action that now has him climbing over the wall to the back of the Pink Moon's pawn shop. Stumbling and barely catching himself on the other side and now heading to the door. This was the extent of the plan, but notices the door ajar. He is listening closely for movement indoors, but he cannot hear anything or see anyone. A rush of guilt and second thought is washing over him, and he feels sorry for the owner for having his property both vandalized and seemly broken into. He takes a deep breath and enters with caution.

Inside is dark, but he has no concern as he is bee-lining to go fetch Tristessa from the shelf. He unzips her and inspects her closely. The wind flows through the streets, as do the people and traffic. Ben finds the stub, placing it on the counter with the money before exiting the same way he entered.

*

The pen tapping on Marty's lip isn't helping him figure out the crossword puzzle.

"A wordsmith's chip off. Two words beginning with W?"

The quiet repeat of the clue to himself wasn't helping, and now, neither was the sound of struggling in the corner.

Marty looks over to see Jimmy Hall attempting to wiggle free from the chair he's tied to, grunting and trying to sense any presence in the room as he is raising his head, attempting to see under the pink fluffy sleep mask.

Marty leaves to fetch Swan, which scares the tied-up man.

"Who's there? What the fuck's going on? Let me go, you fucker." Jimmy says.

Anxious and scared. He's trying to hear what's going on by sitting still with an ear out to the air. The sound from the door has him jumping in fright and uncertainty. The vast space is now quiet and eerie.

*

The place has Bee overwhelmed. Lost yet excited with the number of records; one being played over the heads of the store's visitors who are roaming with content or sitting in small groups where they sip coffee and smoke thin cigarettes. She hears one of the coffee dwellers tell a friend the tune is Curtis Mayfield. The friend heard it, but it's Bee who has interest. Not the music she has been shrouding herself in, but another new and exciting avenue to explore. Bee feels good, that she does not feel out of place, not like she has felt or indeed been in other places, even feeling like a stranger in her family home. She scratches her wrist, now free of bandage and healing quickly. Hardly an ounce of evidence to suggest any wound was even present. There, in the corner, record players are for sale. Bee needs one if she was to play the records apparently exchanged by Paul for her weed and, of course, whatever she was to purchase today. She has already decided she wants some Curtis and heads for the section she hoped he will be in. Sure enough, she finds the Superfly soundtrack and carries it under her arm, now heading back to the record players. The area feeling ever more warming with the scent of coffee and with people appearing to not care, or have perhaps, conquered the art of just letting go.

*

Swan and Marty are ignoring Jimmy, who is throwing threats and insults like he has nothing left to lose.

Swan has searched the free paper for information while Marty is still attempting to complete the crossword in it. A good habit he had since adopted, to give the daily puzzle a go. He was hoping today would be the day he fully completes one. Only three words off.

"You're fucking with the wrong man. You two-bit bastards." Jimmy says.

Trying to loosen his tied hands.

"Where's little league?" Swan asks Marty.

Marty is shrugging. "She left with that kid."

"And the other two?" Swan asks.

Again, Marty shrugs. "Don't know boss."

"Plastic gangsters." Jimmy shouts.

Now laughing in a mocking manner.

Swan nods his head toward Jimmy whilst keeping sight of his associate. Marty takes his time to wander over to the tied man. He'll use this opportunity to vent frustration for the crossword.

He digs Jimmy in the gut while Swan gently cleans the face of the retrieved watch with a small soft cloth, feeling that the crook has tarnished it, and, to his credit, is taking the hits from the big man well.

The springs and the material of the mattresses spread along the warehouse walls mask any noise coming from the unit.

"Who do you work for and where'd you get the watch?" Swan asks.

Jimmy is attempting to make himself small. Crunching his body together, but the attempt is failing as Marty swings another fist into the gut.

Jimmy cries out.

"I'll ask again. Where'd get the watch?" Swan says with a more of a demand to know.

Jimmy is looking in the direction where he thinks Swan is standing. The sleep mask is doing its job.

"Is that what this is all about? A stupid watch?"

Marty jabs Jimmy in the face. Blood now running from his nose and lips.

"Fuck man. I found it OK. And who says I work for anyone?" Jimmy shouts.

Angry with the response, Swan rushes to Jimmy. Grabbing him by the throat.

"Last chance to talk straight. Otherwise, we'll start getting real heavy." Swan says.

The men's cheeks mere inches from one another.

Jimmy is trying to free himself from the grip. Swan lets go.

The warehouse is now quiet, but only for a second before Swan tells Marty to go put the kettle on.

Swan lights a cigarette. A well needed rest from it all.

"Fuck. You're not gonna scold me, are ya?" Jimmy shouts with a panicked tone and is now squirming more than ever to get loose.

"Calm down. It's for tea and not my style. No, I find the way I do things works well. I mean, if it ain't broke, don't fix it, right? Speaking of which." Swan says.

"What? What's that mean?" Jimmy asks.

"You know what your Pollex is, Jimmy? Here's a clue. You have two of them. Which is funny because I have two questions and if I don't get the answers I'm looking for, I'll break em. So, Question one. Where did you get the watch? Question two, who do you work for?"

Jimmy stays quiet. Swan crushes the cigarette onto the floor with the tip of his shoe and walks behind the tied man.

"You see, us humans have become reliant on the Pollex over the years." Swan says.

He grabs Jimmy's left thumb. Holding it tightly.

Jimmy is clearly in pain. Trying to conceal it, whimpering and biting his bloodied lip.

Swan slowly bends the thumb the wrong way. Jimmy can't contain it and screams in pain as Swan asks again where he got the watch from.

With the fear of broken bones, Jimmy cries out that he will tell his captive what he wants to hear. Swan lets go and walks round to face him.

"Talk." Swan says.

"I took it from an old man. He owed money to my boss. Got wind he was in hospital so went to pay him a visit. He collapsed when I was there. So, I took it and left."

"You killed him." Swan shouts.

This makes Jimmy cower a little, only to be taken over with sternness.

"Bullshit. I never touched him. The kid had a dodgy ticker."

Blood is spraying off Jimmy's lips as he angrily tells Swan what he thinks.

"You soft for the old man?" Jimmy asks.

He listens for a response. The silence is telling.

Swan is now throwing fists at the blind and tied man.

Marty returns with two cups of tea. Quickly leaving them on the table to hold Swan back from knocking teeth out.

"Don't need a dead man in yer warehouse, boss." Marty says.

Then turning to the battered man and placing a grip on his shoulder.

"Come on bud." he says to Jimmy.

"I'll talk. Just stop hitting me." Pleads Jimmy.

"Good man." Marty says.

Swan sips his tea. Barely keeping his emotions at bay. Conflicting sadness, anger and guilt and he thinks about calling his fiancée.

*

Clutched in a firm grip is a crumpled generic ceremony leaflet. There are small spouts of creaking floors as Sam walks to see Swan, middle centre of the church. The head injury surprises him, but it is healing well but still has a purple, brown colour with spikes of red thunder bolting in her eyes.

"What happened to you?" he asks.

"Pork and salad sandwich." Sam replies as she sits and looks over the area.

"If this is a state funeral, I want to die broke." Sam says.

Only for a reaction. However, there isn't one. Instead, Swan is excusing himself. Feeling weak and overwhelmed yet keeping a hold of himself long enough until out of view, however, the civil servant is now starting the ceremony. The curtain at the front opening, exposing a dark pine casket.

"Today we celebrate and concern ourselves with the life and sad passing of a new soul, known now to our good lord as one of his brothers."

Meanwhile, Swan is dabbing his face with cold water. He grabs a paper towel as he watches his reflection, appearing to mock his actions.

"Fuck." he says quietly but loud enough. He dabs his face dry.

"Hello?" The church worker shouts from a locked cubicle.

"Sorry. Didn't realize there was anyone in here." Swan says.

"Do me a favour, will ya. Grab me some toilet paper from the next cubicle." The church man yells.

Swan scrunches the paper towel and throws it towards the bin and leaves.

"Hello?"

The church man hears the door creaking closed. He sighs hard.

"Son offa bitch." he expels.

Meanwhile, Sam is lighting a candle as Swan arrives back. Arms in the air as he looks around.

"That's it? It's done?" Swan asks.

"Fraid so. He was rolled away just now." Sam says in a harsh tone.

It was not intended but may have appeared that way.

"How long was I gone?" Swan asks.

"The ashes can be collected in the next couple of days, pending on paperwork." Sam tells Swan as she was advised by the civil servant.

He nods.

"You lit a candle?" Swan asks.

Only for a change of subject.

"Seemed like the right thing to do." Sam says.

The intrigue of the freckled lady's presence, not only in his office but here, now in the church, was burning Swan's gut. So why does a lady with her qualification and a sense of entitlement have Swan so keen on her to be around?

She was magnetizing and happy-go-lucky, has no sexual attraction to her, but can see why people may find her attractive but now wonders who the real Sam is, and what is an act? Whatever the case, he still feels he can talk to her like an old friend. They watch the candle flame flicker for a few seconds.

"You want to hit my house for a coffee? Or perhaps a drink at a bar. For Wesley?" Sam asks.

"I got a few things tied up at the office." Swan says.

"You need a hand with anything? I am employed by you after all, right?" she asks.

Swan smiles.

"Right. But no. Come round tomorrow, though. I'll get you working hard, and you can tell me all about that."

He points to the injury on Sam's head.

"Nothing to tell. Take care Swan."

Sam turns to head out of the church. Halted by her new boss, calling after her. She spins on her heels, producing a crude screech which echoes around the shell.

"You OK?" Sam asks.

She can see that the man named after a bird wants to say something and that she has a few guesses what it might be. She waits a few more seconds before she blends her freckles with a reassuring smile.

"I know." she says with a caring tone.

Swan dips his head a little down and to one side before he gives her an appreciated nod, now left alone watching the candle flame dance again. Seeing paper and a pencil on the table near the suggestion box, he takes a slip and writes with some hesitation. He then folds the paper, again hesitating. This time, placing it to the flame, letting it turn to ash. Never to be known, told, and already forgotten.

Meanwhile, on the upper-level, Ben has been tucked away. Only noticing Sam below when stretching his legs. He had watched her for a moment, wondering what relation to the dead either of the two had. The guy at the table looked dapper, Ben thought. Sam looked like Sam. He also wondered if it was in bad taste for him to be up there scribbling while a man rolls to his heated demise. He places his notebook in his coat pocket and heads towards the small stairs. Leaving quietly.

*

Just outside the church, Ben scans the street, hoping to spot Sam. He sees her at the lights so shouts over to her, jogging as he does so, and instantly has the urge to prod her injury. Sam edges away.

"Does it hurt?" he asks.

"Of course it hurts."

Ben rolls a cigarette.

"Just come from the church. Peaceful places churches. Quiet." he says.

Sam doesn't respond. Instead, she's watching the traffic lights on the other side of the road.

"Thanks for coming to the hospital. I was told you hung around a while."

Silence between them. Again, Sam is watching the lights across the street. Ben lights his roll up, looking up to see Sam crossing the street just as the red-light hits. Cars halt as a sea of shopping bags sway together across the neon and concrete. A constant buzz and whirl of pollution from both a natural and man-made stir. All the cars are the same make and colour. Everybody a nobody.

"Where you heading? I got some nice coffee at home if you want to come back for a while?" Sam asks.

"You got a phone I can use at your house?" Ben asks.

"Sure." Sam says.

They walk in time with the others, all the same but all strangers, whether protester, shopper, valentine, copper or Sam and Ben.

*

The church man is going to miss the smell of spent wax lingering. The candles dripping and the sheer peace and expectation of a church, but now he is thinking of the fat envelopes that are slipped into his grip and that are stirring up the notion and belief in karma. He was a crook himself, just as bad as those who bullied their agenda, resulting in the church man holding items that were to be secure and hidden in the small drawer under the stage step, but to his despair is now sitting empty. He shivers with the thought of consequence, laps of theories pounding his head.

What will be the consequence of this? The church man accepts karma's decision.

His greased palm has invested well, so he's going to skip town. Today. After all, he wasn't responsible. Only he knew that he would have to answer to someone.

*

The item from the vet's little envelope exposes a small gem, which now completes the set of ten.

The items from the church sit on the desk. The money, around 2000 notes, at an experienced glance, will go to charity. The drugs, Swan has no interest in. Some cocaine in a matchbox. A few bags of weed. Never did Swan have any desire to bulk his back pocket with narcotics. Too messy, too over-saturated. He took the drugs purely to piss off the pushers.

Wesley's watch ticks heavily on the desk like it was stirring attention from Swan. He takes a deep breath in and closes his eyes. His mind swirling and conjuring memories, seen before, many times. Seeing himself in his younger days. A stranger in that world. Just an observer of the sad tone and natural happenings of reality, watching a good-looking, well-built teen in a black suit and tie. Shiny shoes, soon to be dusty and scuffed, as Wesley will sprinkle dry mud over the coffin of his youngest. There is pouring of sympathetic eye and soft touch to all attending except for the young Swan. Adult Swan wants to reach out or shout as he's repeating that day. No care or sharing emotion for Swan. He was alone, though he is suffering as well. The man he had long become wishes to not see what was to come. For the last physical contact Swan had from his father was a sturdy barge before Wesley left the freshly dug hole.

Swan shakes himself out of the thought. He is breathing heavily and is feeling sick while life outside goes on with an unknown ignorance or care.

*

Henry is shuffling a deck of cards at the table as Marty is still struggling with the crossword puzzle. Swan enters, looking around the warehouse. He looks tired and has since flushed the drugs down the toilet, not realizing weed floats, but with the four healthy shots of dark rum in him, he doesn't care.

"Shall I cut you in, boss? Twenty-coin minimal mind." Henry says.

He deals the cards three ways.

Swan sits and lights a cigarette. Digging in his pocket to pull out a few coins and placing them on the table. Marty drops the newspaper down and the pen on top. He too, gets some coins from his pocket, placing them in a pile before taking his cards and arranging them in order.

"Thinking about writing a book." Marty says.

Henry is laughing. Shaking his head as he decides on his wager.

"What's so funny?" Marty asks.

"What have you got to write about?" Henry asks.

Swan isn't paying any attention to the other two. Instead, he's again looking over the warehouse. Casually arranging his cards.

Each one of them throw some coins in the middle.

"It's just you can't even finish a crossword puzzle. You've been at that thing most the day." Henry says.

He then takes a card, then chucks them down.

"Fold." Henry says.

"Don't even think about telling me the answer." Marty says.

Throwing his cards down too.

"I won't. Where's the fun in that? Though the clue yer stuck on and this talk of writing…" Henry says.

"What?" Marty asks.

"Well, the irony hasn't escaped me." Henry says.

Henry now has eyebrows raised with a duping delight smile. Suddenly, there's movement in the corner. Followed by groaning. The three men all look toward the noise. Swan rises from the chair and scrapes his winnings up.

"Let's get the kettle on, shall we?" Swan says.

"Sure thing, boss." Marty says.

Now heading to the exit.

Swan claps his hands hard and rubs them together.

"Right. Let's start from the beginning, shall we?" Swan says.

With a fluffy pink sleeping mask, a broken thumb and a sense of doom, Chris Walker sits tied, confused and uncertain of his future.

*

Bee is sitting in pyjamas, stoned on the sofa in her shared living room while Miles Davis plays on a record player. The box, packaging and instructions are on the floor. She is in some discomfort, like she's sitting on something hard. Simone is asleep on the chair. Now used to the scent of herb and with the desire to run and explore losing its appeal. The front door is creaking open slowly. Ben and Sam are cautiously entering.

"Ben. Nice to see you again." Bee says.

"Hi Bee."

"Yes. Yes I am." Bee says.

"Those Paul's records?" Sam asks as she slips off her coat.

"Yeah. You seen him lately?" Bee asks.

"I'm sure he won't be hard to find." Sam says.

She points to the phone.

"Help yourself Benny boy."

"Thanks." Ben says.

Bee is paying no attention. Instead, she is looking at an album sleeve. She arches her back. Again, in discomfort.

Sam is heading for the kitchen but stops as Ben shouts over at her as he's dialing a number.

"Hey what's your surname, by the way? They asked at the hospital, but I don't know it. Just your first name and address."

Sam turns and stands in the doorway.

"Mine? It's Rosiemon. Samantha Rosiemon." she says.

Bowing like a royal introduction and now vanishing into the kitchen.

Ben hangs up the phone and heads for the kitchen as well.

"I think we need to talk Sam." he says.

Bee looks over the top of the vinyl sleeve to see an empty room.

Now pulling an agitated look at whatever is digging into her and investigates, pulling Sam's bat out.

Confused about the item, before dropping it to the side of the sofa and finding a light to hit the pipe.

*

# 3 MONTHS LATER.

Swan felt bad brushing his father from his trouser bottoms, but after much thought and frustration, he was finally scattering the ashes down by the lake and park, around twenty miles east of the city.

He and his family had visited this place a few times when Swan was a young boy, with his little brother always at his side. Either wanting approval, or to not be alone. The ashes floated in all directions from the overpriced and somewhat heavy cylinder with a crude purple design of flowers. Perhaps that was the purpose. Swan thought. To cloud over and disperse to all ends of the land. Swan never thought this way before and wondered if the scattering of his dad could also be a dedication to his younger brother, although none of this mattered.

Swan was now feeling relief and with less guilt for the past. Now, he is worried about the future.

The wedding was only a few days away. The mundane chat of everyday life and adult conversations about the weather being surprisingly nice and a chance to hang clothes out to dry will be spoken once more over pasta and wine.

He was lucky to have Marie, but worried about telling her about his past, and why there is dust in his hair.

*

The kitchen of the Rosiemon's residence has an aroma that cannot be beat. A homely scent mixed with the familiarity of cigarette smoke and home-made dinners. Ben is sitting at the table, confused why there're handwritten notes in between the sheets of his finished novel.

Bob puts three bowls and spoons on the table and points to the notes.

"She was at it last night." he says.

With a wisp of a grin.

He then cracks two beers as the front door slams. He cracks another beer for Sam as she is shouting from the hallway.

"I smell moo moo stew." she says as she is entering the kitchen, surprised, yet happy to see Ben.

She points at her notes as she goes to kiss Bob on the cheek and take the beer. Ben rises from the chair with a handful of papers and gets a hug from her.

"You've seen my notes then, Benny boy?" Sam asks.

He looks over at Bob, who is clearly avoiding all contact by having his back to the two, stirring his beef stew that's simmering on the stove.

"Yep." Ben says.

Hoping that was to be the end of the subject.

"I thought we could look over a few things after dinner?" Sam suggests.

She goes to the cupboards.

"Any bread?" she asks.

Bob takes the stew pot to the table.

"Where it always is."

He gets it from the bread bin.

"You named it Ben?" Bob asks.

Referring to the finished book.

Ben puts a dripping piece of bread in his mouth as he waves an index finger in the air. Sam is dipping some bread into her stew also, which drips close to the typed pages.

Ben slides them closer to himself.

"I was thinking a considerate heavy for a title?" Ben says.

Before taking a swig of beer.

Bob nods before following suit and sipping his beer too.

Sam slides the pages back over to herself and flicks through around halfway. The room falls quiet with a comfortable feeling. The air humming with good food, stale smoke and a good-looking future.

\*

# Chime of a city clock.

Professor Ziegler is leaning heavily back in his chair with interlocked fingers to his mouth with a wide stare towards his office door. On his desk sits a beautifully crafted wooden owl with copper lines and marble eyes. Next to it, an open briefcase. With the first attempt failing, Professor Ziegler was lucky to have re-investments and tight-lipped associates to ensure the second attempt would work. It did, but after underhand dealings, quiet phone calls and meetings unknown, he had finally succumbed to the reality of consequence. So having just got off the phone to the third complaint today, he thought it would be best to have a meeting with Edward Salone, the company lawyer, and Connie Hamilton, one of the company's representatives. The phone is ringing again as he is lighting a cigarette with a shaky hand. He lifts the receiver and promptly drops it back down, making ash fall over his expensive tie and as he coughs up grey fumes, is now flicking in his head the final preparations for plan B. He places the cigarette in the ashtray before taking out a single malt bottle from the bottom drawer and pours a generous amount, spilling a little as his almost transparent hands shake. A combination of age and an uncertain future. The clink of glass on his teeth does not disrupt what has been playing on his mind for quite some time now, thoughts that have since been recorded. The quiet intention known only to him will soon be in motion. Dragging with it the deep facts and truth that lie hidden behind media influence and persuasion, scientific jargon, and financial gain. He retrieves paperwork from the top desk drawer along with a VHS tape, the words 'C.O.A.C.C' stamped on it. He slips the tape into a padded envelope as the door is swinging open without a knock, and in slides Edward Salone with youthful arrogance, holding the door for Connie Hamilton to also enter. The professor places the envelope in the case, clicks it shut and leans back in his chair.

*

Soon after leaving his office, Professor Ziegler is semi-conscious in his car. He can hear sirens and shuffled speeches from who he assumes are paramedics and the rubber necking, wide eyed strangers becoming obsessed with the damage to the car. The Professor is not hurt too bad but is being treated with caution by the sweet-smelling young doctor.

"My briefcase. It was on the passenger seat." The professor whispers.

"Don't worry about that. Let's just look after you right now." The soft tone replies.

A cop is now relaying back his findings and advises down his radio of a hit and run with victim now conscious and will soon be taken to the hospital. All Ziegler can do now is wait. His patience and shock held by warm, soft latex on his cheeks.

*

Hoppers' bar is always busy. A smoky neon-drenched jazz dive with known names, small time hustles, dealers, and hang-ups. Nevertheless, it was not common to see violence or disruption in the place. Now, a new face is standing in the centre of the bar with expensive attire and a clean scent. The regulars follow with drunken love eyes as Tabby Yenta is approaching the booth where Dale Lander is sitting. He has that look that life is winning, however, still driven, and wise to the world.

Tabby clears her throat.

"Dale Lander?"

Dale looks up from his notepad.

"Yes. Hi. Ms. Yenta, right? Please, sit down."

He's flicking to a clean page in preparation of taking a few notes. As he does so, he watches the good-looking lady place herself elegantly between a sticky table and worn material. She flicks at each fingertip to help loosen the grip of material and puts the gloves in her purse.

"So, what can I do for you Ms. Yenta?"

The file was supposed to slide as Tabby pushes it. Instead, it gets stuck on the unwashed table.

"I'm asking for your assistance to document the actions of one Albert Katsav."

Tabby takes a cigarette from her purse.

"I ask contact from yourself three times a week within the duration of two weeks."

Tabby plays with the still unlit cigarette. She continues to lay out the request.

"If your work is satisfactory, then I may require your assistance further."

Tabby takes an envelope with a healthy amount of money from her coat pocket and drops it onto the table.

Dale offers her a light.

"That's a lot more than my usual fee Ms. Yenta." Dale says.

Now lighting his own cigarette.

"You want the case?" she asks.

Dale slides the money into his inside top pocket.

"Great." Tabby says.

She elegantly exits the booth. fixing her attire and stubbing her barely smoked cigarette.

The band is now tuning up and the bar is rumbling with human noise and clacks of pool balls. The TV floating like a plastic star with its glare catching few eyes with silent hypnotic frames of colour.

"All the information you need for now is in that file." Tabby says.

Holding her hand out. Dale grips it gently.

"I'll be expecting your call Mr. Lander."

"I'll be in touch Ms. Yenta."

He watches the attractive lady walking to the exit. As do other eyes, filled with drunken love and confusion. Her perfume lingering behind.

Inside the file are details for Ms. Yenta. But no picture or information of the man she searches for. He opens his notebook and flicks to a page. It reads:

CASE 1 Nick Benton. Writer's club owner, Meeting Cafe 2pm Tuesday. Settle the bill.

He begins to write a second case:

CASE 2 Katsav. Who, what, when and why! Ms. Yenta. To Do: Contact Charles Reeves for information. (addresses and connections relating to 'Katsav').

The band kicks in. Rattles of percussion with a bounce of a floppy riff by the double bass. The brass player is a new neon drenched face in the bar. New to the band. Young and sullen, 20 years younger than his fellow musicians who are well in their 60s. His trumpet rides in with a slow high squeal. Dale sinks into a natural sadness, a feeling he welcomes and has been enjoying regularly, now more so than ever. One might find Mellon collie to have no appeal, but Dale was tired, defeated yet grateful to feel something. He knew he was not alone. The guys on stage were digging into souls themselves, with the tools of music.

*

Nick Benton had hired Dale to establish whose slack hand was working for him, even after advising it was more a police matter rather than a Dick's job. Turns out it was the new girl who needed to feed a habit. She was once a good painter according to Nick but now no longer works for him for obvious reasons. The shaky hands of the bulky man have not gone unnoticed by Dale as Nick speaks with passion of the written word, once an accomplished writer himself but since dipped from any relativity in this ever-changing world so now runs a club for artists to attend. Whether musicians, painters, or writers, they sip on coffee and smoke little weed pipes. A generation lost to Nick, nevertheless, it keeps him indulged and happy seeing varying art still loved by many. Dale lights a cigarette as the hefty man talks of a political thriller he was working on for some time, before dropping it completely. A world with consequences for those that do not fit with or have desire to meet common expectations of the human condition. Dale liked the sound of it and thought it was a book he might like to read. He wondered how he had become friendly with the man who clearly has passion and talent. To befriend an ex-client was not the norm and indeed found himself side-eyeing the big man, like there was something underneath the pleasantries and the offer of free coffee and with his obvious talent for writing.

*

The information given to Dale was promising. For a few notes and a drink, Charles Reeves would provide an address or two as requested. Dale had used Charles's services previously and is keen to keep him on side for the time being. Especially now as he clicks his 35mm Konica behind a tree as the person he assumes is Albert Katsav is leaving his house. As he steps down towards his expensive silver machine, he stops dead. This pushes Dale fully behind the bark like he was certain Katsav knew he was being watched. Then again, the green leaves, well-kept gardens and birds chirping have Dale feeling like a carrot at a mushroom convention in this quiet and peaceful part of town. His stubble and tired eyes with a second cigarette hanging from his mouth as the first still burns at his feet. A well-groomed lady in her 50s taps on heels with a poodle tapping along beside her. Both side-eyeing the strange man as he peers back round the bark to see Katsav's car sinking out of view through dipped branches. His eye now catching the residence once again as a freshly made-up lady pulls the heavy curtains open, exposing expensive decoration and a piano. Dale clicks a few more off the roll towards the presumed Mrs. Katsav. Not noticing Albert Katsav has since crept three corners to park behind to observe him.

Albert glares with intent, and with a crease of confusion.

\*

The slim young man has not long been with the production company, a job that pays well, has its own parking space and a relevantly nice office, not as flash as the floors above but impressive enough. The problem was, Tommy Henderson still did not know how he got the work in media and television, not at this level. He wondered if he should start paying more detail to his work, feeling like he would be deemed a fraud any day now. He was not even wearing a tie but wearing a nice sharp suit.

Alongside Tommy is a fresh-faced lady around 23 years old. Tommy knows she is a temp as she has around her neck a company ID badge that only allows access to certain parts of the building. They are smiling at each other, but his smile is cut as he can feel a sharp elbow in his ribs as Albert Katsav is squeezing between the two, towering above the petite lipstick. He looks Tommy in the eye as people are piling from the elevator. All dressed the same, only recognized by the slither of colour hanging from their necks and what access they possess around the secure vast building. Albert steps into the elevator first. Tommy holds his hand out to gesture for the temp to go in next. He then follows as the doors are closing.

No one is talking and Tommy's floor cannot come sooner. The doors open, where Tommy turns and flicks his index finger from his forehead.

"Good luck Ms." Tommy says.

Glaring hard at Albert as the doors are closing.

The ninth floor has windows from the floor to the ceiling and a thick red carpet.

Albert is stomping heavily over it after watching the backside of the young temp walk off to find the reception for directions of where she needs to be. In his office, Albert uncaps a single malt from the bottom drawer. The doctor told him not to drink, but the advice was ignored by Albert and instead, swallowed down. He then dials a number. An automated answering service rings out. Albert hits one on the pad before having to go through the options. The generic 'on hold' music has him removing the receiver from his ear and is now pouring another scotch.

The automated voice vibrates on the desk.

"Pharm-Tech Corp is proud to be leader in modern science... Please hold and we will be with you shortly..."

Albert slams the phone back in the cradle as there is a soft tap on the door before it opens.

"Mr. Katsav."

The temp is smiling and tucking her long soft blonde hair behind her left ear.

"I've been briefed, so I'm here to help."

"Just answer any calls, take messages and, a little later, I'll take you to lunch." Katsav says. His eyes running slowly up her body.

"Thank you, but the girls have invited me to the cafeteria for lunch." The temp says sternly. Her words have gone unheard and Albert waves her away as the phone is ringing.

Her smile dips as she turns to leave.

"Katsav here."

The voice on the other end tells Albert he has what was asked for and they arrange to meet. Katsav is ready to hang up. But not before the caller demands more than agreed, as the job was not one that he would usually involve himself in. Albert reminds the caller of the agreed fee, then hangs up. Tapping his glass and sucking the scent of scotch, he scans his options. He dials a number.

"Dr Burroughs, Albert Katsav. We met a short time ago. Yeah, well, I need to see you. Yeah, I have the money. How soon?"

Albert hangs up.

*

From the booth, the band are mere silhouettes as neon drapes around them with regular intervals of light shining from the street beyond glass. This dank lighting, however, cannot mask the strung-out redhead with sunken eyes, sipping on a gin through a pink straw that is doing nothing to soften her dry lips. No concern for anything and no care for others. Just another face in a crowd, though Dale thought the petite frame and splashed freckles gave her an edge that some may warm to. She begins to beeline for him, more so the seat on the other side of the booth table and he is reverting his vision as she approaches.

"Mind if I sit?" she asks.

"Be my guest." Dale says.

Thinking now she looks more sober than she did mere seconds ago. He again reverts vision, now watching people enter and leave the bar. His knowledge and experience of this place and the occupants crowding the walls will prevail soon. The lady will no doubt tap him for a smoke or money or a favour of some sort. Instead, the freckled lady puts her own cigarette in her mouth and lights it with a book of her own matches.

"I'm Maddy."

She holds out her hand, which has on it dried paint. A streak of red and a fading splat of black on her thin thumb.

Dale grips the hand gently. Surprised at how warm and soft it is.

"Dale."

"You waiting for someone, Dale?"

"Is that a line?" Dale asks with half-closed eyes before clapping as the band is stepping off stage for a break.

He has seen a dozen a week of people like Maddy. Nevertheless, he was more intrigued by this one and wondered what she looked like in the natural light.

"What do you do for bread, Dale?"

He is unsure whether to tell her but does not see any reason to lie.

"I'm a private investigator. Just starting out." Dale says.

She bangs the table and smiles widely. Her freckles blending.

"Well, I'll be. I've never met a P.I before. Not that I know of anyway. Tell me more."

"Nothing much to tell, really."

Dale smiles and shrugs.

"Oh. I get ya. Loose lips and all that." she says.

Now tapping her nose and winking. Only then to sniff hard and scratch her arm. Another typical gesture witnessed by Dale plenty of times when he was on the force. Kicking concrete and trying to be fair to the community.

"You drive Maddy?"

"Yeah. Why?"

"How about another drink? My shout." Dale says.

He is leaving the booth holding his glass up and checking he has all his belongings. He's hoping to get a ride around with his new asset. Never judge a book, Dale. He tells himself as he is walking to the bar. 'But keep them at arm's length, too.' He smiles and watches the freckled lady through the mirror tiles behind the bar area, thinking a car of his own was to be the next investment. Perhaps use the fee from Tabby for a nice cheap roll around.

*

In the busy, elegant cafe Elaine Katsav had been expecting her husband for the last forty-five minutes and giving him the benefit of doubt that being high in the TV and media game, she expected him to have late nights and business meetings. But she was wise enough to know there was something not right. For the brief time she had known Albert and been married, she had suspected he was unfaithful and that something just does not add up. Especially when he insists on having nothing to share from his past and, at times, has become defensive when questioned on such a subject. So, while pouring cream into her coffee, Elaine wonders again, what reason did they each have to rush into marriage? She did not find her husband attractive. In fact, she regarded him unpleasant but still thrived to make his life comfortable. Caring what he thinks but for her to not have merit for her actions. The trip to Italy the third week of knowing one another was a nice touch, but was only to charm, blind her from reality and show off his wallet. Now, no silk, diamonds or plane tickets are going to take away her reality. She has begun to roll with the crudeness, accept it, for now she is finding solace in home furnishings and decoration magazine subscriptions. So, after finishing her coffee, Elaine made up her mind. She takes a calling card from her purse and heads to the old-looking telephone booth with light varnished wood and clean glass. Elaine found it very fitting with the rest of the café, with its dark green decoration and brass throughout. Inspiration for her kitchen, she thought. Admiring the environment as she is dialing a number.

Meanwhile, Dale runs up the stairs to catch the ringing phone. His clients assume he has his own office, car and at least one telephone. Instead, he is relying on the payphone in the hallway of his rooming house.

"Pink Moon private investigators. Dale Lander speaking."

The quick response pulls Elaine back. She now staggers for words.

"Erm...yes, erm..."

Dale takes his notepad from his pocket. Pulling the pen lid off with his teeth.

"Can I help?" he says with a mumble.

"It's my husband. I'm sure he's having an affair, or flings. I don't know."

Elaine is watching the steam expel from the coffee machine. The bell at the top of the door rings as a young couple enters. Wrapped around one another and smiling.

"Do you have an office I can visit? There's no address on your card."

"How about the Station Cafe? We can meet there." Dale says.

"That'll be fine. I need proof. I can pay whatever you need."

"The fee is minimal at this time Ms...?"

Dale is ready to scribble the name down.

"Katsav. Mrs. Elaine Katsav."

Dale's inhale is sharp, but he has time to take the phone from his mouth. He replaces it to his ear and keeps composed.

"Sorry, did you say Katsav?" Dale asks.

"That's correct. Is there a problem?"

"No. No problem. I just want to make sure I have the correct details, that's all." Dale says in a reassuring tone.

"So is 1pm tomorrow OK with you Mrs. Katsav?" he asks.

"Yes. Thank you."

"Can you also bring with you a picture of your husband? A recent one that he won't miss. Thank you." Dale hangs up.

He's staring at a hole in the wall for a few seconds and then heads for his room. A small compact rectangle, no bigger than a prison cell tucked away on the second floor of the 12-room building.

*

The wind is howling for the plague of gagged screams and shouts from faceless visitors slipping from under locked doors with contouring bodies and with arms stretched. Their presence is blistering the air and whistling around corners while scraping on concrete with blood stains and grinding dust. Tommy is swept off his feet, now watching the twirling sky and its static heat from the wet street below it, with its dim streetlamps only managing crawling slithers onto the buildings. Suddenly, there is a loud bang and a glaring light. Popping Tommy's ears and blinding him, and although numb and senseless, he is aware that breath continues to flow. Tommy now shakes awake from the nightmare. The feeling of death is in slumber with damp sheets and his familiar surroundings. He writes the trauma down in a frantic manner, rushed as he is recalling the nightmare, then shaken from his scribbles, as metal is being manipulated. Someone is trying to break in. Quietly, he climbs from his bed, slowly walking to the front door of his one-bedroom apartment. The baseball bat leans on the wall. Through the peephole, there is a man in dark clothes bending over as he is digging at the lock. Tommy takes a step back and is in shock as the door clicks unlocked. The baseball bat is now in both hands, raised in the air and ready to be swung. A shoulder now protruding into the apartment, Tommy jabs the bat blindly through the gap with contact made harshly, the shoulder disappearing back into the corridor of the modest and overpriced apartment building. Scampering feet now dispersing. With the adrenaline pumping, Tommy flings the door open and is running after the chancer, only when reaching the stairs, he cannot see nor hear anyone. Even heading to the corridor window, no shadow or heavy steps are on the quiet street

*

Professor Zeigler has just arrived home after being treated at the after-care unit of the private hospital at the insistence and expense of the company. Even the taxi driver was over helpful as the Professor scrapes himself out of the cab and is steadying himself with his stick. The professor frees himself from the grip and tells the cab driver he can manage on his own as he is observing a TV repair van, wondering why the two occupying the vehicle are not repairing anything. The driver takes a 20 note and after being told to keep the change, he sits in his cab and watches the Professor enter his home.

Inside, the darkness has a red piercing light through it in the corner as the twelve messages on the machine are trying to attract attention. He hears the first one, something about insurance. He deletes it before picking up the phone. Now it was his turn to contribute to flashing lights of urgency by leaving his own message.

"Ms. Yenta. Professor Zeigler. I'm hoping you are close to fulfilling my little ask?"

He drops the phone down and pulls the cord from the wall and flicks the lamp on. The bottle of malt was ready for him, as was his groove in his favorite chair. He pours a healthy amount of whiskey and goes to draw the curtains, the TV van now slowly passing with dim lights and glares from the two inside. He decides he will not spend long at home and will find a hotel for a night or two.

*

The station cafe, named purely as it is the first caffeine fix for those arriving in the city, was never quiet. Luggage were obstacles for those consuming with the waitresses seemly experienced in balancing trays of hot beverages as they maneuver between and around cases and legs, with dipping accents asking for everything from a simple flat to salted and spiced drinks. All rebounded with a sweet smile and a polite point to the board of choices. Nimble slim fingers matching their waists and flat feet. Dale is watching one of the slim workers blow hair from her vision as she dips teabags into a small silver pot. The waitress flustered and had better places to be but at the same time her demeanor still shining with warmth and innocent professionalism. The steam whistles and bellows as Elaine enters.

Dale could see that Mrs. Katsav, previously known as Mrs. Tyler, was a looker in her younger days but now has to pretend he did not know what she was to look like.

"Mrs. Katsav?" Dale asks.

She nods and they shake hands before Elaine slides her long expensive gloves off and sits. The steps of the waitress find their way to the table. Dale opts for a strong black coffee where Elaine looks with a squinted vision at the board of choices before deciding on a flat white. They both thank the waitress as she heads to make the order. Dale leans back to retrieve cigarettes from his inside pocket.

"Now, how can I be of assistance?" he asks.

"Just like to confirm my suspicions." Elaine replies.

"You been married long?"

Dale offers her a cigarette, but it is waved away with an expensive hand. Her wedding band is elegant yet crude in price.

"Couple of months. It's embarrassing really. I guess I missed company after my first husband passed away suddenly. I was silly to rush into things." Elaine says.

Her tone was sounding rehearsed.

"Loves' complicated Mrs. Katsav. We're conditioned to some extent. And I'm sorry to hear of your loss."

Dale lights his cigarette and is watching Elaine to get a better angle of her.

"May I ask what happened? To your late husband?" Dale asks.

He did, however, know what happened to him, as did anyone who had the newspapers a little while ago. He also had associates who had worked on the case.

Elaine is stumbling for words.

"Erm. It was sudden. His heart."

"I see. Well, in relation to Mr. Katsav. I can follow him. Document movements. Let you know where he frequents, who he sees. That sound OK?"

"I appreciate it. Thanks."

Elaine pulls a picture of Albert out of her purse along with a piece of folded paper.

"This is his work and our home address. My numbers are on there too. Only call during the daytime if you don't mind. This is him."

She slides the picture across and taps twice on the forehead of the suited round man.

"Consider it done Mrs. Katsav."

He puts the photo and paper in his inside pocket as the waitress arrives with their order.

"And the fee?"

Elaine now has a palm full of money.

Dale stubs his cigarette.

"Don't worry about the fee for now. Call this a welcome gift."

Elaine slides the crisp notes back into her purse.

"If you insist. Thank you."

The two now share a quiet moment amongst whistling steam, out-of-town accents, and clinking cutlery.

*

The streets at dawn on this side of town can be vibrant, but this morning, the air is still. Only shallow wisps of traffic and litter sucking onto Maddy's hub caps as she is composing herself well after her last hit. Dale is approaching the beat-up car with caution. He wants to be sure he's not climbing into a trap. Especially with his Nishika N8000 camera around his neck. It was not worth much but had some value to him personally. He climbs in.

"I was half expecting you not to show."

Dale now looks around and into the review mirror.

"Because my sort are unreliable?" she asks.

Maddy scratches her arm. Then wipes her nose on her sleeve.

"I need the money." she says sternly.

She is embarrassed and fed up.

Though Dale was not buying it. He had seen many Maddy's before, and no trick was new to him. She did indeed stick to her word, however. Even if it were just for the need of money. Dale just hoped she was not too high to kill them both or to be pulled over by a fellow ex-colleague. She starts the car, which coughs dirty smoke from the pipe of the brown beast into an already dirty air. She lights a cigarette as Dale scratches around for a seatbelt.

*

The coughing rusty beast has eventually got a mirror on Katsav as Dale is fishing two Co-codamol from the glove box for Maddy, who is now crashing. She swallows down the pills swiftly with a heavy gulp as without water they would quickly fizzle and dissolve.

The coughing exhaust takes a rest as Katsav parks up behind a row of warehouses. Cigarettes are lit, belts are clicked free, and windows are down. Maddy slides into her seat with half-closed eyes.

"What's he doing?" she asks.

Her cigarette ash dropping on her shirt.

"Looks like he's waiting for someone." Dale says.

Maddy chucks herself forward to aim her ash towards the tray.

"Wanna hear a joke? It's about a politician and a whore." she asks.

"I thought all jokes with a politician involved a whore?" Dale asks with a smile.

His attention was still on the expensive car with an expensive suit inside. He throws his cigarette out the window and winds it up slightly. Leaving an inch gap.

"Go on. I bite." he says.

Maddy stubs her smoke and sits a little more upright. Her lips are dry, but she is not thirsty.

"So, a politician goes to a whorehouse. Under his arm he has a big jar of pennies. Well, the girl gets on with her thing right, until she looks over to the jar of pennies and asks if she's expected to take them as payment. The politician assures her everything will be fine and then encourages her to continue with her trick. So, after a short while, they both get dressed. The politician takes a good healthy number of banknotes from his wallet and places them next to the whore. She counts it and tells him it's too much, that it's more than the agreed amount. The politician puts the jar of pennies under his arm and says before leaving, 'Sorry, I have no change.'"

Maddy is now sitting with a cracked smile and eyebrows raised, waiting for a response.

Dale has pursed lips as he thinks about the joke, but his attention reverts to Albert, who now has company. Dale focuses through the camera lens and sees an attractive blonde. She's kissing Albert on the cheek, which has Dale's finger tapping rapidly to capture the action. Only after she heads to the front of his car, we see a thin man with stubble and a faded white shirt. It is Charles Reeves who is handing Albert a padded envelope and a handful of papers. He is a sharp contrast to the female who is blowing and popping bubblegum and trying to catch the eye of the two men loading a van in one of the bays. Charles dips out of sight and Dale assumes he has gone.

"Son of a bitch. What a storm of piss." Dale says.

This shakes Maddy from nodding.

Albert and the young blonde climb back into his car and leave.

"Let's go." Dale says.

Ensuring his seatbelt is clicked in fully.

*

Elaine's reflection in the French doors shows her styled hair, but she is wondering why she bothered. She's aware Albert has events to attend, but not once did he talk about them with her, let alone invite her. In fact, she was assuming she did not need an invitation, assuming being married was the invitation. As the birds sing and the bells on bikes chime, Elaine wonders, was it her that made people treat her in certain ways? She has never been unfaithful, not even in her school days, and never talked of anyone in a negative light as she learnt well to cope with her emotions. Her attention turns to the items on the table. There is a newspaper clipping with the headline:

'POISON SUSPECT FOUND NOT GUILTY' and 'DILAUDID POISON POSSIBLE!'

Flicking through the small leather-bound address book she finds a number and address for 'Clothes of sand' escort agency but what really catches her eye is the address for Dr Burroughs. '110th Belford East. 3rd Floor. Elaine writes this address down before returning the items to Albert's study. Replacing them exactly how she found them and puts the copy key back inside the small penguin ornament on the bedside table. She wondered what the other items were in those desk drawers, but felt ignorance was bliss nowadays. At least for now.

*

Albert's car parks up outside the River Man. A grand hotel west of the city. Pillars on each side of the entrance and large windows with draped, thick curtains. The concrete above the door has the date 1938 chiseled into it. A man in a hat and white gloves welcomes people in as Maddy's car is passing. She's looking around the street in confusion as the difference in tone, people and scent is foreign to her as opposed to life east of the city.

"I'll park up somewhere." Maddy says.

"You mind waiting for me? I won't be long. Just wanna see what the score is. In and out." Dale says.

"Sure. But yeah, be quick. I feel like a hot dog at a lobster convention round here." Maddy says as she is parking up.

"Who is that guy anyway?" she asks.

Dale climbs out of the car.

"Ask no questions, tell no lies. Sit tight." he says.

He slams the door, making the tin shake.

Maddy takes a deep breath, looks over her shoulder while her mind is playing against her. The regular digging at her eyes and unhelpful thoughts do nothing but have her wanting a hit, to hush the noise and to once again escape. The guilt of picking up the pin again hits her gut, the same way a hit does. She drives away from the clean streets with nothing but heroin on her brain.

\*

Lounge music waves over in small intervals as Dale is venturing into the hotel lobby, bustling with businessmen in button downs and journalists. The board resting on an easel type shelf at the reception has times and names of guest speakers and live entertainment for the 'Media and Hospitality' conference.

Dale Spots Katsav's name on the board. He clicks his fingers while looking to see a sign above, directing him toward the bar. As far as anyone was concerned, he was just another hack from another rag that no one reads. Through the thick wooden door, the bar is as busy as the suits checking in. There, in the corner, Albert Katsav sits with a scotch in one hand with the other on the leg of the same bubble gum popping blonde from the warehouse units. Dale orders dark rum and with just a lick of coke, then wonders how much it was going to cost. As it's served, he leans in and tells the barman to put it on Albert Katsav's bill. A nod from the bartender has Dale smiling. During this time, the grey suit is now talking to a heavy-set man with a deep stare towards Dale. He knows he has been rumbled. But how? No time to dwell, Dale thought and hurries his drink as the two men leave with the young blonde hanging off Albert's arm. Dale thought he was in the wrong business. Whatever business this was.

Two gentlemen are manning the main conference door. They stop the only man with no I.D and four-day stubble.

"I.D please sir." The one on the right asks.

"The boss has it. He's already in there." Dale says as he attempts to slip between the two men.

Resembling a slim car through the two buffering posts at a car wash.

"I'm afraid no I.D, no go." The monkey says gently yet sternly.

Dale sees Albert pointing over at the door and his gut is telling him something. Time to go. Nearly at the exit. Dale turns to see the heavy-set man heading for him, along with a friend. He's then grabbed, and his camera is being lifted over his neck.

"Be cool or be hurt." The heavy-set man says.

Dale is being ushered back into the hotel. The action is drawing attention, but the young skirts and rich suits are just keeping their business to themselves, only occasionally leaning and whispering for a short moment as the three men are passing. Dale lands in a heap inside what he has established as a cleaning closet. Mops, brooms and chemicals. The door squeaks closed, with a lock ringing out as well. He rushes to the door, kicking it and shouting to be let out. An ear to the door proves no one is returning and the chance of being saved looks slim, as is the window. No chance he will get through. The vent, however, appears wide enough after Dale eyeballs his belly, then the gap. He is smiling at the cliché as he steps upwards. Lifting the metal grill and scrambling in. The hatch swings back into his legs, trapping him for a second as he crawls on his hands and knees. The thin metal sheets clunking and dipping with his weight.

"I have no change..."

Dale stops crawling.

"Shit, that is a funny joke."

Suddenly, the metal sheets creak and slide apart. Dale falls through and lands on hard ground in the lady's bathroom. With the added chaos of females screaming as debris showers the ground. A few of the ladies are hurling past him for the exit, while others stay in their cubicles. After rolling a little in agony, Dale gets to his feet and dusts himself off.

"Ladies." Dale says.

Flicking an index finger from his forehead and then leaving promptly with a limp and a hand cupping his back.

*

Charles Reeves is cautious. His feet pounding on the concrete of one of the quieter streets east of the city. Reluctant to head to the neon and forever traffic but as he knows nothing of the bag of pharmaceuticals he has stolen from the post office, and as he has no desire to entangle himself in substances that he is unfamiliar with, feels there is no other option but to risk attempting palming off the various pills and liquids to someone on the main street. He was becoming ever more anxious as sirens whaled over the cloudy sky, bouts of people hitting the walls of the establishments, one being a head shop. Outside stands a thin man licking up a tailor made. Slim and unwell looking. Charles takes a breath and, without missing a beat, gets the attention of the smoker.

"Hey man." Charles says quietly.

Now looking around the street, but no one looks at all interested. Instead, they go about their own self ways.

"What can I do for you, my friend?" The thin man asks.

Lighting his cigarette.

The flash of flame shows how dark and dead his eyes are.

Charles was unsure if the man had misunderstood, that he had something Charles may want.

"Looking to get rid of some stuff. Don't care where or what price." Charles says.

"What you got?"

Charles holds the bag up. He then eyes the man up. Certain he would have no issue with overpowering or getting advantage on the dopey kid if he had to defend himself.

Charles opens the bag, exposing a box addressed to Dr. Burroughs and one addressed to a pharmacy north of the city. The bottles of liquid clink against one another and range in size from a single dose to 250ml. The pills, in blister packs and thin boxes. The thin man gestures for his seller to follow him to the side road. Charles does so with a cautious step or two behind. Halfway down the alley, the thin man slides around and faces Charles.

"I've got no interest in what's in your bag."

He cups Charles's crotch gently.

"I do, however, have an interest in other things." The thin man says.

Charles punches the thin man in the face and backs up a few steps. He then rushes the startled bloody man, knocking him cleanly to the ground. Litter is blowing as the thin body is struck twice more with sharp jabs. The lip bust with a cut eyebrow. The nose swelling but not broken. The thin man is limp.

Going through the pockets of the barely conscious kid, Charles finds a small address book. As he flicks the pages, he sees the name 'Dr Henry Burroughs' 110th Belford East.' He looks down at the man who is now more composed, shaking, and uncertain. Charles, for the second time in a short while, feels guilty and disgusted with himself. He walks away quickly before setting out on a jog toward the doctor's office.

\*

The office was not what Charles was expecting. Hit with stale smoke and dust as he is stepping further into the space, not noticing sat in the corner, Dr Burroughs watching the uninvited man and is now quietly sliding his works down the side of the chair. He had barely had a fix, just enough to take the pinch off his hip and continue with appointments before hearing someone approach, then be surprised to see someone enter. Charles, now feeling like he is being watched, spins to face the old man dipped in the chair.

"And who may I ask are you, young feller?" Henry asks.

Composing himself well, considering he's just sunk junk into his barely pumping vein.

Charles is looking over the office. Dusty frames on the walls, newspapers, and reference books stacked below the window and on the desk. The name Dr Henry Burroughs badly stenciled on the rigid glass door.

"Got your address from a friend, says you might be able to help." Charles says.

Henry has since lifted himself from the chair. The arm of it bearing weight and he is now using his walking stick to hobble toward his polluted desk. He's not convinced of the explanation of the uninvited man with a bag that is rattling a familiar sound. And although the man was leaner, quicker, and most likely no better than anyone else who passed the threshold, he had no concern for his safety. The heroin would help bounce off any pain upon him anyway.

"A friend you say."

Henry drops in to his chair.

"I've got these."

Charles tips the contents of the bag. Boxes of pills bounce off papers with the bottles of liquid rolling until abruptly stopped by an item on the desk. Charles sighs. As if relieved to not have them on his person anymore.

"How about a drink?" Henry asks.

He's fumbling to his feet. The heroin is now deep in the system. Seeing Henry struggle, Charles offers to pour the gins. He helps himself to a healthy, overpolite amount before handing the Dr one who has since sat back down and is looking over the items.

Some of which have his address on or for back alley pharms he often writes scripts for. He decides, however, to let this slide. Keep as much of the peace and a desk between them. Life was too short for the old timer. He knew, however, that the stranger needed something, his professional bet, that something was booze, especially as Charles was getting his third glass of gin. His dry complexion and scent were a big giveaway. Henry catches sight of the logo on the stained shirt above him.

"Thallium. Sealed too. A few of these are squares. No use to junky nor man. This, however, is of interest."

The doc picks up a bottle of Dilaudid.

"Your name is on a few of them my friend. So, I figure it's only fair to pay me for the safe return of em, right?"

Henry continues to play it safe but sees an opportunity to gain from this strange meeting. He unlocks the desk drawer, taking out crisp notes and dropping them on top of the copy of G.P monthly magazine. Charles was now harshing Henry's mellow.

"I'll pay you this much for the items here."

Henry is holding the money in the air. Exposing his almost transparent hands.

Suddenly, the door creaks open. Henry checks his watch. Charles is surprised to see the familiar suit and red cheeks of Albert Katsav but plays ignorant with the two just staring at one another as Charles was leaving. Closing the door behind him.

"You have my order?" Albert asks the doctor as he sits down.

Henry opens a small rectangle leather case, exposing a set of scales. The other drawer has various drugs in it. He takes the opportunity here to place his new purchases of substances into it. He weighed out a little short of the order, knowing full well the dope wasn't for Albert, and was indeed clueless to it all. Henry wraps the gear in a small plastic bundle as Albert counts out some money, splashing it onto the desk.

"See ya doc."

Albert leaves.

Henry waits a few seconds before picking up the phone and dialing.

"Hi. Dr Henry Burroughs here. Are you still requiring a particular substance...Yes, Dilaudid. I must advise it's going to be a little on the expensive side."

He lights a cigarette as the voice on the other end advises there is no issue of cost and will visit Henry within the hour. Henry agrees and hangs up. The dust now dancing with the light from the quick sinking sun, gleaming on the frames of the hanging pictures and certifications. Henry reminds himself, not for the first time, to lock the door between appointments.

*

The newspaper reads '5-year-old still missing!' Elaine's attention is on the headline as she listens to Dale on the phone. He is trying hard to be delicate but knows he must lay facts down. He advises he had documented Albert entertaining a young blonde at a conference, but at this time can't say for certain there was anything too untoward.

"I'm sorry for having to break such news. Perhaps the notion that circumstances may be of an innocent one." Dale says.

He knows the words he had just spoken were not to be true but thought it best to say something remotely positive.

"Well, in the grand scheme of things, I shouldn't have the right to complain." Elaine says.

"Pardon me Mrs. Katsav?"

"In the papers. That poor child is missing. I bet his parents are beside themselves. Poor things. I have no right to complain about my life. I mean...I know you, well."

She then falls sharply silent.

Dale feels the strange tone from Elaine. But he understands what she was attempting to get at.

"I'm going to waiver the fee for this assignment, Mrs. Katsav. I just hope whatever you choose to do with this information will have you see a better future for yourself."

"That's very kind but I really don't mind the fee."

"Forget it. Really."

Dale decides not to push further about Albert. Tabby Yenta did not ask him to document his affairs, so he did not think bringing anything else up was beneficial. Just allow Elaine to deal with what she knows, or thinks she knows of her husband in her own way.

"All the best Mrs. Katsav." Dale hangs up.

*

The streetlamps are pouring slithers of light below onto Albert, who is leaning through the window of the passenger side of Maddy's car. Between his fingers, a bag of heroin dangles. Done to tease and mock Maddy, who is sitting slumped at the wheel. He is tapping the small bag on the inside of the door.

"You don't deserve this you know. You haven't done what was asked." Albert says.

A twisted face at the redhead.

Maddy's arm is reaching out slowly to take the dangling treat from the thick fingers, but the small wrap is flipped out of her grasp.

"He's no further forward, right?" Maddy says.

"No thanks to you. Who is he anyway? What does he want?"

She lights a cigarette. Her attention still on the baggy, now hidden from sight.

"Can I get my payment?" Maddy asks.

Her arm is outstretched with an open palm.

Albert looks around the dirty streets and gives her the dope.

She inspects it and puts it in the glove box.

"His name's Dale. A P.I." Maddy says as she is starting the car.

Albert is beside himself now. Red faced and angry.

"He's an investigator?"

Albert climbs into the passenger side and grabs Maddy by the hair.

"You stupid bitch! Who hired him? What does he want?"

His grip tightens.

Maddy grabs his wrist and gets free.

"Get off me." she says in a stern tone.

"I was just playing along with what he asked. Thought it best. I'll get more out of him next time I see him. I cannot just ask random questions, you know. He'll get suspicious."

Albert gets out of the car. Again, he leans into it.

"Find out what he wants, or you'll be crawling the streets again for your drugs."

Albert now leaves.

Maddy rubs her head to ease the pain of having her hair pulled. Her lips pursed.

"Prick." she says.

She drives off.

*

Jane Crawford hands Dale a coffee. He takes a polite sip before placing it on the coffee table and takes his notebook out. As he does, he admires the warmth and decoration of the lounge. And the family home itself, with the mantel piece housing framed pictures and porcelain figures.

"So, I understand your little boy Johnny was, er..."

"What is it you want exactly?" Jim interrupts.

"Jim!"

Jane is giving her husband the generic look of disgust and embarrassment.

"This is the private investigator I told you about Jim. He may be able to help."

Dale is now stashing his notebook away as he gets up from the chair.

"I'm sorry. I didn't mean to intrude. Perhaps I just leave my card with you."

He flicks one out of his pocket and puts it next to the coffee cup.

The room falls quiet, only broken by heavy breaths from Jim.

Dale is now heading for the door while Jim is quietly yet sternly talking to Jane.

"Have you forgotten what I did for a job? Besides, we can't afford a P.I Jane." Jim says.

"I'm sorry. I should have advised you on the phone. I'm not looking to gain financially from this. There's no charge for this service, Mr. and Mrs. Crawford."

"Why offer your services for free Mr..."

"Lander."

Dale goes to scoop his business card up from the table. Holding it in the air between his index and middle finger before holding it out for Jim to take.

"I'll be in my study." Jim says.

Now gripping his wife's shoulder gently before leaving the room.

"He feels helpless." Jane says.

"It's understandable. A parent's worst nightmare. I assume he's been asked not to involve himself in the case. Because of being a retired detective?"

Jane expels a belated and relieving heavy breath with tears streaming.

"Mr. Lander. I'm beside myself. We were suspects of this."

She walks to the coffee table to tear out a tissue from the box.

"Our child is missing, he may even…"

Again, she is crying hard. Her shoulders bouncing up and down as she sobs. Dale can only follow Jim's example and gently pinches her left shoulder.

"I know this is painful, Mrs. Crawford."

Jane just shakes her head and wipes her tears away.

"I'll be in touch. I'll see myself out." Dale says.

*

Throughout the years, the bar had established a stronghold on bands and musicians, nowadays, only crackled jazz hits the walls from a record player. Once named 'Achilles Last Stand', the place is now known as 'the writer's club.' So called because the only occupants being poets and authors along with hang ups that dominate the damp and cramped space. Free coffee on the counter and scattered books across tables and glossed bookshelves. Paul Duval is rubbing his trumpet with a soft yellow cloth as he is watching two young ladies, no more than eighteen years old, who are flicking ash from long cigarettes and picking at their teeth. Paul's own cigarette drops from his lips as a rolled-up copy of the daily newspaper clips the side of his head. Followed by a click of fingers.

"Hey. Casanova. You need to blink, my friend. Or else you'll get eye strain. Or a reputation." Nick says.

Dale enters. Seeing Nick and heads for the table.

"Good to see ya, Dale boy. Let me introduce you two." Nick says.

Nick sits up a little and holds his arm with a flat palm towards Paul.

"Paul. This is Dale Lander." Dale. This is Paul Duval."

The two are squaring each other up. Dale just nods an appreciation at Paul. Paul returns a nod back.

"Excuse me a minute."

Paul stands and replaces the trumpet into the ragged edged case before heading to the counter for some sugar.

"Something I said?" Dale asks with a sarcastic tone.

He lights a cigarette and looks over the questionable room.

Nick just shrugs and sips his coffee. He wipes his chin before deciding to answer.

"He's an odd one. But aren't we all?"

"You know him long?" Dale asks.

"Not too long, no. He's looking to get back into the scene."

Nick points to the trumpet case.

Dale is watching Paul with a questionable eye. The music man dressed well, with sharp clean shoes to match. The eyes of Paul fixed on the two girls with their long cigarettes. Their thighs shine in the dim light hanging over them. Nick is now scanning the room of his club. He is aware of the damp and the old man that sits quietly and frequently in the corner. Only there for the small warmth and safety from the streets that growl and grunt around them. He catches Dale, who has a deep thoughtful stare now. Dale feels the stare.

"Your friend may need to wear shades if he's gonna stare so hard." Dale says.

Without a joking manner.

"You said he's odd, right?" Dale stubs his smoke. "How odd are we talking?"

Nick is just giggling and shrugging before pouring a coffee.

"The rain falls on us all, kid." Nick says.

*

Later that night, Dale is in Hopper's bar. The pull of the female vocals is fresh and inviting and welcoming, along with the familiarity of the band. This is interrupted by Charles, however, who has not just blocked Dale's view but is now shouting over the beautiful sounds.

"How you getting on. My info bang on for ya, my friend?" Charles asks.

Stumbling over his own feet.

"Good enough, though I think I'll hit up a few other connections next time, conflict of interest you see." Dale shouts back.

Charles has some clue that Dale knows something, but the booze makes him forget he should care or at least think about enquiring further about Dale's comment. Instead, Charles just tips his head, raises his glass, and is now stumbling away.

"Wait a minute."

Dale takes his small notepad out. Writes Tabby Yenta's name on a sheet and tears it off and hands it to Charles.

"Need information on her. Can you do that?" Dale asks.

"What about your other awesome connections, eh?"

Charles takes the piece of paper, looks at the name and places the slip in his pocket.

"Half now." Charles is demanding.

Dale gives Charles some money. This too gets slid into the dirty pocket.

"Tomorrow. 2pm. Here." Charles says as he stumbles away.

Dispersing through the smoke and neon, now being replaced by an unsteady and high Maddy. Sipping gin through a straw.

"Hey Dale."

Her eyes dripping over her freckled cheeks.

"How you been? Still gumshoeing?" she asks.

"Yep." Dale says in a tone of annoyance.

"So, you haven't forgotten who I am then? On the account of leaving me to walk for miles. With a bad back no less."

She takes one of his cigarettes and lights it with a confused expression.

"Huh?"

"The hotel Maddy. You left me there. Ring any bells?"

Maddy clicks her fingers and exhales a cloud, which cuts the dim light above the booth.

She answers like it's no big deal.

"Oh, right yeah. You were gone a while, Dale boy."

She flicks her ash and looks over the bar.

Dale is counting a small amount of money out. He holds it up in the dirty light before slapping it on the table.

"What's that?" Maddy asks.

Pointing to the money.

"For the ride. Gonna need you again in fact. When ya little more sober, that is."

He finishes his drink.

"I'm straight Dale boy. Like an arrow."

"If you insist."

He gets up awkwardly as his back is throbbing in pain.

"Where you going?" she asks.

"I dunno, west side I guess."

He heads for the exit through the crowds, smoke and vibrant jazz. The female vocals still tingling on his neck. Maddy slurps the rest of her drink and then follows.

*

Maddy's car is parked at the corner of the Katsav residence. The leaves blow gently with calm air around. A family in the small park plays and laughs and Dale watches them with an emotionally cracked smile.

"We look outta place. Like mushrooms at a leek convention." Maddy says.

Her comment snaps Dale back into the space, where he chuckles before nodding to agree with the freckled face. Her high is still present but clearly dipping now.

"So, what's the plan Dale boy?"

He is in pain from his fall, from the worn seat, and just irritated with everything else.

"I have no idea." he says.

Again, now looking towards the families in the park.

"Why you following this guy anyway?" Maddy asks.

"Sorry. Confidential."

Dale lights a cigarette and rolls the window down. Now hearing innocence from across the street. He exhales the smoke, more than a by-product from defeat and loss rather than trying to rid the toxins inhaled. He arches his back and lets out a whimper. Maddy reaches into the glove box and takes two pills from a capped bottle.

"Here. Take these."

She is holding out a cupped palm with two pills in it.

"No way. I ain't needing downers kid. No thank you."

Dale is again watching the family and flicks ash out of the window, which flutters back into the car and onto his thigh. He wipes it away.

"There only 500's. They'll take the nip from ya." Maddy says with raised eyebrows, dragging eyes with her freckles pronounced in the clean heat and pale skin.

"What are they?" he asks.

She shrugs her shoulders with pursed lips.

"Don't know. Co-codemol. I think."

"You keep them. You need them more than I do." Dale says as he flinches with a tingle of pain in his lower back.

Maddy is not convinced, but she will not push, so she just puts the pills into the holder between seats.

"How long you been a P.I then?" Maddy asks.

"A few months."

Dale is stubbing his smoke into the full ashtray.

"How long you been hooked on horse?" he asks.

"A few months."

Albert is dipping into his expensive car and paying no attention to anything. So much so, he was lucky to not hit the golden retriever puppy and her owner from five doors down. This shocks Maddy. She gasps as she is grabbing Dale's sleeve and squeezing it. The innocent creature is unaware of the near miss and is continuing to waddle and pant with her ears flapping in all directions. The owner watches the car roll out of view and strokes the family pet before going to tell his wife of the incident. Gossip for the next week or two for the click.

"Now what?" Maddy asks.

Dale is fed up with assignments. He also needs to contact Tabby, which he has no desire to do. He had nothing really, and he should cut ties with the junky sitting next to him.

"I'm gonna call this one a dead issue kid. Let's head off." Dale says.

Maddy turns the engine, met with a splutter. Another attempt, however, has the beast roaring, but there's smoke bellowing from behind. As the car rolls off, Albert slowly creeps up from behind. He parks up and watches Maddy's car sink to a dot.

"You stupid bitch." he shouts.

Banging the wheel before heading in the direction he had just come from. Leaving the streets again quiet except for the light breeze blowing the bubbles of the child's excitement, exploration, and wonder.

\*

Charles called Dale instead of meeting him in the bar as arranged. He still wants the other half of the money, even though he has not found a sniff on Ms. Tabby Yenta. He tells Dale there is no record of her, either in the residential files, or business and services records stored at the sorting office.

"Why don't you get one of your old cop friends to dig around for info?" Charles asks with an innocent tone.

"They're busy solving crime, that's why." Dale says sharply.

"Yeah, well zero, nada, nothing, I'm afraid. Who is she anyway? You're not stalking an ex, are ya?"

"How far afield did you look? I mean, is it rare to find no info on someone?" Dale asks.

"You tell me. After all, yer the investigator, right? So, when do I get the rest of my keb?"

"When you've earned. Stay breezy kid." Dale says.

Sharply dropping the phone back into its cradle.

*

Maddy keeps looking down at the paintbrush in her hand. The size of fifteen brushes in one. She only needs to slit a delicate few lines, no use for the giant brush like this one which is now dripping a deep red, forming a puddle which has Maddy surprised, yet delighted to see. However, on closer inspection, she realizes it is blood. She checks her hand and body with confusion, frightened now at the sight and the source of the blood streaming, harder and faster, now a spray. Holes in her arms burst.

Maddy drops heavily awake. Sweating and gasping as she is trying to gain a grip on reality. The light is heating her cold body from the slit in the curtain, making her have a sudden hard shiver. She lights a cigarette and focuses on the painting she has been spending the last few days on. The paint dry, and crumbling on the palate, just like the smack on the once shining spoon, lying on the worn carpet. A strong coffee is what she needs to help get more awake, like a tool to help against visions and vivid dreams that she cannot deny have scared her. This nightmare has shaken her to her core. Making her question what it means. Making her feel dirty, but a shower was never to be of any benefit. She is fully aware the feel of water will only resemble a storm of pins on her skin, each drop piercing her as the liquid splashes and rolls over her dehydrated body.

\*

Dishes lie dirty in the sink as the Chet Baker record collects dust, which only adds to the mood in Dale's room. Paper clippings lie on the unmade bed. One headline reads:

'COP'S DAUGHTER REMAINS FOUND; SUSPECT STILL UNKNOWN.'

Another has a picture of Dale in a police uniform. Dale scrapes the clippings up and puts them back into the shoe box. He then takes a small pile of photographs out of the box. One by one, he slowly files through them. They are of him, his now ex-wife Fran, and their four-year-old daughter. Fran. Named after her mother. Her Golden hair with a red ribbon and eyes large and wondrous like green marble. Without exception, Dale is sad. He cannot forget, but remembering is a heavy burden to bear as well. He places the photos carefully back in the box and slots them back into the gap in the cupboard. Suddenly, the door rattles as a heavy knock rings out. Dale turns Chet down.

"Who is it?" he shouts.

"It's Tabby."

A heavy sigh expels from Dale as he is looking over the room, ashamed of the state of it. Reluctantly, he opens the door to her. A cigarette in her left hand held at the waist side and although her hat may be oversized, it suits her well, along with her gripping perfume. There she stands, expecting an invitation. At the same time, Dale stands with raised brows. Like he is expecting her to enter.

"Well, you coming in, or shall we talk in the hallway?"

Tabby walks in with elegance, dropping her coat off at the shoulders. Dale catches it and lays it on the unmade bed. Tabby rests the oversized round hat next to it.

"You're not sticking to the brief, dear boy."

He rolls his eyes.

"Did you just roll your eyes at me Dale?"

"No. I was just casually looking up at the ceiling, Ms. Yenta." Dale says with a clip of sarcasm.

Tabby lights the smoke she's holding and sits reluctantly on the bed. Dale hands her the ashtray, which she holds in her spare hand. Her legs now crossed. Dale doesn't hide the pain as he leans on the counter. Rubbing his lower back.

"What happened to you?" Tabby asks.

"Took a tumble."

"So, what do you have so far on Katsav?" Tabby asks.

"That's he cheats on his wife, visits expensive hotels, and attends business conferences. A boring man in an elegant suit, Ms. Yenta."

"That's no surprise, that he's a cheater. But that doesn't concern me. I mean, who is he associating with? Have you witnessed or documented him with anyone or see anything?" Something catches Tabby's eye. A thin slice of shadow points and shifts on the carpet, protruding from the hallway. Dale takes this moment to really see who his client was. No doubt she was charming and elegant, but cunning and sharp at the same time. A mix that scares men and that most could not pull off but Ms. Yenta. Dale admired her. But more so for the intrigue and mystery of the well-to-do sweet enigma who is now sitting in a bedsit on an unmade bed, like caviar in a fish finger factory. Out of place. Her domineer now twisting, her cigarette burning in the ashtray while she monitors the door.

"You OK Ms. Yenta?" Dale asks.

She holds her index finger up to him. Then leaning forward before sharply pointing twice toward the door. Dale does not take one more second, knowing exactly what to do. As quickly as his aching back allows, he rushes to open the door. Hoping to surprise whoever was there, instead the hallway occupies no one. Dale then hangs himself over the banister. No movement below and no slam from the communal door. He returns to his room and holds the door open wide. Tabby is tapping on the walls.

"You trying to contact ghosts Ms. Yenta?"

"You see anyone? That a fire door?"

She is referring to the only door Dale has.

He smiles.

"I hope so. The landlords' gonna have a lawsuit if it ain't."

Tabby is now looking out into the hall. Dale closes the door after she goes to sit down.

The Chet Baker record is now finishing. The room now thudding as static rushes and tangles itself on the needle. Dale is rubbing his back before turning the record over. He then goes to get the rum from the cupboard and is pouring two glasses.

"Do you have an assumption of who may have been at my door, Ms. Yenta?"

Aware that he would not get an answer. He hands her the drink.

"It's your room Dale."

She lifts the glass up as a gesture of thanks before sipping it gently. Her red lipstick shines from the moisture. Then dried by a slide of her index finger.

Dale is grateful to have Lament humming from the speakers. His mind now wandering between Chet Baker and the freckled red-haired junky. Tabby is tapping her now empty glass. He pours her another. Hoping he could squeeze some kind of information from the untraced and undocumented enigma.

*

Professor Ziegler is watching outside. From where he stands, he is only a dot to those below. His attention is on the parking lot where the same TV repair van that was parked on his street the other night is now idle. He limps with a strain on his face, reaching his chair just in time as he is unbalanced. Slumping down into soft leather, he taps the plane times and timetables for public transport. He is at the point of no return. Random people following him, stolen evidence and now letters lying on his grand desk. One headed by an investment company. The ink is red with a demand for either explanation of loss of funding or for twenty-two million to be paid back with the pre-agreed 12% interest. A second letter is less concerned with formalities and instead demands two million for the guaranteed return of the contents of his briefcase, snatched at the hit and run. The letters are bright and mismatched from cuttings of various media sources. He still feels a safe escape is possible, surprised that the authorities were not yet hounding him. He was in debt with many, but the savior of hearing of no consequence for his greed was still being controlled well by Edward Salone and Ms. Hamilton. He composes himself a little. Clearing his throat and rubbing his drooped eyes while his glasses hang from his fingers. He gets the whiskey bottle from the second drawer and pours a generous amount. He picks up the phone and dials. There's a short wait before the person picks up.

"You got it yet?" The professor asks with urgency.

He doesn't like what he hears, so he slams the phone down. Sipping his drink, he feels his legs heavy and his head hurting with anxiety and a million thoughts. He takes a deep breath and dials another number.

"Professor Ziegler here. I need the full amount from all investments for the 'C.O.A.C.C' to be deposited. And a counter sign from Edward Salone. From legal. It's a priority, so please, right away."

The professor hangs up, pours another sharp and friendly amount of booze before calling another number. As he is waiting, he empties items from the drawers. Paperwork, files and the daily pack of complimentary cigarettes that always appeared on his desk every morning without fail. He caps the whiskey bottle but puts it back in the drawer.

"Salone. Where you been?"

"Out to lunch. That new place, west of the city. They make the best egg mayo sandwich. The lettuce never fails to keep that crunch, you know? You need a good crunch with such a moist filling."

"Young man. I have no desire to hear about your eating habits. Now listen, the time has come. You need to countersign the papers heading your way. When you do, I will arrange your 10%."

"Well doc. I've been thinking."

Edward is picking a sesame seed from his teeth.

"I feel 15% is more desirable. Having this burden to bear, you know." Edwards says.

He has sought the seed and is dropping it into the bin.

"There will be some explaining to do if this still goes belly up, doc."

Professor Ziegler had no strength to barter or disagree. Take the hit old man, he told himself. Or maybe not. Play the game now, and cheat later, the Professor thought.

"OK. I agree with that. Get it signed and I'll do my part here too. Hurry on it."

He hangs up.

Zeigler has packed all he needs into his new brown leather briefcase. He nods an acceptance and with eyes tightly shut and with a pale complexion with beads of sweat trapped in his frowning, he quickly taps six digits into a communication beeper. Instantly, the phone rings out. He swoops it from the cradle. Knowing who it was to be.

"Ms. Hamilton. This is it. Chime of a city clock."

The other end clicks to end the call while the professor stares blindly. Feeling alone, no longer accepting, or decisive, but scared and evermore frail.

*

Moments later, Ms. Hamilton's Love 85' heels are slowing her pace, as is the struggle of getting her I.D card from her pocket as she approaches the door at the end of the sterile corridor. Inside is a vast area. Generators buzz, computers bleep with commands and prompts on various things as they expel a plastic, man-made and unnatural heat. Ms. Hamilton takes a pair of ear protectors from the hook and a white coat, along with a badge with the code 'A1' on it. She puts the code on to the sheet that's hanging on the wall and heads slowly for the rear end of the room, a contrast from the rush she was in mere moments ago as now, the reality of potential consequence and the sheer responsibility of the task in hand was dragging. Her love 85's too, dragging along the buffered shining floor while staff hurry by with their own agenda.

Ms. Hamilton taps on the glass partition of the administration office where Dr. Fred Derry is sitting, shooting the breeze with two other white coats. The sight of her has them now upright and stumbling as Ms. Hamilton's conventional, yet elegant attractiveness was a struggle for the men. Her smile is wide and showing bright pearls behind red lipstick that shines under the artificial light. The males working in the many labs and long corridors always found the ear protectors nothing short of adorable over Ms. Hamilton's light blonde hair, but now they hang from her wrist. She enters, again her expensive heels scraping. For a moment, there is silence.

"Say boys, perhaps you'll be so kind to get me a milky coffee?" Ms. Hamilton asks.

"Of course, Er..." One of the white coats is attempting to play it cool.

"Two sugars, right?" The other white coat asks.

"Well remembered." Ms. Hamilton says with slight fun in her tone.

The two gentlemen head out of the office to fight about who gets to give her the beverage. Leaving Mr. Derry alone with her. She is now stern with her features and a fixed stare on Fred Derry's face.

"What can I do for you, Ms. Hamilton?" he nervously asks.

Realizing now she is holding the first key, he knows what is to come. He averts his vision by turning his back to her.

His action gives Ms. Hamilton a chance to take a breath. She assumed she was showing some vulnerability, presenting herself slightly unfamiliar to the scientist.

"You have the second key?" she finally asks.

"In the safe. By your knees." Fred says.

He turns himself back into the room and goes to open it.

Ms. Hamilton scrapes her heels out of the way as he kneels in front of the steel door and taps in six digits. He is soon back on his feet, holding the key into the air.

"Is this a drill?" he asks.

Ms. Hamilton's face says it all. Derry then purses his lips, only then to chuckle. Nerves and uncertainty now have him weak. He swallows hard. Eyes wide and with another slit of a smile. Again, through nerves and not from some sick thrill. The two stand for a silent second.

Ms. Hamilton now nods firmly with tight lips.

"Let's go." she says.

Taking the lead and waving him out of the office as her heels are clipping the sterile floor.

Derry is stepping behind her and looking over at the scientists and co-workers of the vast area. His pace now slows down with reluctance and guilt. He would never have put himself forward for this privilege if not for his demanding wife and expensive school fees.

"These people are not what they seem, Freddie. There are mere subjects, numbers. You know what they are." he tells himself quietly.

Gripping the key hard in his pocket.

*

Jane Crawford stands looking out the living room window at the media and journalists that litter her usually ordinary street. Dale is unbuttoning his coat as he looks at the framed pictures and ornaments on the fireplace. He is more than aware that by now, the likely hood of a positive outcome was slim to none. Both professionally and personally.
Jane pours coffee from the tray.

"I hope those outside were not too much bother for you when you arrived?" Jane asks.

"Not at all. I just ignored them."

Dale takes a cup and sinks into a comfortable armchair. The air smells of laundry and the birds are singing above the humans outside. He thinks that the lost little boy has a good family. A little older than the conventional caregiver, but love was certainly present.

"So. How are things?" Dale asks.

Mrs. Crawford holds a cup with her eyebrows raised.

"Well, we're no longer suspected of any foul play. And the neighbors have been ever so kind. Too kind."

She pulls a big smile.

"It's easy for people to be a little too helpful. They mean well." Dale says.

The lounge door opens slowly and enters Mr. Crawford, who is bee-lining towards Dale with a hand out. Dale lifts himself from the cozy seat with his right arm as he is keeping the coffee cup in his left. He felt strange sitting while shaking a client's hand. Especially in the client's own home.

"Mr. Crawford. How are we?"

Dale shakes the hand.

Mr. Crawford points to the chair as a way of inviting his guest to sit again. Seeing he needs a seat and is in pain, but he won't ask what the cause of it was.

"I owe you an apology." Mr. Crawford says.

Dale is waving it all away with a soft hand in the air.

"Really. If anyone need to apologize, it should be me."

The two men give a look to one another. A practiced skill shared with common and familiar roles within the police force. The look goes unnoticed by Mrs. Crawford, who is again at the window, watching the small crowd getting restless.

"Er, I don't wish to be a burden, Mrs. Crawford. But I wonder if I can trouble you for a glass of water?" Dale asks.

"Yes, of course."

She turns quickly before stopping and turning back to face the men.

"Oh. How about some sponge cake?... Yes?" she asks.

"I really don't want to put you out." Dale says.

"Nonsense young man."

Mrs. Crawford smiles wide and leaves.

Dale cannot sit with the words he was to expel. He needed to stand and talk right into the eye of the man. He puts the cup on the coffee table. He's reluctant to talk further but feels it is important.

"I'm sure you are aware of the likelihood of a safe return, Mr. Crawford."

Dale is looking at the door, hoping the soft-toned lady isn't over hearing.

"I may mirror others, and I..." Dale stops talking.

He is out of words. The hurt he carries was fading, but the world kept turning and getting seemly dirtier. He could say nothing else to help and hoped their shared experience was met.

"I'm fully aware of the stats." Mr. Crawford eventually says.

He turns to speak more but stops as the lounge door swings open, bringing with it a strong scent of lemon with the sound of ice cubes clinking on long glasses. Mrs. Crawford's smile is wide but forced. It was clear to Dale that she was not coping well and felt he should leave. Instead, he accepts the glass of water with a slice of lemon and politely sips it.

"I wonder?" Dale says.

He takes another sip of the water.

"Do you suppose the circumstances have something to do with you being a detective at one time, Mr. Crawford?

"Needle in a haystack, young man. Well, you know that."

Dale is a little taken aback by the client's response but is understanding, due to varying circumstances. Dale sips again and places the glass down.

"Of course. I'm sorry to ask?"

Dale puts his arms around his back and nods slightly forward to Mrs. Crawford, then to Mr. Crawford, which hurts his back.

"Thank you for your time. I'll be going now."

Dale clears his throat and heads for the door. Unsure what else he can do or say for the parents, for the reality of it all.

*

Information on varying levels is tacked to the corkboard on the fifth floor. Sketches of wanted people between well-being classes and reminders of retirement parties or a birthday. Dale leans into one of the wanted sketches with squinting eyes. It's Charles Reeves alright. The description seals that certainty, as it outlines his last known occupation as a postal worker. He rips the drawing from the pin and is folding it into six as Detective Sally Longdowne calls from down the corridor.

"Hello stranger." Sally says.

Her fingers gripping the door frame. Arm stretched way out and crossed feet. An attractive smile and matching eyes.

They hug and enter her office.

"Still cracking skulls, Longdowne?" Dale asks as he's looking around the office.

The window is wide, covering at least half the left side wall and the view is typical of mid-town. No cars or people seen, only heard. The chime of the city clock shakes the glass.

"Shit. Can't use the excuse of not knowing the time round here, can ya?" Dale says.

He is now sitting and is stretching to catch an eye on the large face of the clock towering above even the tallest of buildings that traps litter and people between themselves. He lights a cigarette and offers one to the Detective.

"No thanks. Sorry my friend, I have nothing to give ya. Only a few files here, but if I brought in everyone with a crooked smile, I'll have to answer to the taxpayer, and the suits upstairs. As it's a copper's relative too, his associates are told to keep lips tight. You know the score. I've only just heard of this Crawford guy too. From you."

"Yeah. He took early retirement. I'm guessing the kid is leverage or revenge on him. Karma if you like. Who knows?"

Dale is now looking for an ashtray. As he's doing so, the view catches him. He goes to stand at the window.

"Or maybe just a dirty stain on society." Sally says.

She is sighing hard.

"Dale?"

He does not turn to face her.

"You know as well as I do, the boy is likely dead. Time frames, resources, stats..."

Again, she gives her visitor a moment to respond but is still met with silence.

"I'm surprised you're working this case, I have to say."

Her face was now twisting with frustration.

Dale's silence was now insulting. The only sound is the lips puckering around the cigarette butt, hissing of toxins expelling from the smoke. Sally catches herself before talking again. She felt she was being harsh. Now seeing that perhaps Dale is needing to do this for himself. She did not know.

"How you doing Dale?"

Her tone is now a little defeated but genuine.

She holds her mug up for Dale to drop his smoke into.

"I'm O.K kid."

He picks up a file and looks at the first sheet. The name Jack Sugarman.

"Wait. What? I know this guy. Only not by this name." he says.

"Oh?" Sally says.

He flicks over a few more sheets before returning to the first page. The mug shot is of Paul Duval.

"No convictions or cautions for the last three months." Dale says before dropping the file and picking up another.

"Check the other files will ya. We're looking for the name Duval." he says.

The name, however, is not in any of the other files. Dale assumes it is an admin error. Though that didn't matter too much. The fact Duval was in the system was enough for him.

"What we thinking Dale boy?" Sally asks.

He taps the 'Duval/Sugarman file.

"Can I get a copy of this?" he asks.

She rises from her chair. Grabbing the file from the desk.

"A please would be nice."

"Sorry. Please."

He playfully pouts his lips and gives her sad eyes.

Sally inserts the sheets in the copier at the back of the office. Her certificates hanging above it.

"You eaten?" Sally asks.

The copier is doing its job and spitting out duplicates. Sally hands them to Dale, one by one as they slide out of the machine.

"No time to eat."

Dale takes the last paper, kisses Sally on the cheek and is now leaving.

"Say hi to the family for me. Thanks for this too."

Sally flicks her index and middle finger from her forehead.

"Yeah, see ya Dale." she says with a concerned tone.

*

Dale enters his room. He spots something on the floor, a note. His back is aching as he leans down to pick it up. Turning it over, he sees words cut and stuck from a newspaper.

'BACK OFF LOOKING FOR THE KID OR IT WILL GET WHAT YOUR DAUGHTER DID.'

He quickly leaves.

*

In Albert's car, sits a small bag of heroin between his legs. He doesn't for a second attempt to conceal his disgust for Maddy who is slumped in the passenger seat. Black paint on her hands and a smear on her chin. This, however, does not retract from her posture and clear signs of being high.

"Look at you. How do you function in that state? How do you not get knocked over, or worse?"

Now looking around, over his shoulder and through the rearview mirror.

"I can't answer that one, man." Maddy says.

She cannot get comfortable. Though her body appeared to not want stillness. Her nervous system is twitching from inside her shell. She lights a cigarette.

"What sort of business you in any way? Why you got a P.I after ya?" Maddy asks.

Katsav winds down his window, takes her cigarette from her mouth and throws it out.

"Well, I guess you were supposed to figure that out, weren't you? For this?"

Katsav holds the smack in the air.

"Well, you don't have to worry about him anymore. I think he's done with ya." Maddy says.

Her mind wandering and her vision squinted. She rubs her eyes. Trying to correct her vision.

"That so?" Albert says.

"Yep. I guess that's the end of our working relationship. So, if you don't mind paying my last wage, I'll be on my way."

Albert is winding the window up.

"You think you've earned this?" Albert asks.

Again, he holds the dope in the air.

"You're lucky I'm in a good mood." he says.

He throws her last pay into her paint-stained denim lap.

"That shit will kill ya. Trust me." Albert says.

Maddy stuffs the baggy into her jean pocket.

"I'm sure he's not gonna bother you anymore." Maddy says.

"Get your drugged up self out of my car. You fucking degenerate." Katsav says.

Maddy climbs out with some urgency, nearly stumbling as the rise in blood pressure has again caught her a little off balance. Albert revs the engine and drives off. His car a diamond amongst rotten apples this part of town.

*

Albert was always looking to gloat or show off some expensive item. This occasion, the new piano. So now there is thirty or more people downstairs, including under-paid waitresses and caterers. Upstairs, in the en-suite, after checking her reflection, Elaine sprays on some more of the fresh Avon order. And, for the third time today, checks the bottle of Dilaudid is still under the homeware magazine in the drawer in the bedside table. She decided to hide a while from the fake laughs and common pleasantries, but more so, from her husband. Albert was in a mood when he arrived home. Complaining about the lack of housework, which Elaine had spent much of the day doing, tidying, and ensuring food orders had been met and that the workers were to be on time. She takes a deep breath in preparation of returning to the guests, as she does, she hears someone at Albert's office door, and assuming it was Albert, she waits for him to enter before heading down the stairs, instead, through the gap in the bedroom door she sees Tommy, though to her, just another strange guest in her home. The office is locked. Suddenly, a slither of material dashes from Elaine's sight as she sees the guest heading down to the party.

Back in the lounge, Tommy is weighing his options, as Albert is tapping an uninterested employee on the chest while pointing at the backside of the young caterer. His actions are being witnessed by Elaine, who is now standing in the lounge doorway and before she can interrupt his rude talk, she dips into the room and bumps gently into Tommy as Albert is excusing himself, now heading out of the lounge and up the stairs.

"Evening. You must be the lovely Mrs. Katsav. I'm Tommy."

He gently shakes her soft, warm hand.

Elaine can't help but admire his watch. A gold shiny strap and a bright white face.

"You have a lovely home here." Tommy says.

The comment was unexpected, and Elaine is a little embarrassed.

"Why thank you. A labour of love." Elaine replies.

A half-cut employee is hammering the piano. Elaine points toward the noise.

"Not so much that, though." she says.

Smiling and looking at the newly laid brown carpet being crushed by the unwanted noise maker.

The pair each take a drink from a tray as it passes.

"So, what do you do at the company, then?" Elaine asks.

"I ensure we are running as smoothly as possible, Mrs. Katsav." Tommy says.

He shrugs which prompts the host.

"Are you unhappy with your work?" she asks.

"It's not what I was hoping for. What can I say."

He shrugs again.

Suddenly, Tommy is pushed slightly, lucky not to spill his wine on the brand-new carpet, as an attractive lady is now leaning in and kissing Elaine on each cheek.

"Elaine darling. Love the new piano." she says as she is looking over the small crowds.

Tommy raises his glass in a polite manner and is about to excuse himself.

Elaine holds her hand out again, and as he shakes it, he can feel something in his palm. Elaine nods slightly.

"You take care young man." Elaine says.

He smiles and establishes the item, now in his pocket, is a key. As he turns to leave, his elbow pushes into the gut of Albert. Tommy just raises his glass and walks away.

"What's that perfume you're wearing?" Albert asks Elaine.

"I bought it from Avon. Thought you might like it." Elaine replies in a quiet and reserved tone.

"It's vile." he replies.

Walking toward the backside of the young waitress.

*

The first hit from the fresh score sinks firmly and pleasantly into the bloodstream of Maddy. Slump and consumed by a soft cushion on the tattered sofa. Paint smeared on her fingertips and smoke rising from a burning cigarette in the ashtray. But now, the familiar sinking and glow is being replaced with confusion. Maddy feels her veins throbbing, her lungs grabbing at non-existing air and panicking. The dizziness is intense, which makes her feel sick. With some effort she tilts forward, ready to mess her rug with bile and churned coffee. The sheer weight and imbalance has her falling forward, banging her light body on the floor, vibrating the contents in her room. The folded cardboard used to steady and level the old easel has become loose. Tipping it before collapsing in on itself. Maddy's face is now pale. With a panicked, wide stare. Her breathing sharp and quick with desperate attempts to catch oxygen. She rolls on her back. Still wide-eyed but near blind, now accepting what she believes to be her fate. She takes her last bout of recycled air. Now still. Her stare ending on a beautiful half-finished portrait of Dale.

*

The door unlocked with a small creak from the hinge. Tommy looks around towards the stairs before sliding into Albert's office and closes the door quietly. Small bouts of party attendees rumble below as he heads for the large, dark pine desk. The drawers are locked, but this is to be expected. It took no time, however, for them to be picked. The smooth grinding of metal being released felt good to him. In the top drawer, letters cut from newspaper as well as newspaper clippings slipped in a brown file. Headlines reading:

'IS SHE A BLACK WIDOW? 'WOMAN INNOCENT OF HUSBAND'S DEATH'. 'POISON SUSPECT FOUND NOT GUILTY' and 'DILUADID POISON POSSIBLE.'

A picture of Elaine under the clippings. He can hear voices from outside as he finds what he is looking for in the second drawer. A VHS tape, some paperwork, and a hefty stash of cash. He is slightly concerned and questions why there are small sachets of rat poison and a baggy with dirty dust in it.

He slips the VHS into the small of his back, with his belt doing well to hold it in place. The papers are folded and slipped into his inside pocket, the money, into his trouser pocket, making it bulky and obvious. Tommy did not care; he was sure he could leave with no issue. Albert would be happy for him not to be there anyway. His plan now, to stash the key somewhere, allowing Mrs. Katsav to know where. That way, Tommy was conscious free.

*

Edward was not expecting to see Ziegler as he opened the professor's office door. In fact, he was expecting never to see him again. Long gone. On the desk, next to the beautifully crafted wooden owl, with copper lines and marble eyes, there are two envelopes, one for Edward and one for Ms. Hamilton. Edward takes a few seconds to watch over the city. Feeling reflective and burning time. His mother had always told him the law game was full of sharks and corruption, and he had promised her the day he graduated from law school, he would always do the right thing. Now, as he reflects on the past few months, he has only guilt and remorse to carry with him. He splits the envelope open and sees a cheque. There is also a note:

'10%. TAKE CARE, Z'.

"Son of a bitch." Edward says through gritted teeth.

He suddenly must compose himself as the office door swings open. Stuffing the note and cheque into his pants pocket.

"Ms. Hamilton." Edward says.

She says nothing, instead bee-lines to the desk to pick up her envelope. She looks over the office and then goes towards the cityscape with the clouds looking close enough to blow. She is placing the envelope in her inside suit pocket as Edward is looking through the desk drawers. A nice whiskey sits in one of them.

"Well, I guess the old professor won't be needing this." Edward says.

Now walking to the door with the bottle in his hand. He turns, index finger on his chin.

"What?" Ms. Hamilton asks.

"Just wondering how you feel about all this?"

"Nothing." Ms. Hamilton says as she heads for the door.

Looking at the floor, as if to avoid eye contact.

"I guess this is goodbye, then?" he says.

"I guess so." Ms. Hamilton says. Still looking at her heels.

"Take care of yourself." Edward says.

Flicking an index finger from his forehead as her heels disappear behind the closing door. Now left in silence with short bursts of city living below. He takes a deep breath, thinks of treating his mother to something nice, and then leaves the building while wondering where Ziegler has ended up.

\*

All the way from Hopper's bar and along dark streets on the edge of the east side, Dale follows Paul. The chime of the city clock retracts behind them as he is keeping a trained and experienced distance, passing polluted concrete, barking dogs and voices from various corners with dim light appearing to only help hide the decaying houses. Dale stops in the shadows and watches Paul approach a house, kneeling before straightening himself up only mere seconds later, looking around and quickly dashing away. Dale waits for a beat before slowly and cautiously approaching where Paul has just come from. A small house. A two up, two down. He can see a note protruding from the gap at the bottom of the door and with a firm scrape, retrieves it. The words:

'2 DAYS THEN I TELL!'

Written in newspaper cut outs.

Dale folds it and puts it into his pocket as he quietly steps on dead plants towards the front window. Darkness. He takes a coin out. Heads he will enter, tales he will leave.

*

The air and aroma feel distant, yet not too unfamiliar to Tommy as he's looking down at the aisles of the stone building and up towards the stain glass as he's wiping sweat from his brow. He feels unwell. Two elderly ladies are standing near the entrance, and a dirty bearded man in a pinstripe suit, nodding in the far right.

Tommy spots the Bibles displayed on a small bookcase. He places money he had taken from Albert into them. As he puts the last bit of money in one, the nodding man approaches. Looking Tommy up and down.

"You look like money, son." The dirty man says.

Tommy assumed he was referring to the money in the Bibles. He points to the bookshelf.

"Take your pick, my friend." Tommy says.

Now heading to the exit before he's ushered back with a tug at his arm. It's then he sees a small blade.

"What's that mean? You a religious nut?"

The dirty man was anxious, uncertain whether this was worth a score. Until he spots the watch shining from his victim's wrist.

"Give me that watch boy." The dirty man says.

Stepping forward and showing the blade.

Tommy is holding his hands up to show no threat. He is unfazed with the situation but is sorry the world is in this state.

"I hear ya. But could you maybe put the knife away? Will you do that for me?"

"What?" The dirty man says.

One of the elderly ladies is scraping her feet slowly towards them.

"Put it away. Now!" Tommy says with a quiet, stern tone.

He hovers a finger along the bookcase and picks a Bible up.

"Here you are Madame, is this what you need?"

The old lady smiles and nods as Tommy hands her a Bible.

"Thank you, young man." she says with a wide grin.

Her eyes squinting, expelling her creases and crinkled skin. Unsteady on her feet as she turns to make it to the seat where her friend is waiting.

"You can have the watch my guy. That's no problem."

Tommy unlatches it from his wrist.

"But I'm not too happy with you waving a blade around. Not in a place like this."

The dirty man takes a beat, then flicks the blade into the handle and pockets it.

"Good man. Here."

Tommy hangs the watch off his index and middle finger and holds it out. The dirty man snatches it and slides it into his pocket.

"You gonna hock it? Don't take less than 3200 for it." Tommy says.

"What?"

The dirty man is confused, thinking this was the strangest mugging he's ever involved himself in.

"You believe in God, my guy?" Tommy asks.

Looking over the church.

"Nope." The dirty man says sternly.

"But I'll tell you this for nothing. The guys who strung yer boy up. Capitalists. Yep. Your boy was a Commie. Think about that." The dirty man says.

"That sounds reasonable." Tommy says.

"And resurrection? Bullshit. Impossible."

The dirty man is now looking down at the floor. The cold concrete warmer than his feet.

"I guess you gotta see it to believe it right?" Tommy says.

Sliding close to the dirty man and slipping the watch from the mugger's pocket.

"Take care of yourself." Tommy says.

Leaving the man staring at his shoes, while the old lady is screeching with surprise at the money she has found.

*

The penguin ornament on the side table shakes from Albert's coughing. He's sitting up in bed, finding it hard to catch breath. His vest soaked in sweat, a pale complexion over his usually red cheeks.

"You alright Bert?" Elaine asks.

Now she is sitting up herself.

"Can I get you some water?"

Her care is faint. Only becoming less concerned when he waves her rudely away and coughs loudly again. He stumbles to his feet and heads to the en-suite. The light from the bathroom spreads along the bedroom carpet. He runs the cold tap and dabs his face. He coughs again, noticing spats of blood on his hand and dotting around the sink.

"Bert?"

"You've…"

Albert can't catch enough air to finish talking. He tries again, but with half a breath.

"You…"

Now holding his throat as the water swirls into a pinkish flow as the blood drains away. The mirror above the sink never lied. Gaunt, sunken features, his eyes once brown, now pin size. Lost in hollow sockets. He rips a piece of tissue off the roll and wipes his mouth as he rests on the side of the bath for a second, attempting to get a steady breath.

Attempting to stand, his legs are dense and difficult to manipulate. All motion now set back with his body heavier with each small movement, like lead in his veins. It was at this point he panicked. This didn't ease the difficulty of catching air into his seemly scarred lungs. He whimpers again for Elaine as he takes one uneasy step, resulting in falling face first onto the stylishly designed bathroom floor. His nose breaking, the pain intense, but the scream unheard as his windpipe is shrinking. A cold and repulsive complexion has now washed over his scared and horrified face. Deep, quiet gasps are now being taken over by shallow hits before becoming limp. Lifeless.

"Bert?"

Her curls loose as she climbs from the bed. She's nervous about what she might witness because of the noise Albert had made hitting the tiles, followed sharply now by an eerie silence. Slowly she approaches the doorway but can't face looking in. She is blocking the light with her back to him. She gasps as the doorbell rings out. A welcomed, and somewhat perverse distraction for a second, but wonders if she can avoid answering it. After all, it was past midnight. Perhaps it is just her neighbor, Harriet and her poodle running free again on the quiet and clean street or scampering in and around the residents' gardens. Elaine checks in the drawer under the homeware magazine to see again a still unopened bottle of Dilaudid.

She was confused and still faded with the over-indulgence of wine and her sleeping pills still absorbing into her system. Again, the doorbell rings out followed by stern knocks. Elaine heads downstairs to answer the persistent visitor.

From the bottom stair, she can make out three men standing outside.

"Mrs. Katsav? Mrs. Katsav, we can see you standing there."

The voice shakes Elaine. Like a jolt to the spine.

"If you can just open the door. We can talk properly."

The voice waits for a second or two for a response.

"Mrs. Katsav?"

Elaine gingerly steps towards the door, flicks the outside light on, and presses her night cream face to the glass.

"Are you police?" she asks.

"No. We're not police. We're aware of something that needs our attention. This will benefit you as well, Mrs. Katsav. We just need your cooperation, so, if you'll be so kind."

The voice is waiting for either the door to be opened or a response.

Elaine opens the door, which has two of the three men burst in but not to any extent to scare or harm the lady of the house. They separate, one scopes the ground floor, while the other searches upstairs. The third man calmly closes the door and turns to face Elaine.

"Mr. Katsav? Is he...?"

The man upstairs interrupts him.

"Right here boss." he shouts.

"I didn't do it. Please believe me, please." Elaine pleads.

Her eyes filling with tears, which are now running, separating her glow of skin.

In one of the man's hands, holds a foil bag around 12 inches square. They each nod at the third man and close the front door.

"What was in that bag there? What's going on?" Elaine asks.

The third man smiles sympathetically.

"We need to talk, Mrs. Katsav."

*

After best of three with the coin toss, Dale is picking the lock of the small dark house with ease, not proud however, of his personal best and wondered what was on the other side of the door. He creeps in slowly. Sliding his picker into his pocket, he is now standing still to hear his surroundings. An open plan area, lounge to his left, worn in sofa, coffee table with dried stains, newspapers, cereal boxes, and cigarette packs. The dining room to his right has boxes on the table with newspaper clippings spread out. Dale breathes through his mouth as the smell of dirty dishes and ashtrays is turning his gut. On closer inspection, the clippings are centered on missing children. One headline catches Dale's attention.

'COPS DAUGHTER'S KILLER STILL AT LARGE.'

Below the headline, a picture of Dale and his wife Fran. A quick inspection of one of the boxes, he finds photographs of the Crawford home and materials and supplies for cutting and sticking paper and cards. Dale's ears suddenly prick up. Now fully aware there is someone behind him.

"You lot think you're above it all. Don't ya?" The voice says.

The voice is familiar to Dale. Hoping he was wrong, he turns to face the homeowner, Nick. He has in his right hand a small axe handle.

"I thought you'd be more concerned with this?" Dale says.

Holding up the note he retrieved from the floor.

"I figure this is to be the second note. Your good friend Paul dropped it off." Dale says. Checking his exits and weighing up his options. He lights a cigarette.

"Mind if I smoke?" he asks.

Dale is now looking around the table. There is one more box on there.

"I got a note too, Nick. Though you know that already."

Nick is looking uneasy on his feet. He is shaking a little and is wiping sweat from his brow.

"I can't let you leave Dale." Nick says.

Dale is not at all fazed by the man, met similar many times when a cop. Even before his time in the force. School had him tough, and he rarely dipped out from some little dick playing the hard on. However, he was preferring the big man opposite not to be tooled up.

"Put the stub down my guy."

Dale warns the heavy sweaty man.

The demand is being ignored. Instead, Nick is slowly closing the gap between them, looking somewhat hesitant as he does so.

"Sorry Dale." Nick says.

Dale quickly flicks his cigarette into Nick's face. Followed by a swift kick to the shin and as expected, Nick was slow. The axe handle drops to the floor as Dale then jabs the big man in the face, the lips now bloody before Dale slides behind Nick and grips the man into a choke hold. Squeezing tightly.

"Go with the flow, big man. Float to sleepy town." Dale says.

The big man becomes limp. Dale lets him go. A heavy thump as the unconscious man falls into a heap. Dale stamps on his burning cigarette. The smell of singeing carpet for him is foul. Noise above. There is someone up there. He picks up the axe stub, sticks his foot into Nick's ribs three times and quietly heads upstairs.

Three rooms up there. Silence. Dale thought he would check the room where the noise came from first. As he swung the door open, there sits the little lost boy, Jimmy. The sight hurts the gut of the giant who is standing over the innocent child. No reason for anyone of any age to have to experience such a thing. Whatever that thing might be. Dale knows, however, that this will be lived with, most likely for life now. No time for tears though, hard man, Dale thinks. Just smile with a soft tone.

*

The little boy's eye sockets are like puddles as they hold tears. His pink lips pouting as Dale is carrying him down the stairs. Nick is gone. Dale puts Jimmy on the sofa, placing his finger to his lip as a sign to stay quiet. The boy looks small and vulnerable again, making Dale both sad and angry. He takes a breath. Composes himself and begins looking for the missing man. The kitchen is the same as the rest of the house. Dirty. Dishes in the sink, cartons sprawled. Spoiled milk on the counter. The back door is open. Dale looks out and searches through the garden with a long, slow glance. Nothing. He heads back to the little boy, who is still sitting. The tears dry and his pout less pronounced but now with a more trusting wide stare that is hitting the soul of his rescuer. Dale finds the phone and calls Sally Langdowne.

"You're OK now, kid. You're safe." Dale says in a soft tone.

"Yes, detective Langdowne please." he says down the phone.

He looks towards the little boy as he waits to hear her response.

"Sally, it's Dale. I've found the Crawford kid, alive."

He picks up an open letter and reads the address off to her where she advises she is on her way, and not to touch anything. He hangs up and begins rifling through drawers and the rest of the boxes on the dining table. A red ribbon. Dale knows what it is. He is, however, reluctant to accept it as fact. He grips it tight, holding it to his lip. Tears forming. Again, he takes a breath.

"Tough guy my eye. Compose yourself, Dale."

He slips the ribbon in his pocket and goes to pick Jimmy up as sirens are approaching the address.

"Come on kid, let's get you home."

*

The bar appears denser. Not with the number of people occupying the space as the band set up, but more so, of a different level. As if there were more souls lost with a sense of hopelessness, hooked on substances and self-pity. Always there, but with no direction. Dale had rarely wondered why he contributed to the dripping taps and yellow staining walls, but tonight, feels reflective and puts the hurting gut down to the emotion of the last few weeks. Especially as he is staring at the newspaper headlines on the table again.

'EX-DECTECTIVE'S SON FOUND SAFE & SOUND.'

Below is a picture of Dale with the little boy Jimmy and Sally Langdowne. He downs his first shot and splits the bitterness with a sip of cold beer.

Tommy is now standing with a rum and coke in one hand and a briefcase in the other.

"Mind if I sit?"

He points to the seat opposite before sliding into it. Placing his briefcase at his side.

The band starts up. Fast tempo with keys spiking. The female is comfortable on stage. Dominating the lush and hang-ups.

"Hey…" Tommy picks the newspaper up. Tapping the picture of Dale.

"That's you. You're the one who found that kid. The guys' still blowing in the wind, right? As they say."

"You a reporter?" Dale asks.

He is leaning back now. He cannot find a light for his smoke but sees a hand holding out a booklet of matches with the River Man Hotel written on it.

"Me? No, my friend. I'm…" Tommy stops talking. He realizes he is unsure anymore.

"I guess you could say I'm now not economically viable."

"That's quite profound, I must say." Dale says with a little sarcasm.

"So, what brings you this part of town, erm…?"

"Tommy. What makes you think I'm not from around here?" Tommy asks.

The band finishes their first tune. A broken applause breaks out around the bar.

"That suit for one, the briefcase for two, and let's not forget that weight around yer wrist." Dale points to the watch.

"Not cheap on all accounts."

Tommy is now coughing. The table shaking as he is trying to compose himself. Dale waits for the man to stop expelling his germs around the place. Silence between them until Tommy speaks.

"I apologize. I've interrupted your night; I'll be leaving now. Nice to meet you."

Tommy quickly finishes his drink and slides from the booth.

His insistence and pace have taken Dale by surprise. He sees the briefcase and shouts over the noise but can only watch the well-dressed man leaving. Dale stubs his smoke, grabs the case, and heads for the exit.

Outside, the frequent scent of hot dog onion and the stench of cheap plastic ornaments are being palmed off from the side street stores. Dale opts to go left as it just felt right, leaving behind the smooth tune of Jazz and now blinking in time with dirty neon flashing and constant honks and blares of car headlights. Only dipping when he turns a corner. The city clock is chiming. Dale sees Tommy. He shouts after him, but it's unheard. No choice now. Dale jogs. Shouting once again for the stranger. As Dale turns the corner, a strong wind blows fragments, cold and sharp, into his eyes. Landing on his lips, too. Dale spits and grabs his mouth with urgency. On closer inspection the material gathered in his fingers appears to be some type of small metal grains. He places a few in his pocket. Now looking around, his eyes sore from the lashing of the material. Tommy has gone. Thin air. The briefcase won't be returned tonight and Dale wished he had probed more, maybe got a second name from Tommy. Perhaps the information he needs is in the case.

He looks over the street, just about to look in the briefcase as a car is heading up towards him. Dale closes his eyes to avoid blindness from the headlights. As he does, he scurries into a doorway as the car pulls up near him. Three men climb out. Moving slowly from the doorway, Dale conceals the briefcase the best he can, wondering why he was the one feeling he was under suspicion, as the three men are up to something. Two of them are now looking over the concrete and up at lit windows with various noises protruding from them. The third man is standing smoking, watching Dale scurry out of sight around a corner.

*

Dale had visited Hopper's bar hoping to see Tommy return for his case, but after three whiskies and two pale ales, was now back at home. And after two flips of a coin, the contents now lie on the unmade bed. A VHS tape with 'C.O.A.C.C' stamped on it, a transcript named '1st attempt', with some of the information redacted, an envelope with 'Read last' written on it, and an envelope containing some money. All of which interests Dale, however a note addressed to him has him beyond intrigued. It contains the hope it finds him well, and the contents of the case, to be considered how Dale saw fit, signed by Tommy.

Dale pours a drink, then tunes the TV in. The VHS slides into the recorder, where it begins to play. The tape is loose, making both sound and vision slack until it corrects itself. On screen, Professor Ziegler is rustling leaves of a plant, concealing the recorder. A knock then hits the office door, shaking the Professor in hurrying his action before allowing the visitor to enter.

Dale is looking over the paperwork labeled '1st Attempt.'

*'All six are unaware and unfamiliar with the failed attempt. All staff to conduct, continue and to present as 1st attempt, without this knowledge shared within the six subjects.'*

Dale's vision is now back on the screen where an elderly man sits at the desk. He's admiring the wooden owl with marble eyes and finely carved lining before his attention turns to six envelopes on the desk. The office door creaks open.

"Professor Zeigler, nice to see you again."

"04. Or perhaps I should call you Henry Burroughs now. How does that name suit you, anyway?" The professor asks.

"Not my first preference, but it'll do." Henry says.

A slight confusion again rushing over him. Ever more intense as the situation sinks deeper.

"So, you'll be giving an address for your office. There, you will conduct business as any G.P would. You will have patients and will treat them accordingly."

"OK." Henry says.

Professor Ziegler was expecting a little more from Henry. He assumed a lot more questions from him would need answering. Instead, Henry is looking keen to leave, like he has somewhere else to be. He will, in a few days, but now, Henry Burroughs, or 04 as he was originally 'labeled' was still the property of the Professor. 30% investment and ownership, however, was owned by many other corporations and business types.

"Last-minute check is all, Henry. I'm doing the same with the other five."

"Who are the other five?" Henry asks with an innocent tone.

"I'm afraid the terms of contract still stand 04. Breach of this will only end badly. How are you feeling?"

"Well, I truly remember nothing of my life, nothing at all."

"And how does that make you feel?" The Professor asks.

He was genuinely interested in knowing. No answer met, however, only a shrug and again, the sense Henry is keen to go.

The professor now picks the fourth envelope from the left and holds it in the air. Henry takes it from the thin pale hand.

"What's this?" Henry asks.

"Open it." Professor Ziegler says as he is looking over the grey sky, then looking at the draped plant on the shelf.

His thoughts falling on other matters at hand. Much more important than his success, part of which is sitting opposite him and is now ripping open the envelope.

Henry's confusion is visible on his brow, and he is squinting.

"What the hell is this? Why?"

"Is it relevant?" The Professor asks.

Still adverting his vision towards the city sky.

"Considering you're asking me to kill this person, yeah, I'd say it's fairly relevant."

Henry leans back. He crosses his arms and is waiting for a response from the frail old man.

The professor is now steadying himself as he is standing, clutching his walking stick, and is slowly hobbling toward the vast window. He takes a deep breath. An exhale of frustration and old age. He has no concern about what Henry will do with the demand, or the other five subjects for that matter. He has his own agenda.

"And what if I decline this ridiculous ask?" Henry asks.

The professor is still looking over the city landscape.

"That is your choice 04. I cannot make you. You are a free man, with a new start. Do what you see fit."

Henry says nothing. He is not keen on the old man's response, like it was a weak threat or some kind of reverse psychology. He was certain of one thing though, that there would be some consequence if he did not fulfil the request. After all, the contract outlines all assignments require the utmost importance and will need to be served as required.

"Are you asking the other five to do the same?" Henry asks as he is slipping the paper back into the envelope.

"Again, I cannot discuss anything of that sort, because of contractual obligation."

"Yeah, yeah." Henry says with a dismissive tone.

"So now what?" Henry asks.

"Now nothing. You'll be taken to your new home in due course and will live a normal life for the time being."

"Until I kill a stranger, unless... Is this someone I once knew, at one time?"

The professor is now thirsty, heading back to his desk for a whiskey.

"Again, sorry, contracts." The Professor replies.

The room falls silent, only the booze hitting the glass is heard. This is frustrating Henry. Waiting for the Professor to say something. Instead, he watches the old man slump in his chair and sip at the drink.

"Anything else I need to know?" Henry asks.

Now standing, stuffing the envelope in his inside pocket of the expensive suit supplied to him.

"You know all you need to know, 04. I mean Henry. I'll see you in a few hours."

The air is still thick as the door closes. Professor Zeigler goes to turn the camera off. Then only for it to flicker back on to reveal him looking ever more tired and deflated, and drunk.

"My name is Professor Jeremy Zeigler. This is my confession."

The VHS tape is straining and flickering again as he continues to speak.

"This second attempt has worked, millions of other people's money invested." He stops talking and swallows hard before reaching for his drink. He sips it slowly, like he's buying himself time. His tone is with some frustration as he speaks again.

"Quacks wanted to witness human condition where the white coats wanted to see practice through theory. Corners had to be cut; you can't please everyone. This is to be detrimental to me, no matter how successful the experiment is, or seems to be."

He swigs the drink and continues to vent.

"Under the table payments to those untrustworthy. You think you can trust those who, for a small fee, will dig up six strangers, no questions asked? Confabulation, ironized radiation…"

There's a knock on the office door.

The tape strains with the audio squeaking, as the visuals are fizzling until the tape snaps. Dale is too slow to save it and presses the eject button, dragging the reel of tape into a thick line that is trailing to the floor.

Dale notices a napkin tucked in the small pocket of the inside of the case. It has writing on it. Dated November 2nd, 1938.

'Six people were once criminals on varying levels. Six people who had been alive but have since passed. Six people will be extracted and brought back to life. Promise of change and fortune, assignments to be fulfilled. Recompense? For what has been done, karma? Paid for the services to fulfil a role, assassination of a world leader, build armies, companionship for the lonely. Allow people to buy back time with a loved one now gone!'

Dale opens the only thing left in the case. The note in the 'Read last' envelope. Dale did not know what to think after exposing the words 'Kill Paul Duval.' He needed air, someone to talk to, not about any of this, however, just breeze blowing. He wondered if Maddy would be at Hopper's bar.

*

# Two weeks later.

The heat alone, even in the out season, was of contrast to Dale. 3,000 miles from his hometown of Dalton West. His small case by his feet. The air smells clean too, with minimal traffic and people along the clean concrete with small bars and businesses shrunk under the large hotel, which is dominating one side of the street. Dale watches the taxi disappear behind the bright sun. Wiping his neck with a handkerchief. He looks up to see a plane heading in the direction he has just come. He lights a cigarette. Not his normal brand, ones bought on the plane. They taste dirty to him, and he needs a drink of water. Bottled, he reminds himself. He is checking the address of the hotel. He cannot help but notice the smiles of the locals, the warmth bouncing off his cheeks and clean buildings, thankful for having the money Tommy left to fund this trip.

The lobby is bright as he enters, and the relief of cool air has Dale feeling good. The receptionist again has a local accent and is nothing but pleasant. Her skin soft and moisturized, as opposed to the stranger opposite. She spins the sign-in book around and hands Dale the pen. He signs and pays for the next few days, not really knowing how long he was to stay and heads for the second floor.

After getting to know his surroundings, both inside the hotel and around it, Dale sips a rum and Coke in the dining area, people watching as he waits for his club sandwich to arrive. He has fresh clothes on and has fluffy over-conditioned hair. The hotel was generous with toilet paper with two of the rolls already in his case.

After another rum and a tickle of coke, Dale again is thanking the sweet young waitress for the beautifully crafted club sandwich. Only the crusts remain, and sprinkles of salt from the thin and crunchy fries.

Down the corridor has a dancehall. Empty and haunting. And a swimming pool further down, behind sterile glass doors, with its water swaying on the walls under the dim light. Only one man is making use of it currently. Dale needed to buy shorts if he was to ruin the man's harmony. A man who swam with ease and with no apparent care.

Onto the second floor. It mirrors the first, with only room numbers differing and the privacy of the guests behind those numbers. Dale knocks on room 27. The red hair ribbon fluttering on his wrist. He can hear movement from inside.

"Who is it?" A shaky voice shouts.

"Professor Zeigler? I wonder if I can have five minutes of your time?"

*

# Heating the nation.

The gas and electricity are running off a payment card, with the green screen on the machine showing low credit. On the sofa, Zoe Lewin is wrapped in a blanket and reading the free newspaper that she picks up every morning before getting on the ever-busy bus to work. The headline shouts about the rise in energy prices and those who are struggling.

Jerry kisses Zoe on the cheek.

"How was work?" he asks.

"Same old, same old. More importantly, how was yours?"

"OK yeah. Want me back tomorrow night. I'll tell the agency tomorrow."

Jerry slips his coat off and drapes it over the chair at the desk in the lounge's corner.

"You hungry? You eaten?" Jerry asks.

Heading to the kitchen.

"That's good, right?" Zoe asks.

Wrapping herself more tightly in the blanket.

"What?" Jerry shouts.

Clattering around in the cupboards.

"The job. Sounds promising."

Jerry is now standing in the doorway, seeing Zoe wrapped up.

"I'll put the heating on."

"No, it's fine. Warmer in here than work is, that's for sure." Zoe says.

Jerry goes to check on the pre-paid gas meter. Even though it's running low, he puts the heating on.

A short while later, he is sitting at the desk. Toast crusts and bean juice on the plate next to the open forensic psychology course book. Surprised by what he has just read, he turns to tell Zoe, but she is asleep with the blanket sagging off her. He pulls it up to her shoulders and turns the TV down.

*

Bright lights buzzing above like noisy and annoyed angels. Jerry always thought the blinding light was on purpose. He is snarling toward the man in the corner, nodding. This has not gone unnoticed by the employment coach, who is calling out from the doorway.

"Jerry Fenn?"

Jerry sits and watches the jobs' worth waddling around to her chair. Bigger, more cushioning with a headrest. Unlike the flat board on four thin pegs that he was resting on.

"Hows' the job search going then?" she asks.

"Got a few weeks in a kitchen, through an agency." Jerry replies.

The lady opens a drawer. Not finding what she needs.

"I have to go get a form for you to fill in; I'll only be a minute."

She pushes herself away from the desk on the wheels of the chair which is squeaking as it recovers from bearing her weight.

To Jerry's left is a girl, no older than 17 years old. She has with her a pushchair with a child no more than a year old who is crying. The young mother has no patience for the child and is ignoring its cries. To Jerry's right is the nodding man from the waiting room, now putting his case forward to a job's worth.

"Just got outta jail, need some money." The nodding man says.

He pulls his trouser leg up to show a tag around his ankle.

"When was your last employment date?" The civil servant asks.

"Never worked, my guy." The nodding man says.

He then turns to see Jerry looking over.

"Fuck you looking at?" he asks.

Jerry looks away. Mumbling under his breath at the waste of space to his right. And now, to his left, as the lady with the form returns, dipping into the chair and dragging herself back under the desk.

"Ok. So, you need to fill this in. The day you start the work, the address and manager's name. Any overpayment will need to be paid back."

Jerry is looking over the form.

"It's asking how much national insurance contribution I've made. I have no idea."

The job's worth rolls her eyes.

"You'll have to contact the number at the bottom of the form." she says.

Jerry looks over the room. What a sorry looking lot, he thought. Including the workers.

*

The neon lights and traffic splashing around the ankles never seem to cease. Jerry has just finished another shift at the restaurant and, as he is leaving, sees a group of teens following a man down the street. The man is aware of this and is now quickening his pace, looking over his shoulder as he does so. He hits lucky and jumps on a bus just before the doors close. The group sprint, now banging on the bus window and are shouting obscenities. Jerry walks the long way home.

*

The underpass is unoccupied, and the lack of noise is creeping Jerry out as he heads through it at a quick pace. Suddenly, he hears steps behind him and ignores the voice that is now echoing around.

"Give me ya loot, or I'll chuff ya." The youth says.

Jerry turns. It's the same group that were chasing buses on the main street.

"Just keep walking, Jez boy. Just keep walking." Jerry quietly says to himself.

He reaches the other side and is heading up the verge as another group is coming down the verge on the opposite side of him. The two gangs are now clashing. He can only hear the fighting as he heads quickly to his block entrance.

*

The late-night current affairs show on the TV is loud as the audience are clapping and agreeing with a man sitting centre of the semi-circle, facing the presenter and her two guests. The audience member, with his growing courage, now stands, and wants to know why nothing in his community is being done to sort out the drug problem and anti-social behaviour, and why there is no rehabilitation in prisons.

"We're soft on crime." he shouts while holding his hands out, scanning the audience for support and approval.

They clap, but the presenter is looking at her guests. A look to say, 'how are you going to get out of this one then?'

The crowd quietens down. The guests look at one another until there's a throat being cleared.

"What do you advise we do? We can't force prisoners to engage with the relevant resources to establish any degree of satisfactory rehabilitation in the public eye. There is much more to just re-offending here. Other factors must come to light." The guest says.

Collectively, the same question is echoing.

"Why can't you?"

Again, throats are clearing. More so to buy time.

Another man stands and points to the stage.

"We need to take example from other countries. One that deters crime. Makes an example of the crooks."

"Chuck em in a pit." A voice shouts.

The comment is met with a cheer and a clap.

The presenter places her index finger to her ear to hear the producer a little clearer. She finds camera two and advises they will return after a short break.

The presenter removes the earpiece and is now walking out of sight behind the stage. Mumbling to herself.

"You wanted live boss. You got live."

Jerry comes into the living room. Slipping his coat off.

"Zozo." he shouts.

Zoe is in the kitchen making beans on toast for them both. Stirring cheese into the pan.

"It's kicking off tonight, kid. Fucking youths. I was nearly robbed you know?" Jerry says. Looking down out the window and looking at shadows from the dim light near the underpass.

"What? Are you OK?"

Zoe stops stirring the pan.

She then holds his cheeks, looking him straight in the eyes.

"Yeah, I'm fine. Got lucky it seems."

Jerry pondered as blue lights hit the ceiling.

They are catching Zoe's attention too as she slides bread into the toaster. Jerry watches the youths scatter into dark gaps and away from the police. All except two, now being shuffled into the paddy wagon.

"They'll be out by morning. Back to the same shit circle of life." Zoe says.

Sorting the cutlery.

"That's it then." she says.

Jerry stirs the pan, turning the hob down.

"What's it?" he asks.

"We said that if one of us gets threatened or hurt or doesn't feel safe, then we find a way out of here." Zoe says.

Jerry kisses her on her cheek.

"Easier said than done." Jerry says.

He knows something needs to be shared just by the look from Zoe.

"Go on?" he says with a reluctant tone.

It takes a beat, but he has a good guess what Zoe is going to say.

"Your dad, right? Offering a deposit on a flat?"

"The offers' there, Jezzy." Zoe says as the toast springs from the toaster.

*

A short while later, Zoe is reading the free paper.

"Says here, elderly people aren't putting their heating on, because of the cost of it now."

Jerry hears Zoe talking, but not what she says. He has his attention on a case study in the forensic psychology course book.

"No one can afford to live now." Zoe says.

"Two incomes, no brats. We're doing alright." Jerry says.

Zoe replies in a playful, sarcastic tone.

"And how were your beans on toast tonight sir?"

"Not as good as last nights, I must say."

Smiling into the course book.

He taps the page of a case study that talks of three homeless men who planned on robbing their 19-year-old dealer, only the dealer stabbed two of the homeless men, as a result one died, with the other discharging himself shortly after being admitted to the hospital, where he refused to talk to the cops about the incident. Eventually the dealer was lifted, however, at his third police interview, his lawyer presented a written statement, the dealer pleading not guilty to any offence and was claiming self-defense, so it went to trial. He walked free after time served for the possession of a bladed article with all other charges dropped.

"What do you think of that?" Jerry asks.

"Good lawyer? I don't know, really. His age might have something to do with it. That kid needs some attention. Harm reduction, or a new lease on life."

"Won't happen kid. You said yourself. Back to the same shit circle of life."

Jerry reads on from the coursebook.

"According to this, prisons have poor rates of reducing re-offending and within a year of release, at least half will re-offend."

"So what's the answer then?" Zoe asks.

Jerry shrugs and heads to the kitchen.

Zoe shouts through.

"We're on emergency credit now."

Lighting a joint and wrapping herself up in the blanket.

\*

The bar is a dive, and Jerry loves it there. A sense of hostility where at times, something will happen, whether a scuffle over money or a game of pool or a woman. Jerry never gets into any trouble there, though. He is a familiar face that shows no threat. Nor is he seen as an easy target. Jerry watches the horses on one of the TV screens being pushed into the starting gates, some with reluctance as he is waiting for his friend Tyler to arrive back with the drinks. The other screen has a show where people talk about their business in the hope of one of the rich people on the panel picking up on their idea. Jerry was unsure what was being said as a pillar and pool cues blocked the subtitles. Tyler returns and puts two pints down and sits, lights a cigarette.

"You know it cost the taxpayer 40,000 a year to keep a murderer in prison. You know that?" Jerry asks.

"Nope. Why do you know?"

"Forensic psychology degree." Jerry replies.

"Oh yeah. How's it going?" Tyler asks.

Jerry rolls a smoke. Looking over to the TV screen where horses are being whipped and with text crossing over the bottom of the screen.

"In all honesty, my friend, I'm jaded by it all. Zozo keeps bringing the free press home too. Headlines never ending about the shit in the world. And to top it off, I wash dishes for a living."

Tyler giggles.

"Sorry I asked."

He sips his pint.

"How is Zozo?"

"She's good. Still at the old folk's home. Seems to like it. Well, I say like. She's not a complainer. Just gets on with it."

Jerry lights his smoke.

"She's a diamond." Tyler says.

"She certainly is. Er. I can't return the drink. No pay till next week I'm afraid." Jerry says.

Tyler is waving away the comment as a man runs into the bar. Blood running down his head, dripping on the stained bar floor. A beat later, two police officers crash in behind him and in a split second, one has the man by the neck while the other officer is hugging the legs and is charging the man to the floor. Rolling him over and cuffing him. Punters are shouting and making a nuisance of themselves with one of the cops shouting for them to get back while grabbing his pepper spray as a threat. In a moment, the bar is back to the same noise. The jukebox playing generic tunes, punters smashing pool balls, and loud over excited drunken jive talk. Jerry and Tyler have seen it all before, and Tyler goes back to the bar for two more beers.

*

Jerry is paying for gas on the payment card. As the shopkeeper is sorting the payment, Jerry can't help but think how protected and secure everything is. The cigarettes are behind a shutter, and the booze is locked beneath the counter with three inches of plastic. Smeared and greasy separating the worker from the customer. The newspapers are not protected, however. And Jerry reads the first few sentences of the article about a 52-year-old man who was given a two-year suspended sentence six years ago, has again been spared jail after being in possession of indecent images. Below are two small articles about the absence of clues and leads relating to a job centre employee and manager of a garage. Soon to be filed as cold cases. Jerry and the shopkeeper share a beaten smile before Jerry leaves to heat the flat.

*

The shared tower block entrance is quiet but smells of weed. Even the stairs are unoccupied by rolled up sleeves and spit. However, pins and caps still litter the stairs to Jerry's floor. Music is blaring out from each of the levels, nearly merging into one thick, messy noise as he ascends. He favoured the stairs over the lift. Always being teased by Zoe of his reluctance and fear of being trapped in a metal tomb. He smiles and is looking forward to seeing Zoe, but that happiness suddenly turns to concern as he opens the flat door and sees her on the phone, panicking and upset.

"Like hell there isn't. Which hospital?" Zoe demands down the phone.

Jerry is pulling his brow down and has open arms.

"I'm on my way now." Zoe says and hangs up.

"My dad, he's had a heart attack." Zoe says as she hurries with her shoes.

"I'll call a taxi." Jerry says.

He skips through his contacts to find the taxi firm he has used many times, only being advised by the cab office that they are not driving into their estate because of the trouble over the past few weeks.

"Shit." Jerry expels.

Hanging up the phone.

"The taxis aren't coming up this way cos of the fucking yobs out there." he says.

The clock reads just after eleven. He goes to hug Zoe who's in a panic as she can't find her purse. Her coat is half on and dragging on the floor.

"Missed the last bus, kid. I'm gonna go see if I can flag a cab down on the main street. Call you in five minutes."

Jerry heads to the front door and kisses Zoe. Gripping her hand firm and with a smile.

"I'll wait outside for you." Zoe says.

A few moments later, Zoe is outside and calling her mother again. The wind is picking up, which is blowing noise towards the walls of the tower block. No answer from her mother and she wonders if she should make her way to the main street. Zoe hangs up and is watching a car's headlights coming toward her. The car pulls up where she notices Jerry in the driver's seat. She runs over and leans into the car.

"What the fuck, Jez?" Zoe says.

"Just get in." Jerry says with urgency.

Looking over his shoulder and in the review mirror.

Zoe too, is now cautious, looking around before dipping into the car.

He speeds off toward the hospital.

*

It's just gone one in the morning and Jerry is arriving back in the stolen car. He is alone, as Zoe wanted to stick around the hospital. He parks the car a little further from where he found it. He looks around before climbing out. As he does so, he's hit in the head from behind. Instantly going into fight mode and turning to face the fist. He's too slow though, and is now hit in the jaw, landing heavily on the ground with no time to compose himself, feeling this is going to be rough. Instead, verbal torment. The man standing over Jerry is calling the police. As he waits for a response, he continues to fling abuse at the thief on the ground.

"Yer lucky I listen to my wife yer twat. Otherwise, I would've broken yer legs."

Jerry is now composed and sits on the small wall. Running was not an option, and a crowd of nosey residents were now out, shining their phones, and shouting over to the hard hitter who was now telling the police the address of the crime. Jerry felt nothing, but something had now knocked him to dreamland.

\*

The next day, Jerry is standing in court. His eye swollen, seen by the judge as a threat and violent life, rather than an unfair beating. Four officers are now approaching the hurting man and closing him in like a trapped, bruised banana. The judge is around sixty-five and has a sour snarl on his sagging, pale face before he stares hard at Jerry as he speaks.

"I read your statement. I can't condone your actions, though some patience is due. However, in this instance, I take your history into consideration and feel an example be set by yourself, that you serve 17 days in prison. Good day."

The judge snarls and lifts his nose toward the ceiling before disappearing behind a heavy wooden door.

Jerry cannot believe what he has just heard and has become limp as two of the officers march him out to the wagon.

\*

Zoe is in the kitchen with the phone between her shoulder and neck as she is spooning sugar into a coffee. Jerry tells her he is doing fine, but she knows him too well. His tone is slow and drawn out. He is tired and still hurting from healing wounds.

"How's your dad?" he asks.

"Still in hospital. Hoping to be let out later today."

Jerry feels useless and has let Zoe down.

"I'm so sorry kid." he says.

There's a beat. Jerry wants to cry, but circumstances and environment have him taking deep and heavy breaths to compose himself.

"Mum wants me to stay with her until dad gets home. But I'd rather stay here."

"Are you safe at the flat?" Again, Jerry feels less of a man.

"Of course, bloody kids have discovered knock and run though, as well as some flavoursome words through the letterbox. And now have a habit of messing with the lift."

"They sound young." Jerry says.

Looking over the space and watching the other prisoner's movements.

"You sure you're OK in the flat alone? Perhaps you should go to your mums?"

"I'm closer to work from here. I'm fine, really Jez."

The two fall silent for a second or two.

"I'll be home soon. Reckon I'll only do another 5 days or so." Jerry says.

Suddenly, the phone goes dead. End of call.

*

Returning to his cell, Jerry sees his cellmate with watery eyes and dabbing blood from his nose with the sleeve of his sweater. The prisoner from a few cells up is cooking rice in Jerry's kettle. He ignores this and turns to leave but before he can gain any ground, another prisoner stops him. Blocking the doorway.

"How you get the shiner?" The rice cooking chef asks.

"Burnt the wife's toast." Jerry replies without thinking about it.

The response is ignored, however, with another question from the rice chef as he is stirring herbs and salt into the kettle.

"You got any batts for me?" he asks.

Now getting closer to Jerry's shiner.

"I quit." Jerry says.

Two others now enter the cell.

"Proper nosh boys." One of them says.

Jerry takes this opportunity to leave. As he does, his cellmate is following but is called back into the cell.

"You still owe me guy." The chef says.

Jerry's cellmate just nods and quickly leaves the uninvited men laughing and eating.

\*

The bookcases are tall and chained to the wall. Behind the desk sits the librarian with a walkie talkie and four small screens monitoring the library as a prison warden paces the floor. Two other prisoners are sitting quietly, and Jerry feels the atmosphere is calmer and safer than any other room in the prison. He's looking at the section labelled research, looking for similar content he was working on when free. However, no coursebooks or workbooks about forensics or crime appear available, which Jerry feels to be ironic. He decides on a book titled 'Business and Plan B' which he takes from the shelf, not really knowing why he picked it up. A far cry from where his interests lie. Though if pushed, he would admit he had few interests. As he is heading to the lady behind the desk, an Orderly enters, pushing in a trolley of books. One wheel is staggering along the floor, making it difficult to steer.

Jerry spots 'One flew over the cuckoo's nest' novel on the trolley and asks the Orderly if it is OK to take. It's fine by him and hands him the book. Jerry gives himself a challenge to finish the novel before being released from this awful place.

\*

The shiny black Range Rover pulls slowly into a parking space outside the tower block. Looking like a gold bar in a compost factory. Out of place and vulnerable in the area. From the back of the car climbs Zoe. David climbs out of the passenger seat, followed by his wife Christina from the driver's side.

"Where you two going?" Zoe asks.

The underpass now echoing voices.

"We thought we'd come up. See how the place is getting on." Christina says.

"The flat is fine. I'll be five minutes. Just pack a quick bag and be right back down." Zoe says.

But with sirens blaring and voices getting louder, Zoe feels it is probably safer for her parents to come with her, but plays it like they have got their way.

"Suit yourselves." Zoe says.

Now walking the same pace as her father and ensuring his stepping is OK over the uneven pavement. She decided staying with them for a while would be a good idea. Warmer at the parents' house at least. And if asked, she would admit she was feeling lonely.

At the entrance of the block, a group of lads around ten or eleven years old are taking turns to kick the lift door. They are all wearing the same type of tracksuit and expensive sports shoes. They stop as the three enter. One boy hits a vape and passes it on, then tapping his friend on the chest as he is pointing at Zoe. They file out the door, being kept open by Christina as Zoe is helping her dad to the lifts.

"That yer boyfriend?" One lad shouts out to Zoe.

"I would fuck you girl." Another one shouts.

"Charming." Christina says with a disgusted tone.

Suddenly, a more still and calm moment washes over the area as the voices disperse down the dimly lit path. Zoe pushes the button for the lift before heading back to the door to check on the car. Knowing full well that type of vehicle is easy to boost.

The lift doors are now sliding open with a slight shudder. Zoe thinks about the stairs, but her dad could not manage them, and it would be easier to just get the lift. Quicker too.

"What were they smoking there?" David asks.

"A vape dad. They were vaping." Zoe says.

"What happened to a good old ciggie?" he asks.

Now stepping a little unsteadily into the lift.

Christina is shaking her head at her husband's comment. Zoe points down toward her dad's shoes and then runs her finger up near to his chest.

"This happens, dad." Zoe says sternly.

The doors close, but the lift only rises a few feet before halting abruptly. The light above them is flashing before it switches off. Being replaced with the small emergency light shining dimly on the metal walls. Zoe taps the buttons to entice the lift to move. The doors clamped shut with no life seemly behind them. Zoe gets the torch on her phone.

"You guys OK? mum?"

Zoe points the torch toward her mother's face.

Christina is finding it hard to catch her breath but nods that she is OK. Zoe now pans around towards her dad. The two ladies take a step back as he is pushing himself into the corner on the floor and clutching his chest.

Even with the artificial light, he is clearly pale and in pain.

Without a second thought, Zoe calls for an ambulance and is banging on the lift door in the hope of someone helping them, sooner rather than later as her dad flops unconscious.

She hands her mother the phone and begins CPR the best she can.

\*

Jerry returns to his cell to see it empty of his cellmate's stuff. The top bunk now stripped. It's still early, and he is thankful for the quiet time before the rest of the population gets up for the 5th day. The slim sunlight was doing nothing to warm the cold steel and hard interior, so he wraps his bedding around himself and starts passing the time by reading the business course book.

A little while later, halfway down a page with the heading, 'No idea is a bad idea.' There is a knock, followed by a shout for Jerry.

He opens his cell door where a slim, yet healthy-looking young man walks in. He can't be a day over nineteen years old. Jerry thought.

"Governor wants to see you." The screw says.

"What for?" Jerry asks.

The screw just shrugs.

"Now?" he asks the screw.

"I guess so." The screw says with a sarcastic tone.

"This is your new cellmate." The screw is pointing to him. "Jerry."

"Jamie. They call me Jammy, though."

The two shake hands and take a second to get the measure of one another before Jerry follows the screw out of the cell.

"Good luck my guy." Jamie says to Jerry.

"Thanks."

*

The phone goes straight through to voicemail, so Jerry leaves a message for Zoe, telling her he was going to be released next day, and is looking forward to seeing her, also putting forward that he hopes her dad is OK as he has not heard from her. He wants to just keep talking to the machine. Some normality for a moment. The charge dips however, and the call ends.

Back at the cell, Jamie has made himself at home and is lying on the top bunk with pictures of family members on the wall. It is Jerry's toothpaste that his Bunky has used to stick the pictures up, but Jerry does not care. He knows by tomorrow night he will be in his own bed. With his beautiful Zozo.

The cell door swings open. Jamie now sits upright, instantly recognizing the kettle chef, who launches towards him as his mate stands on watch. Jerry does not think twice and grabs the kettle, swinging at the chef's head before he can get a hold of Jamie. The kettle cracks, but Jerry strikes again. The chef falls on the floor and in a split-second Jamie jumps forward, kicking the chef's mate in the face, carrying on with a barrage of swift and fast punches to the face, belly and ribs. The cell falls silent. The mate wipes his face and sharply leaves, for many reasons. The chef, however, is fighting consciousness. Jamie grabs him by the scruff and shouts for him to clean the cell.

The chef is barely splattering a sentence, but Jamie hears it.

"With yer jumper. Do it now." Jamie says.

The chef composes himself. Jerry heads to the door to keep a crowd forming. The last thing he needs is to be questioned for GBH but is sure the chef will not grass.

The chef's top is blood stained, and Jerry feels bad. Though wonders why. The guy is a criminal and a bully. If it wasn't him and his new cellmate, then someone else would have eventually taken care of business.

Jamie is close to the chef's ear.

"Now fuck off, kettle boy." Jamie says.

The chef limps out of sight, down the hall.

"Think we need a new kettle my guy." Jamie jokes.

Jerry laughs, then noticing the course book on the floor. A calling card drops out of it as he picks it up.

An email address is printed in a small font on the bottom, along with a website.

The words:

'DRAKE MOON'S.'

He turns it over to see the words:

'HAVE AN UNCONVENTIONAL IDEA OR BUSINESS?'

Jerry thinks nothing of it and slips it back into the course book.

\*

# 3 days later.

People gather and scatter around the first floor of the modest three-bedroom house. Food and drink lie over a long table in the dining room. Jerry is filling his plate of small sandwiches and nibbles for himself and Zoe, over in the corner talking with relatives strange to her and strangers to Jerry.

He hardly even knows Christina, who is now approaching him, and he feels the amount of food looks greedy and hopes Zoe will come and help explain the overflow of pork pies and cocktail sausages. Christina takes a plate and begins scanning the table for what she fancies, deciding upon an egg and cress triangle and a slice of shortbread.

"Hello Jeremy."

"Mrs. Lewin. Hello."

Jerry pulls the typical sympathetic smile and bows slightly.

"I didn't get the chance to say how sorry I am for your loss."

He now feels even worse and foolish about expelling the typical speech for this type of circumstance. Her response, however, was positive and is now gently stroking his cheek with a warm soft hand, like it is he who needs soothing.

"Just finish that degree of yours. And take care of my daughter. Perhaps by spending no more time inside a cell." she says.

Christina is looking at Jerry directly in the eye.

Her stare is intense and uncomfortable, how it was intended to be, and Jerry can see where Zoe gets her strength.

"Of course, Mrs. Lewin. I'm lucky to have her."

Suddenly a wave of black clothes washes over towards the two with Christina now ushered away in the middle of them, heading to another group of relatives. Jerry sighs with relief. Soon drowned by admiration for the Lewin family, looking over to Zoe, how beautiful she is. He chomps on a cocktail sausage and puts the plate on the table to head for the toilet.

*

The guest has tried the bathroom door twice now, so Jerry flushes the toilet and heads out. His shiner was still prominent. He smiles at the man, who does not return the gesture, instead just dives rather quickly into the bathroom and locks the door.

Across the hallway is a door ajar. Jerry wipes his hands dry on his trousers and goes to see what room Zoe once had, instead enters Mr. Lewins' study. The walls have certificates on them. A degree in social science and diplomas in extended science, research and theory. As well as certification to teach. On the desk there are a few thank you cards and on closer inspection, see they are from classes Mr. Lewin had taught. What was beside those cards, however, was more of a draw for Jerry and as he is filing through some papers, he's shocked as Zoe has snuck in.

"Came looking for ya. Heard you were hogging the bathroom." she says in a mocking manner.

Jerry picks up a card.

"He seemed well liked." Jerry says.

"Yeah. He was a good teacher." Zoe says.

"Strange how we're sent on, ain't it? Just dust in a box."

Jerry again has his attention on the paperwork.

"You really have a way with words. I wouldn't open with that mind." Zoe says.

She is used to his views; this one, of course new, but she knew he was not being crude, or disrespectful.

He holds her tight and kisses her forehead.

"Mum was asking where to keep him." Zoe says.

"That's what I mean."

Jerry paces over the green carpet.

"Strange to be placed somewhere, right?" he asks.

Zoe just shrugs and has pursed lips as if to say 'it is what it is.' She holds her hand out.

"Come on. Let's get pissed." she says.

Jerry walks back to the desk.

"You know what this is here?"

He picks up the papers of around forty sheets.

Zoe glances at it with no interest.

"I dunno. Maybe an experiment for one of his classes. Come on. Before my Aunt Wendy sips the house dry."

Zoe is now heading for the door.

"Can I take these?" Jerry asks.

Holding the papers up.

"I guess. I'll put them in my bag."

She kisses him on the cheek, takes the paperwork and leads the way back downstairs.

*

Christina insisted on giving Zoe some money. Zoe declined, but had no choice as Christina slid it into Jerry's palm before the cab drove off. This money was to come in handy, now Jerry was unemployed again, but the pair did, however, have brand name beans for tea with thick whole meal toast.

Jerry is placing the needle gently down to hear static before Superfly record begins while Zoe smokes a joint. He had her take another look at the papers he had brought from her dad's, especially after finding a business card for DRAKE MOONS attached to the last page. The same he had found while in prison. One page has a picture of a cigarette, beside it, a drawing of a tin can, the size of a bean or cat food tin. Below are math's workings.

"Oh yeah. I remember this, kinda." Zoe says.

She flicks a few pages before returning to the beginning.

"Dad was messing around with this one day in the garage when I went to visit."

Again, she flicks through the pages like she is reminding herself more of it.

"Yes, that's right. He was seeing how long it would take a tin can to heat using a lit cigarette inside it. Then how long the can will stay warm after the cigarette burns out."

Zoe taps the front page, then passes Jerry the joint, then the papers.

"Like I say. For a science lesson or something."

But Jerry is less convinced as he reads nearer the back of the work again.

*

A restless night for Jerry. He can still hear the echoes of criminals and chancers ringing through the steel and concrete confinements. Lying in bed thinking of injustice. Unable to shake the bitter taste of dealers getting off with a murder charge. Or sex pests never seeing a cell.

Even now, at 3.27am, the chopper was flicking the night air with a party vibrating a few doors down the corridor. He rises from the bed, careful not to disturb Zoe, as her alarm will do so in a couple of hours.

In the lounge, the desk light is warming the bean juice on the plate but wrapped around Jerry is a blanket. The crude brightness of the computer screen is now pouring out the website for Drake Moon's, which is well presented. Deep green and red with options to click. He does so, only now getting a full understanding of what was on offer, and what investments have been made. Investments somewhat unknown to the public. Some underhand, some illegal, some hostile, and some just immoral. Yet they have backing both financially and with networking and marketing from many.

Pages 21 to 26 of David's paperwork looks as if it is talking about the cigarette and the tin can theory in more detail and on a bigger scale with the words:

*'Pugilistic attitude' after about ten minutes.*

Also written are the words:

*'670 and 810 degrees C and 'Full motion start to finish, appx 2-3 hours...*

Jerry lights a one skinner joint and leans into the chair. Plugging an earphone into only his left ear, he finds Massive Attack in a file and fades into 'Five-man army' all the while, stirring ideas and attempting to make sense of the work. He thinks of conducting heat, but for what? What was Mr. Lewin looking to do?

He is suddenly hit with a shudder of chilled air. Then hit with an idea. He scribbles on a pad quickly, and sloppily. Telling himself just to get the basics now. Don't complicate the idea and work on it with fresh eyes tomorrow, but as he looks over his scribbles, he can see the plan coming together. A plan he was certain David had all along. He'll fine tune it tomorrow, but for now, he will look more into the Drake Moons' organization.

\*

# 3 Months later.

The floor to ceiling tinted glass boasts a vibrant view from inside, where trees stand in tidy rows and with their branches draped to form a natural pathway to the electronic gates. Zoe is watching the branches tickle each other as she is drying her hair with a soft towel next to the heated pool attached to her new 4-bedroom, 3-bathroom house. The guilt she had felt about the job she left behind, and how beans on toast are more of a want rather than a need these days, has subsided rapidly.

Suddenly, Jerry appears at the door.

"Zozo. Hurry it's on." he shouts.

His voice echoing off the tiles and bouncing off the vast windows as he hurries back to the lounge.

"Be right there." she shouts.

\*

Zoe enters the large lounge with the large TV fixed to the wall. On it, the late-night current affairs show. The guest is Jerry. He is sitting looking small and lost, but smart in his new well-fitted blue suit on the stage. At the bottom left of the screen, Zoe can be seen in the front row.

"Welcome to another show where we have tonight with us, Jerry Fenn." The host says.

Jerry just smiles nervously and bows his head slightly.

The host again takes the lead.

"So, Mr. Fenn. It is said the idea came from generating heat. Could you start with how this came to be?"

Jerry clears his throat. A producer had prepped him earlier that day, so he sticks to that script.

"Well, we can't help noticing there is less crime wherever we go now?" Jerry says.

He is looking at the audience which is met with cheer and applause. This builds his confidence a little.

"That the sheer threat of consequence if you are committing a crime is obvious to us all? Who wants to be put in a Furness for not behaving?"

He continues to talk of the can and cigarette, that energy prices have fallen and those who re-offend and dodge responsibility and rehabilitation, are then to heat the nation for those who need it most. Cleaner and safer streets with affordable cost of living. A cheer explodes from the crowd while Jerry thinks about beans on toast.

*

# Here's how to order.

After polite wipes of mouth corners and a decline in more beverages, Mrs. Truman was interested in hearing more of the investment her neighbour John Holland had spoken of a few days ago in passing. She was hoping, however; it was not the investment opportunity that had arrived through the letter boxes of the entire street as, after communicating with the others on the well-to-do avenue, all agreed it was most definitely to be a scam. Both financially and emotionally. It was unfortunate then, that John produced the same leaflet from his cord trouser pocket and, seeing the lips of his neighbour curl down, he is quick on the defense.

"That's exactly the look I got from number 34." he says.

Throwing his arms in the air in defeat.

Mrs. Truman has always held her neighbour, come friend in high regard, but was now feeling his age of nearly 90 was playing some part in his decision. Perhaps he was afraid of the future and wanted to find a purpose. This, to everyone who knows John, or at least thought they knew him, did not think it was the answer.

"Oh, come on John." Mrs. Truman says with a stern tone.

More so with hurt for her friend rather than a slant of authority or righteousness.

"You don't honestly think that any of this is true, do you? I mean, how can this business prove it true and where's any proof it can and will happen?" she asks.

John swallows hard and is shaking his head.

"I didn't think I would have to explain myself to everyone. I've been around long enough to do as I please, without having to run it past everyone."

"We're just worried John. That's all."

The room falls silent, only broken by Mrs. Truman slowly pouring more tea into her cup. She holds the pot up as a way of offering more to her guest, but more so as a way of keeping the peace and to ensure the two old friends were still O.K. He nods but keeps his eyes away from hers as she is pouring.

John feels a little guilty and remorseful for his actions over the last few minutes but stays quiet as Mrs. Truman leaves to make a quick call.

*

Clive Henderson is wiping sweat from his brow as he is awkwardly climbing into the back of the car after again being threatened at one of his many conferences. He is now certain, after some reflection, that the hate is growing stronger for him and his business. A once simple idea sloppily scribbled on a napkin on a hazy drunken night is now amassing millions a year on the sign ups alone. Bringing with it a mass of problems.

His associate, Simon Pickard, who was keen to stay in the shadows of the conference tonight, has no opinion or suggestion and can only curse himself for being at the point of no return. Too much money, time and reputation invested with great loss if he was to bow out. So, as he watches Clive Henderson sigh in relief with a lucky smile on his face, he will continue to be the silent partner and not share his growing concerns.

"Still, in our defense, there's more at the conference supporting us than there are outside against us." Clive says.

No one responds. Simon is looking out the window as the bright lights flick past on the quiet street. The driver, assigned by an agency, never speaks unless spoken to. A military man.

Tough skin and scars of war. Nowadays he's keeping his nose clean and keeping busy, thankful for the job, and has since been assigned full time by the two wealthy businessmen who are looking like they have things to say to one another but cannot muster the words.

*

The next morning is the same as the others over the last couple of weeks. From the time it takes for the businessmen to arrive back at a hotel to the rise of the daylight, the undesirable and nuisance of the protesters will have gathered around the entrances or stand waiting for a chance to harass and harm Clive and Simon, and anyone else they are with.

Simon is looking out of his window, watching a small crowd unraveling a banner. He doesn't see what it says, as he has someone at his door. Knocking in quick succession for the fourth time. He answers it to see Clive already shaved, dressed, and fed. He invites himself in.

"They're a fucking media nightmare this lot." Clive says.

Simon now knows his associate has also peeked from the curtains of his hotel window to see the people who are clearly against their business and its future.

"Why does everyone have an opinion? If you don't like something, don't invest your money or time in it. It's that simple." Clive grunts.

His tone is a little defeated before taking Simon's croissant, winking and leaving while shouting over his shoulder.

"I'll be hiding in my room. Get that bean brain driver of ours to find a way outta here, away from those soap dodgers down there."

Simon is again keeping quiet. And again, he has convinced himself as he laid awake for most of the night, that it was too late to pull out. Clause 2.8. of the contract. That the investor here named Mr. S. Pickard shall be subject to liability for any cost relating to or referring to outside involvement within the first seven years until 1. A successful and substantial financial claim for Mr. C. Henderson is met. And 2. The death of one Mr. C Henderson, which ever falls first and is legally bound. Simon was, however, richer than he could have ever dreamt, but money was not helping the rope around his neck, contractually speaking. Simon calls the military man on the hotel phone, where he asks for him to call back when he finds an exit free of the protesting crowd, and, with a stutter, also asks if the two may speak privately soon and the military man agrees before they hang up. Simon looks out the window again to see the passionate people below, or as the media have coined them, The 'anti-afters.' A term he and Clive have already grown tired of.

*

Across town, in a very stuffy media office, are men in button-down shirts and ladies with makeshift fans made of folded paper. Feeling the brushing air from one of the girls' fans, Frankie Lowe is paying no attention to his boss, who is dishing out the jobs for the days ahead.

"Frankie, you're gonna share with us what you got on the Henderson story and the afterlife campaign or just sit there looking dumb?"

The comment is followed by a wave of chuckles by his associates, which is no surprise to him. He shares with the bored, hot, and thirsty room that Clive Henderson has escaped jail time relating to various drifting and long cons he has been involved in. The most recent one, auctions that take bids under a business name, the buyer places a bid, then is told they are the highest bidder, then they would need to provide payment for the auction item, the only thing was, the item was not owned by the seller, that being Mr. Henderson. The bids would flood in, and each bidder would be told they won the item. Mr. Henderson denied any accountability and involvement of this con, but was, however, still ordered to pay back over 13,000 in costs but dodged prison. Even though he had apparently accumulated a little under half a million from the swindle.

"As you are all aware, his new venture is cunning. Only viable, however, to those who trust the claims of the business idea, believe in it and can indeed afford it, no matter of the uncertainty and history of the man running the scheme. Whatever the case, the guy certainly has some balls on him." Frankie says.

The room chuckles, for the right reasons this time, and Frankie is smiling, only sharply stopping as his boss is the only one not amused.

"So, the thing appears to be selling well. Why, however, I can't understand."

"Then find out." His boss says with a sharp and stern tone.

This quietens the room ever more and Frankie is watching the boss's eyes following him out of the room.

"Shitbag." Frankie mumbles to himself as he heads back to his desk and after shuffling himself under it, calls one of his connections.

*

The neon lights in the bar are not flattering and do not help to disguise the undesirable lush and the chancers, especially the crinkled man staring with dead eyes towards Frankie. Rarely blinking and skin pale and unconditioned. Frankie wonders why his connection, Henry Holland, insists on meeting there. Not only because they stick out like carrots in a mushroom pack, but that it is miles out of the way of both homes and offices of the two associates. Henry was never on time too.

"Well, I was hoping to have something juicy for ya, my friend, but what I have discovered only last night has turned my gut." Henry says.

"Go on." Frankie insists.

He sips a rum and coke from a questionable glass before getting his small notebook from his inside pocket. However, he slips it back into the pocket as the look on Henry's face does not need or want this on the record for now.

"So, I get a call from one of my dad's neighbours." Henry says.

"OK." Frankie says.

Sipping again his rum and coke.

Henry is being cautious about what he wants to say. Frankie was a friend, but a reporter will always be a reporter. However, Frankie's profession so close to hand may be of some benefit.

"He's bought into all this shit."

"What. The Afterlife venture?" Frankie asks.

He has never met Henry's dad and surprised to hear that a relative of a man who Frankie could argue is highly intelligent was to fall into such a trap.

"Has he paid anything towards it?" Frankie asks.

"Apparently so, yes."

Henry lights a cigarette.

"How much? And by chance, you have a contract or any information only those who have signed up to it may have?"

Frankie feels awful asking but is also intrigued.

"He's paid enough." Henry quietly says.

"And I am hoping to find something in his office, though I'll dig around it when he's out of the house."

The smears of grease on the mirror tiles behind the bar now grab Frankie's attention. Again, as does the grey man, still with a blank expression and a posture looking in need of something. Frankie now looks like he's deep in thought about the circumstances of his associate, but the frown was how undesirable he felt the bar to be. And the people in it.

"How old is your dad?" Frankie asks.

"89. He's still of sound mind, though. And he is still quick to argue logic, never seen as a fool, or be taken for one. He was a lawyer, for gods' sake. So how is it that he's now piling money into a scheme that is utterly bizarre and questionable?"

Henry is keeping his eyes on his associate.

"Apart from this little issue, have you found anything further about the scheme?" Frankie asks.

"They're doing a pre-recorded interview tomorrow, Studio 10 buildings, so to keep the land still. No more live interviews or conferences because of the hate they're getting. At the suggestion of the cops and security firm they hire from. According to my guy, anyway."

The TV is shining above the bar like a square star. The visuals grab the associate's attention. An advert for the 'Afterlife venture' scheme. A number to contact the business and a discount code for group bookings, sold by a Z-list celebrity, has Frankie wondering where he recognizes the has been from, before the colours are disbursing from view and back to some old cheap quiz show.

"No point going to this pre-record. Any chance I can talk with your dad?"

"As a friend or as a hack?" Henry asks.

"Would it matter?" Frankie asks before finishing his rum and coke.

*

The postman is making a racket as he is attempting to shove a forest's worth of mail into the slot. Hearing the ruckus from upstairs, Frankie assumes it is his brother coming to visit. He had advised him he was back in town after some time away, but Frankie is yet to hear from him and wonders where he is. Always a lone wolf and quiet, even as a baby, Tommy never squeaked or became upset, like most kids do.

Instead, Frankie is heading down the stairs to see the envelopes and flyers slowly dripping onto the inside before the avalanche caves and is scattering on the soft carpet.

He scoops a handful up, not quite grabbing the pile completely and is heading for the kitchen, passing framed pictures of memories and the handmade jug, unintrusive and now barely noticed on its own little table in the hallway.

Frankie was never a morning person but the hanging eyes and clumsy actions around the modest kitchen was more than just the sun barely scraping high in the sky, but a sour look of the past, still gripping to Frankie as the death of his wife only seven months ago is nothing but a brutal reminder of how cruel the world is. Frankie slots some bread into the toaster. A mundane and somewhat pointless task in the grand scheme, but as he is waiting for it to pop, looks over the mail with only one drawing his attention. A letter from the life insurance company, attached, a long-awaited cheque for a substantial amount of money. Frankie sighs, dropping the letter on the table as the toast flings from the toaster. If only he could return the money for just one more day with the love of his life.

*

Mrs. Reid is looking around the care home rec room, hoping to grab the attention of a nurse, or another resident or visitor. The greased hair and the cocky young attitude of the salesman were scaring her. With his smoky breath and potent aftershave. He unlocks his briefcase and produces some paperwork.

Now piling the pressure on.

"Mrs. Reid. The contract clearly states you need to keep up your payments, otherwise you dream life will not be obtainable. Now I appreciate these care homes are costly, but a contract is a legal document."

"Who let you in here young man? Who are you?" Mrs. Reid asks.

This was loud enough to alert the nurse, Olivia Walker, so she walks toward Mrs. Reid, who is looking confused at the leaflet she is holding.

"Mrs. Reid." Olivia calls out softly.

The pusher stuffs the paperwork back into the case and straightens his tie.

"Mrs. Reid. Are you OK?" Olivia asks.

Now looking at her seemly unwanted visitor.

"Look sir, this lady has health conditions that warrant care. Who exactly are you and what is your business here?" Olivia asks in a stern and useful tone.

The young, confident man may swindle and coast through life when he is in control, but his inexperience of meeting varying levels of people was still yet to be perfected. So much so, that he was not expecting to be blown back by the middle-aged, petite lady.

"She has a plan with us." he says with a high pitch and red cheeks.

He's now being ignored, and Mrs. Reid has grown tired, now dipping in and out of the situation, carrying no worry or urgency for the last few moments.

The pusher is looking around before smiling out of embarrassment and uncertainty about what to do, so he just leaves the room quietly but quickly.

*

Henry watches his dad striking his millionth match of the same brand he has always used. Remembering the first time seeing the box of magic strikes when he was a kid. The size and smoothness of the box, the smell of the strip and the noise of the wooden sticks rattling, was a memory Henry hopes never to be lost. The question Henry had asked seemed a long time ago now, as he leans in to catch the flame of the match held by strong fingers. Catching also the scent of his dad's aftershave. Another habit he hopes never dies young. That Henry could pick his dad from a crowd with only a scent and a rattle from a pocket.

Henry smiles.

"Care to share." John asks.

"Just remembering happier days, pa." Henry says.

The two share a familiar silence, now being watched by the wife and mother from the bedroom window.

"Remind me. Who's that man on the Afterlife venture advert? He's so familiar. Just can't recall him." John asks.

Henry does not know. Or care.

"You still haven't answered my question." Henry says.

John looks up at the window to see his wife sharply dip out of view.

He wants to speak but does not know what to say, so he just sucks on his smoke and looks at his well tendered white roses with a stain of pink.

Henry, being conflicted, wanted to throttle his dad for such naivety, seeing weakness from a once strong man. But part of him was glowing with a memory of a parent's night when Henry was twelve. Whatever was discussed on that warm spring evening, he did not know but found school easy thereafter. At that age, Henry knew his dad argued for a living but felt there was some other power involved. That was until he got a bust nose and a kick in the ribs from Kyle Port, a kid three years older. John had convinced the jury of some minor detail of some sort, resulting in a twelve-year prison sentence for Port's father. Henry also thought about the woman suspected of poisoning her husband who walked free. Purely because of his father's experience and his knowledge of the law. As well as the human condition. The newspapers had covered the story, long after her supposed proof of innocence.

"I'm going to leave a key for my desk drawer. The'll be a letter waiting for you. Open it only after I'm gone. You hear me?" John finally says.

Henry shakes from his pointless memory and nods.

He is becoming frustrated and feels the best thing to do now is just leave.

John is watching him disappear.

"Take care son."

*

Frankie was asked to attend the care home after Olivia Walker contacted the press but can only offer condensed research and information on the Afterlife venture. Just old paper clippings and copies of a timeline and media reporting. So, after a cup of coffee and the freedom to smoke in the dining area, he leaves the file with Olivia, who was grateful and spoke about looking through it later that day. Frankie, now feeling his karma is done for the day, is ready to leave.

"Your mother lives here, right?" she asks.

He sighs quietly, but it's low and long. So now feels he's being rude, somewhat stand-offish.

"Yeah. That's right. Quite a lady." he says with a familiar and sarcastic tone, which is adding to the awkwardness.

He begins stepping to the door in little bouts while pulling a tight-lipped grin and watches Olivia's round face spread into a bright smile.

"See you around." he says.

"Take care." Olivia says.

In the hallway, the TV is shouting from the room a little further down as Frankie is walking past. The same washed-up celebrity from the bar TV, relevant maybe 20 years ago, but now, shouting of how the afterlife venture is tailored to personal needs and preference.

'To live the life, you have always wanted…Here's how to order!'

Frankie is wondering again where he knows the old face on the TV from, now unconsciously walking to the first floor, room 99.

*

The freshly employed driver is scratching his forearm with short but sharp nails, now creating three thin white lines over his eagle tattoo. He has quickly become used to relaxing with the radio and a smoke while he waits for Clive Henderson to get his end wet. The same girl and the same hotel. Same time and day every week and, although this was not what the military man had signed up for, he quickly reminds himself he will be on his next assignment soon.

Today's timings were as important as the last few drives with Henderson. Usually arriving back at 2.40pm. Then the ten-mile drive to the pre-arranged weekly meeting but for now, nothing was to disrupt him from the silk of Barry White and the smooth whisk of the cigarette smoke before the chaos and boasts of Clive and his actions with the girl from the last hour.

*

Meanwhile, in a more desirable part of the city, the room is warm and smells fresh of laundry, which is folded neatly on the bed. Spoiled with a few empty vodka bottles lying around the room and opened mail scattered around. Frankie looks to see a jigsaw piece on the floor and picks it up.

His mother has options for who might be in her room but is more concerned with the puzzle of a cityscape with silhouette people.

Frankie wonders what piece of the puzzle he holds and what the letters on the bedside table were for.

"Hello mother." he says.

"Not dead yet." she says sharply. Still looking at the puzzle.

"Where in God's name is the last piece?" she says to the room.

Banging on the table, which makes the puzzle scatter a little, and now reaching out to grab her mug.

"Your brother brings gifts."

"He's been to see you lately?" Frankie asks.

She does not answer him, however, and he already feels he has been there too long and can't help noticing she was looking frail and more lost since his last visit a few weeks ago.

"What you here for?" she asks bitterly.

Killing the vodka with a long gulp.

He has no reason to lie. And in fact, there is no reason to be truthful. He remembers playing a game with Tommy one night in which they both tried to remember the last time the woman who openly resented them had smiled. Tommy thought it was when her first drink arrived when she went into the care home.

"The sight of the booze lit her up like a Christmas tree." Tommy had said.

Frankie could not remember a smile. In fact, she could have a gold mine in that rotten hole, and he still wouldn't know.

Her eyes glazed, and wet, which are now brushing over the room, up towards her son and then sharply back to scanning for the booze bottle. Frankie sees no reason to hinder her only delight in life, so he helps her by picking it up from near the letters where he can get a better look. An invoice from some law firm, a demand from a credit card company and a letter from the manager of River Man's care home.

"Well, you going to pass my medicine or stick your business where it don't belong?"

"Money troubles, mother?" Frankie says. Unconcerned.

Suddenly the old lady bursts out with a loud, venomous, yet familiar and somewhat expected shout.

"Get your nose out my rose, you vile man. Fucking hack. Now, give me my bottle."

Frankie has heard it all before. The poison. Both from a bottle and expelling from the pores and breath of his supposed care giver. He uncaps the drink and pours it to the rim before he places the lost jigsaw puzzle beside it. Her eyes are watching him do this but quickly shifts her sight toward the great view towards the small forest and the four acres of green with thick wooden benches and a private gardener who is raking leaves, fallen from near naked branches hanging from the sky. Just like his last visit, Frankie is standing above the old lush but still feels small.

"Your brother would have been there for her. They should have married one another."

This is another obsession his mother had. Blaming Frankie for something completely out of his control. He should tell her that his wife Claire was sickened by her, and how she treated her husband when he was a boy, and that she could not stand the sight of her. That Claire had only met his brother Tommy a handful of times, and even then, didn't engage too much when the three were together. Instead, Frankie is admiring the land outside. Peaceful and unpolluted while his mother is trying to push the puzzle back together with blurred vision and with frustrated determination.

Frankie is now heading to the door, but stops to look at the letter, not addressed to the resident of the home but by the room number. Informing a rise of 125 a week is necessary but done with a heavy heart. That all at the River Man's care home are supporting residents where they can.

"See you, Heather." Frankie says.

Leaving his mother to wipe her wet eyes and dabbing her hand over spilt drink, soaking into her blouse.

*

Simon Pickard has not worn jeans since he was around 12 years old, but now, he wears the attire to blend into the surroundings of the run-down part of town. A duffle bag held tight under his arm. There is sweat gathering and soaking into the peak of his cap with every shout or passing car. The phone booth he is to use is lit too, making Simon even more anxious, as he is alone and an easy target. He dials the number and follows the instructions and notices headlights slowly growing as a car is creeping closer, now at a point where they are blinding him. He hears a voice from down the phone.

"Leave the bag, hang up and keep shut. You'll know when it's done."

Simon is at the point of no return. Like he has been for a long time in life. In this world. He is looking around as he hangs the receiver up, the car's exhaust dripping and growling like a metal feline with its eyes fixed and with purpose.

Simon slides from the booth and is just wanting to run. No harm in that, he is thinking to himself, but would it bring unwanted attention? He jumps in the car he had bought cheap to ensure no trace of him, learned from cop shows when growing up, and had arranged for it to be scrapped tomorrow morning.

*

The manager's office of River Man's care home is well lit with the large bay windows that look out toward the forest entrance and the vast green layout of the outside. All the leaves are free from the hands of the trees and are sitting in bags at the side of the large house. Out of the view of residents and visitors, though, the staff know of the organized chaos along that narrow path, as they would sit and chat with the groundskeeper and have a cheeky smoke.

The military man is savoring the taste of rich coffee before making sure he places the small cup back on the coaster provided by the manager.

"So, like I said. I would like to secure my mother financially for the next year. God forbid she'll be around any longer than that." he says.

The comment does not faze the manager. She knows residents are always someone's burden, not less hers and her employees, and understands the tone of today's visitor.

"I also saw this on my last visit."

The military man is dipping forward and retrieving a brochure from his pocket that he had picked up from the reception area.

"Option 2 sounds good." he says.

The manager, needing to familiarize herself with the brochure, is heading to the coffee table to take the leaflet from the bulky man.

"Option 2 care plan includes everything. Including transport and function room, right?" The military man asks.

The manager is nodding in agreement, like she is familiar with the options, which she is not, until she has the brochure in hand and is glancing at it quickly.

"Well, we can certainly arrange this for you at some point." she says.

"No time like the present Ms." The military man says.

He pulls his folded cheque book from his inside pocket.

"So, it's 2800 for the coffin, service, transport and the church. 200 for cremation and another 150 admin?" he asks.

"Er... yes, I think so." The manager says.

Again, glancing quickly at option 2.

The military man is writing out the cheque, which is making the manager feel awkward, so she heads to the filing cabinet for the relevant paperwork.

The military man tears the cheque off and goes back to enjoying the still hot fresh coffee.

"I'll just put in your mother's details and then we can look over the arrangement and contract where I'll notify the crematorium of your chosen care plan."

The manager is ticking some boxes and counter signing the document.

"Right. So, what room is your mother in again?"

"99." The military man replies.

*

John Holland is enjoying the contrast from his garden with white roses with a tickle of pink on the petals to being drenched in neon lights and the uncertainty of the people in the dive bar. He is walking around with a cigarette dripping from his dry lips and the day's newspaper under his arm. His fourth vodka is soaking his stomach lining and being absorbed into his bloodstream like a sea around a napkin. He thinks he can see a vacant booth in the corner and is now making a bee-line for it. There's a bloke occupying the other half, but this does not faze him, so he plonks himself down awkwardly and heavily. Placing the newspaper on the table and peeling the cigarette off his lip, which makes the skin rip a little.

Frankie is the man sitting opposite. Not surprised at someone taking up private space, not in this place anyway. Frankie can only think how wet and messy the newspaper will be. Now it's made contact on the dirty table. On this day, he could tell you word for word what was on the front page as he was the writer. The headline reads:

'CON MAN HIT WAS 'PROFESSIONAL.'

The first paragraph talks of the history of Clive Henderson, the near miss of jail time, what his life had been like until he became rich, and what his close friends and family really thought of him. Not including a statement or interview from his business partner Simon Pickard, however, as he is not to be found at his home, his office or with anyone he may regards close to him. Frankie found this odd but also assumes the threat to Simon's life is a possibility, therefore, has gone far from anywhere. And of course, not to discount the possibility that Pickard himself, may be responsible for the murder of his associate.

Frankie also loved the calls to his desk by the crusties and left-wing Libbie protesters, claiming to be responsible for the hit. Those claims were dismissed rapidly by Frankie, and the police, for many reasons. Someone with a background in combat and strategic planning clearly did the hit, not a father's credit card and a sense of entitlement. The statement 'money talks, all the truer now though, as Frankie had financial backing, which he spared nicely to get the best press release for years to come.

His attention is now being taken from the paper and up towards the floating TV screen above the bar where the advert with the somewhat familiar man is on.

John is sharing the expression as he too, wonders about the man on the screen.

The booze exacerbates this struggle and Frankie wonders why there are still commercials for the con.

John is now clicking his fingers like he is about to catch the credentials of the advert guy. Pulling a face like a word sneeze is about to explode.

"Phillies at three." John says with certainty.

He bangs the table in celebration.

"Yes. Of course. His name's Leo Scott, right? You know, that's been driving me crazy." Frankie says.

"Phillies at three. Well, I'll be damned. Why, that must be over twenty years old that show now. You must have just been a kid."

"I'm older than I look sir." Frankie says.

John is now chuckling to himself.

"I'm not."

He sips his vodka, which is stinging the small cut on his lip and eventually lights the cigarette.

"The weather is perfect this time of year. Perfect for roses, as it's humid, somewhat pleasant on my skin too." John says.

Frankie cannot see how the weather has helped the skin of the man opposite. Where he sat, he can only see a pale, greying tone with slight lines of pink in the cheeks, and creases along the forehead of the man. The mundane talk is creeping him out, too.

Looking at his watch, he still had an hour before Henry was to meet him there and was likely to be running late anyway.

"I'm I intruding? Are you expecting someone? Yes. Of course you are. Please excuse me." John is getting up from the booth. Somewhat staggered and frail, however.

"No please. He won't be here for a while yet, and he's usually late. Please stay. At least finish your drink and smoke."

The old man nods and spreads a thin smile with appreciation for the kind gesture and falls back into comfort.

"I'm John."

"I'm Frankie."

The two shake hands, now cocooned around noises of all types and from all directions.

"So, what kinda business you in then, Frankie?"

"I'm a journalist." Frankie says.

"Well son, get your notebook out. I've got a hell of a story to tell."

*

# Man in a shed.

Colin, the landlord of the grand house, is a soft-spoken middle-aged man with fraying hair and red cheeks. And, although a businessman with opportunity to make money, he appeared to have some empathy, which I liked him for. I remember meeting him for the first time after finding his number in the back of the local paper. We stood in room 6. A compact rectangle. One wall dominated by the workbench, on the other side, the bed. Stale smoke and a 1950s folding table and a fridge and bookcase. Light, busy sounds occasionally rose from the street, which made the room warm and inviting. We filled the housing benefit application on top of the silent, still fridge as sunshine wished to invade the small room. Halted by clouds and green shiny curtains.

Colin had asked why I needed a room and felt there was no reason to lie. I told him I was homeless and could not crash at various places anymore. We signed a few sheets of paper and arranged a time to meet again the following day. He was also good enough to waive the deposit on the room too. Now, the air is dense and with a circulation of familiarity. The tiled floor of the stern house has no mail for me. The Giro cheque from the job centre still unaccounted for.

I have a coffee and a bowl of cornflakes before heading out in search of answers.

*

Every town should have a place where phony people meet. Dalton West has the small shopping complex with most, if not all, that pollute the benches either claiming welfare or attending the art college.

The city clock chimes like any other chime in any other city, normally with every third car a cab shortly after the 5pm chime rings out. The job centre is the same as any other day too. Bright, warm, and loud. As soon as you enter the second floor, you're greeted by a civil servant with a pen and clipboard. If you have no appointment, it is a case of explaining to the job's worth what you are there for, then only to be told to take a seat and either wait for death or for someone who could help. Whichever comes first. I spotted Adam, the feller I see once a fortnight, to sign on and prove I am 'actively seeking employment.' I took the chance and called out to tell him about the missing cheque and needing food, where he said he would see what he could do. He wanders off, leaving me with employment leaflets and docked out cigarettes in waiting pockets. A few minutes pass when I see Adam again. He gestured me over with his hairy, manly hands. After I advise him again about my visit, he makes a quick call and tells me to come back in a few hours.

*

Only a few skins remaining, stuffed crudely in the dry, dusty tobacco pouch. I roll a joint. Inhaling long, oxygen deprived hits, drawn out with slow, relaxed exhales that bring with it immense pleasure and fond familiarity. The stereo, which I was lucky to find, is constantly on. It was lying next to the industrial sized bin one day when I went to put my rubbish out. A turntable on the top, twin tape decks and a C.D player. The AUX lead was missing, but that is not an issue. I have about seven of them. The speakers have typical chipped corners, but the cables were in good condition. The thing worked perfectly when I got it back to my bedsit. It took two trips. One for the stereo itself, with the second round collecting the speakers and C.D player. The nib of the arm was clean and sharp. Like brand new.

*

I went back to the job centre and was told by the podium prince with his clipboard to take a seat in shame corner, along with the rest of the hopefuls. The constant tap on keyboards and buzzing phones is obtrusive to the senses. I can't imagine working in an office or being tied to a phone all day. Then I remember the phone in the hallway of my house. I do not know who lives in any of the bedsits, but a fellow named 'Pev' has called many times during the past few days and is needing the money for that 'thing'. I tell 'Pev' I do not know who he is asking for and would find myself just hanging up. I should stop answering the phone in the hallway. I hear my name being called and then see Adam's hairy hands waving me over. He greets me as he offers me a seat. With the pleasantries done, he slides over a brown generic envelope. The letter states something or other, and I sign for the cheque in there. Adam reminds me of our next appointment before I leave for the post office.

*

The tall skinny man with a soft tone is sitting near the kitchen swing door. The table stretches down the faded green wall and passes the side of the café counter. It is Nick, my mentor who is supporting me through a BTEC music technology course. It is part of the conditions of claiming welfare for over twenty-six weeks. Apparently, now deemed 'unemployable' the government needs something to keep track of the millions claiming. The course, however, suited me fine. Right up my street. Music, for me, has always been a major part of my life. From crawl, fall and step, music has always been there without judgement. Although some days she may bite, pausing for a reaction. I feel all emotion for it, an emotion I assume some yearn for in life. It is a dominator, and I love it more than ever. A giver and a taker. It can, and will rip you up inside, if you let it, though it does not intend to wound, not long term anyway.

The job centre gives Nick money for coffee and a snack for us both; of course, I take full advantage of this. Coffee with cream, three sugars and carrot cake is my usual. I sit watching the busy roads through the rain dashed narrow window. Rain does not care about anything. It will slap you at any moment.

Nick flicks through the work I have done: Theory of relation, how do some genres take from others' etc, etc. He stuffs my papers in a folder he has and takes a chunk out of the chocolate cake. After he wipes his mouth with the rough white paper napkin, he explains the next module. It involves spending two days writing and recording a track with other people on the same course as me, though he is unsure where or when, but he says he will keep me posted. Nick still has some chocolate on his lips. It is gross, but of course I am ignoring it, or at least trying to, hoping the next bite of cake might get him to wipe again.

\*

I spend a lot of my time sitting in front of the found stereo, rolling joints on my 'record of achievement' folder, given to everyone on the last day of school. It is supposed to hold report cards and certificates, something to take to interviews and all that jazz. Instead, the pages are blank, the plastic wallets crisp and unused.

I examine the weed situation and feel the familiar dread. Running low is always a drag. For a while now, I have been scoring resin from a guy named Liam. A stick thin, tall 22-year-old with brown, sharp teeth in his curved pink mouth. I first met Liam in the centre of town with the guy who originally put me in touch with him. I introduced myself and he played through the whole 'I'm the kid round here' routine before he was happy to deal with me.

I bought a 1/4 block from him there and then and have been since, though he is now proving hard to get a hold of, with little or no alternatives at present.

*

The wind is biting my cheeks as I am heading to cash the cheque at the post office. It is the missing one that had eventually made its way on to the vast hallway floor. I knew cashing it was a risk but needed the cash. The lines in the post office are snaking round and the smell is stale and inhumane. Old coughing beings, not bothering to cover their lined sagging mouths when spluttering an unhealthy spoil from their frail shell. I must leave; I'm edgy about cashing the cheque anyway and the smell is making me unwell.

Outside, I see a potential hook up called Mac. I assume I remember him better than he does me and remind him of the last time we met, a party not too long ago, where he was sorting people with nice blocks of resin. He has nothing on him right now but says to contact him in a couple of hours, so I run back into the stinky post office for a pen and paper and take down his number and he heads off, leaving me in possession of a stolen red ballpoint pen. I take a walk down to the bong shop where I buy most of my smoking goods like eight packs of zig zags, eight lighters, with the likelihood of only four or five working and the occasional piece of vinyl. The store owner is pleasant enough, but I don't trust him as far as I could carry him, a very large, greasy man with a scent of unlawfulness to him.

After hitting the supermarket, I generously divide what little weed I have and try to spread it throughout the day until I can get connected. The scent of coffee haunts the room, and I build a joint. The skins smooth and difficult to manipulate. I sprinkle a small amount of resin that falls into the papers like heavy brown rocks on a thin and precarious highway. The waves from the stereo humming with melodies and good vibes. Universal Reprise, 4Hero. I sip a coffee and take light hits from the fast-burning joint as I look through the BTEC course booklet. A thick yellow A4 brick with each module and timeline in sections, spanning around twenty pages for each part.

\*

With his yellow teeth and an eternal grin, Mac welcomes me into his house. A good-sized mid terrace on a slanted street ten minutes south of the city. An aroma of food and weed. He asks how much I am after, and I tell him 70. I figure, although I have Mac's number, I am not too confident about having a regular score with him, therefore need as much as I can afford. I still need to eat for the next couple of weeks, put a few coins in the electric meter and pay the landlord a few notes towards the rent, as the housing benefit only pays some of it. He offers me a coffee, but I decline as I never feel too cozy sitting in a dealer's house any longer than necessary. Even if it appears rude. He tells me he'll be a couple of minutes and leaves me to watch the news on the TV. Some dog walker has found a dead body and is being interviewed about it. It's always the dog walkers. I'm more a cat man myself.

Mac has returned with a good-looking block of well-rounded brown resin. I give him the money and I'm about to leave before I get sucked in with small talk. After we establish who we may or may not know around town, I thank him and leave, thirty minutes after arriving.

\*

The bedsit is a trap for smells. I add to this while I eat rice and tinned vegetable curry, which will linger for days.

The intercom is now blaring aggressively, drowning the music out and harshing my mellow. A mumbled tone echoes down the receiver. It's Zeb, so I buzzed him in and put a pan of water on the heat.

Zeb is an old friend, known him years on and off and regarded a 'nice guy', well that's what some might say anyway, but not everyone. We had lost contact with one another when I moved away for a while, only to be reacquainted soon after returning to Dalton West. I make toast which Zeb consumes rapidly, and I feel he has not eaten too well over the last weeks, so I placed two more slices of staling bread into the toaster, scraping what little butter I have left and put four spoons of sugar in the coffees. I press play on the tape deck. Squealing tones from the cassette ring through the speakers. King Tubby's 'A Murderous Dub' plays. Zeb would visit in short bursts; you would hear little from him then he will pitch up suddenly. He leaves an hour after arriving. High on weed and caffeine and with a full belly.

*

There is a faint tap on my door, as though the person is reluctant to do such an action, though I am just as reluctant to answer it. I crush the roach in the ashtray and check the end is still not burning. The chancer on the other side of my door knows I am in, because of the level of volume from the stereo and smoke travelling a pointless route, like lost ghost sheep clouds. I pushed my gear under the stereo unit and composed myself. The kid who stood at my door is a wide-eyed 20-year-old with a slight arch in his posture and appears to display no hostility. He introduces himself as Tony with a cautious stare. His T-shirt tucked into his cheap dark blue jeans.

He apologizes for the interruption in which I assure him there is no need. He says that he and his girlfriend Lisa have moved in a few days back and wonders if I have a lighter or a book of matches. I let him take a pick out of the small white paper bag where there are now seven of the eight lighters. Chances are, he'll pick one that's a dud, one where the flint has gone already or, sometimes, the flint being non-existent.

The unwanted visitor flicks his thumb over the cog with a large flame shooting up.

He thanks me and invites me to his room sometime which I tell him I will. Though I really don't want to.

*

One letter I received after scooping up the mail from the hallway floor is a list of dates on which I can attend the two-day recording session. It is going to be in Felling Burn, just outside the city of Salta. This is a 45-minute train ride north on the mainline, however, as I had lived there for a short while, knew people, so if needs be, have a place to crash. I call Nick and tell him I will go at the next available time where he advises to go to the D.S.S where I can apply for a rail pass entitling me to 50% off travel.

*

Steel greets you with bolted down seats, and glass partitions when you enter the third floor of the D.S.S office. A number machine obstructs further entry and so you have two options. I tapped the 'enquiries' tab where it prints a number. The steel seats are cold, and the automated calling screen is loud and buzzing. Number 64 is my ticket with the call screen calling number 12.

*

I need to steal more toilet paper as I am running dangerously low and I'm not prepared to use another newspaper, not after trying it once, and only once before. The idea came to me one day when I had nipped into a McDonald's to use the toilet. The Biro scribbled cubical was free and had a lock, as I like to pee privately when possible. As I did my business and whistled badly, there sat on the back ledge, an enormous roll of unused toilet paper. The problem was, I had no way of smuggling it out. I finished my business and washed my hands before just tucking the beast under my arm, heading back down the stairs for the exit like it was no big deal. It wasn't really, after all, who is paying any attention, right? I remind myself also to bring the toilet paper back to my room with me, after every use, as it will go missing if left in the bathroom. I mean, who would not take a roll that size, and for free, no less? I left my shampoo in the shower cubicle one day, only for it to be gone when I went to retrieve it.

*

I decided that tomorrow I will get an early train to Salta, but for now, the pile of dirty clothes dumped in the corner need washing. The electric meter teases on the red section to show an absence of credit and will soon be empty and, although it may have lasted until the next day, I slot two gold coins into it that will sit idle while I am away.

I keep my word, and grab the pile of clothes from the corner, cupped in my arms. The house is still. Silent all round, not even a sigh from the breeze that you can frequently hear calling from the gaps of broken stone, or the cracked bathroom window.

Someone's garments occupy the washer when I get to the washroom, and I can't work out on the machine how far the cycle has left. I look through my clothes and take the risk of leaving them on the bench.

After a coffee I venture back and find the machine vacant. Inside it lies a small plastic baggy and on closer inspection discover it is a lump of resin which has slightly melted, leaving a puddle of brown fluid swimming at the bottom of the bag. I slip it into my pocket and set the machine on a quick wash for a couple of coins. I wait for it to kick in to action before heading back to my bedsit. I investigate the find from my pocket.

The weed itself is still hard and has a scent of washing powder and I am unlucky to spill some of the resin liquid on my jeans, instantly staining the denim, absorbing the fluid like a deprived lush. I wonder who it belonged to and weighed the options. I have no intention of tapping around the house asking residents if they have misplaced any drugs recently though, so I decide to keep it.

*

The next train should be on platform 5 in 48 minutes' time according to the screen floating above like an informative star. The air is dirty and gaps in noise are non-existent in the dense cocoon. Screeching wheels and crowds of shuffled voices are echoing over the telecoms. I roll a one skinner in the station toilet, being interrupted twice in the process by eager needy toilet users and attendants of the station; why would they knock on the door? I walk outside but do not venture too far, just hit the joint before being greeted once more by the square star in the sky of the fumed filled station.

All who are bound by travel watch our train approaching early, bringing with it polluted shells and stale leftovers.

*

The streets are familiar but play distant. No change attracts my attention, the air dense and trapped. I walk the square of the city centre, regretting it as familiar faces with tired old familiar stories do nothing but remind me of what I had left behind. Mike answers the door when I arrive at Benny's house, where he is sitting and scraping dials accordingly on a Yamaha sequence sampler. Too absorbed to notice my arrival. Mike goes to fetch three beers. Benny, now shaken out of his craft, welcomes me with a handshake.

Later, he serves up some sweet and sour rice in three bowls and we drink some beers while we speak fondly of the reckless times we once had.

*

I approach the reception area of the music centre and I am greeted by a bearded, skinny man in his mid-fifties.

He introduces himself as Geoff. His teeth are yellow with age and has thick bulging eyes. He tells me I am the first to arrive and to sign in the red book at the reception desk. After I do, I head outside for a smoke, during which the rest of the people attending rock up.

We all introduce ourselves in a large room that echoes. The acoustics were good there.

A mild-mannered chubby guy named John talks of playing acoustic guitar and is a fan of 70s rock music when it is his turn to speak. He has long hair down to his shoulders and comes from a village not too far from Salta.

Darren is originally from Belford but now lives only a mile or so from the centre where we sit. He has brown teeth in a pink lipped mouth which sucks on a harmonica as a way of introduction.

Lee is there to learn how to record and doesn't play an instrument. He likes electronic music and produces using Fruity Loops and a Roland 303.

I introduce myself, tell the circle where I live and that I am looking forward to getting something down.

So, then we go into a studio room which has everything set up, ready to rehearse and after an hour we have some rough lyrics and a tune that resembles acoustic blues with indie vocals by Darren. I was behind the drum kit for most of it, just banging the skins and keeping rhythm the best I could, after all the whole affair is new, especially to me.

After an egg-cress sandwich and three cigarettes, we are happy, and as there is nothing more to do, Geoff suggests calling it a day and asks for us to return at the same time tomorrow.

*

A red automobile pulls up outside. I am told it is Mez with Mike riding shotgun. Mez lives with Benny and smells of chemicals when he introduces himself. He tells me he works at a chemical plant; so hence the smell, I guess. Benny asks me to join him at the computer as he wants to show me some tunes he has been working on. I laid down a beat and a bass line later that night and stashed it on Benny's computer. I later learn that Mez handles some of the sound systems and marquee set ups at various warehouse parties in the area.

I decided to head back to Dalton West later that day. Skip the second day of recording. I miss room 6 and my tunes.

*

The bedsit is keen to absorb all the heat it can. The sun today is beating harshly and consumes all that is below. I have no choice. I strip down to my boxers and throw my clothes on the bed. I still feel like a clay mold in a kiln, though. I flick the 14inch black-and-white TV on, something I rarely do and tune it the best I can. Luck of the draw. A Wimbledon tennis match. The phone rings. I ignored it, couldn't answer it anyway, even if I wanted to. Too much hassle to put my clothes back on.

I am not used to facing the TV. Nowhere to sit except on the bed, but that has quickly become uncomfortable, which makes little sense. It is, after all, a bed. The bare minimum you expect from a bed is comfort, right?

The cool, low breeze brushes the green curtains as the phone is ringing once more. I need to pee anyway so have no choice but to redress as I couldn't, no wouldn't brave leaving my room in just boxers to go visit the little boy's room. I answer the phone when it rings again. It is Zeb asking if I want to join him and some others at a bar. Some kid he knows is playing an acoustic set. The beer is cheap too. I agree to go along with him, not really meaning it, and arrange a time to meet.

*

The track from the session has arrived. I'm not too interested in hearing it though and feel bad about not attending the second day. It was also likely I was not on the track.

The resin is now the size of a small pea and Mac is proving hard to catch, and I wonder why I am assuming the worst and that the fuzz has caught him.

I leave the warm, calm shell of room 6 and go to buy cereal, butter, rice, milk, and brown bread. I then take a walk to the centre of town to the shopping complex where the phonies hang out, looking for anyone who might be some help in my quest for weed. Familiar strangers pass, referenced only by appearance and not by name.

I buy some tobacco and skins from the bong shop and head back to the bedsit.

*

Echoes are expanding my footsteps that are beating the wooden stairs. I turn to see a young man heading for the exit. The goatee on his long face suits him. Without shame or care, I ask if he knows of anywhere that I can score. I have nothing to lose. He tells me to knock on room 9 at around 7:30 tonight. I thank him and we part ways.

*

As I twist my key in the lock, a female voice shouts down from her landing. I climb around six steps and see a young lady peering over the banister, her hair hanging over her face.

She introduces herself as Lisa and tells me she is Tony's girlfriend. She wonders if she can have a tea bag, which makes me crack a smile. I can see the confused look even through her long, flowing hair over her face. I tell her I only have coffee but is welcome to it. She takes the offer, and I tell her I will tap on her door in a few minutes.

I put my shopping away and tip some coffee into a small mug. I also contemplate rolling a joint and taking it upstairs with me. I decided against it. No need to be so sharing, right?

I mean, she is already depriving me of caffeine, therefore, I believe, my kind gesture is done.

I tap on her door where she shouts to come in. I put the coffee down on the table and she asks if I want one, filling a small blue plastic kettle. The wallpaper above the window and cooker are creeping away from its purpose.

Silence. Just quick glances and smiles.

Then I asked where the bed was. She looks at me with such confusion and after a while tells me it is next door; her tone is one that took me for a simple man. The front door hides another room when it is open, so I have walked in without noticing it, assuming it is a single room like mine, only bigger and squarer.

I ask where Tony is, if only just to fill the silence where she explains he had to attend the police station of his own free will to explain where some business trust funding has gone.

I didn't want to ask what she was talking about, but it felt right to do so. She told me she has suspicions of Tony smoking a lot more weed than he will confess to. I am glad to not have brought a joint with me. Lisa said she had found some hidden in his jeans pockets when preparing clothes for the wash. She also said Tony owes some money and people were now wanting it back. I confessed to finding some of his stash in the washing machine and that I didn't hesitate to keep it. She laughs at this and slaps my chest playfully. She tells me to call anytime and thanks me for the coffee before I politely but quickly sip mine before leaving.

*

I climbed the flight of stairs towards room 9 with some hesitation. Without over thinking, I tap gently on the yellowing gloss door as the washing machine across the hall is viciously churning someone's clothes around, a deep scent of washing powder lingering in the air, sweet and fresh like a meadow.

He tells me his name is Ali when he answers the door, and he shook my hand. He offers me a seat which I take but I decline the offer for tea. His bedsit is square and has a scent of resin. Same wallpaper as all the others; faded, tired, and aged, with curling ends in the warm corners of the room. I asked if it was OK to smoke and he asked if I wanted to roll a joint. I didn't really. Wanting to adhere to my 'in and out' in ten minutes rule, but he passes me a small wooden box which has resin in. I build one and I am polite with the amount of weed I use. We spoke of what we did with our days, in which he said he works in a convenience store in town. I told him I have recorded a tune with a few people through a government funded music course. Which, of course, is a bit of a lie. He comments he would like to hear it, but I think this is more out of politeness than a general interest.

He asks how much weed I want and tell him a quarter. He opens the heavy 1950s wardrobe door and produces a red money box the size of a cereal box. He's sitting in front of it on the floor and unlocks it. The resin is like a rock on a plastic tray beach, and I can't help but smile. Neither of us comment on the size of the resin, though if I must guess, it is certainly a fresh 9 bar. I put the money on the coffee table in front of me and watch Ali heat the weed with a small handheld flame torch. He heats a knife in which to slide through the weed with ease. Small puffs of smoke rise from the solid block as it reacts with the hot metal. It is no wonder his bedsit stinks of fresh, heated resin. He drops a good-sized block on a battery-powered electric scale and wraps it in cling film. He tells me to knock on his door any time or to visit the shop where he works and let him know I am after him.

I examine the freshly bought score when I returned to room 6 and smile. To think there is a guy renting a room with that much score, living above me, no less. A tap on the door followed by Colin, the landlord shouting out that it was him. I let him in and hand the small amount of rent owed, and he writes it in the rent book. I am certain he knows I am stoned most, if not all the time, though I figure it didn't matter too much to him anyway.

\*

Roadblocks and associates of various offices meet in small groups as I approach the busy street and wait for the beasts to calm down before crossing. A tap on my shoulder. The stranger asks if I recognize him. I vaguely do. His features are big on his face, accompanied by thick-rimmed glasses that sit tight on a bulbous, thick-skinned nose. He reminds me he attended the art college with Benny a couple of years ago in Salta and that we first met when he came to the pool hall one day. Tells me his name is Ben, and he is now doing a course at the university here. Living in the university halls.

That gave me an idea. Students who are new in the town may be looking for something I could help with, for the benefit of me, of course. I ask Ben if anyone is looking to score as I could help with this. He tells me if I could get hold of an ounce, he would pay for and distribute it himself. This is good for me. Take out all the bullshit and unnecessary strain. I take his number that he writes on a small pad and tell him I will contact him later that day. All I must do now is to convince Ali to put the 'Oz' on tick and allow me to pay it back as soon as I can.

\*

I can see Ali having no objection to my ask for an ounce as I live below him and would have no issues hounding me for payment if he must recover such a debt. I tapped on room 9 and told to wait a second. I hear the wardrobe doors closing from the confines of the bedsit, followed by heavy footing getting louder as they approach the door.

I accept the coffee and a seat after I am welcomed in.

Ali asks what I want, and I come right out in asking him for a tick on the ounce where he will get his return later today or early the following morning. He has little issue with my request and soon gets on with the order. The soft brown brick smokes a little, giving the air a dense scent of familiarity with the weed accepting its fate and dividing itself with little effort. He wraps it in cling film, as I could swear the wallpaper is creeping away from the walls before my very eyes.

*

I sit in front of the stereo with a lit candle and a dinner knife. Pink Floyd's 'Dark side of the moon' is an album I can play in its entirety, and I absorb it just like the heated instrument into the resin is doing. I chop a good-sized chunk from it and stash it under the stereo unit. My finder's fee. I then called Ben to confirm we were still on with the plan and to meet later at the halls. He gives me directions and a heads up on the activities of the security that creep and linger in and around the university grounds.

Tony is at my door when I return from using the phone. The wide saucer eyed man standing hunched like a rabbit on a motorway. He tells me that Colin, the landlord, has asked for him to collect people's money from their electric meter boxes. I tell him I wasn't aware of such arrangement and that I am shortly heading out.

You can't blag a blagger, my bunny eyed friend. Not this one, anyway.

*

I meet Ben near the green metal gates. The crunching stone underneath us is alarming the birds, and black shapes now cut the air as they fly in uncertain directions to escape our human noise. We approach a red bricked square building which has uniformed curtains with each window equal in size.

Music and various noise coming from different rooms. We approach number 109 and Ben opens it with a key attached to a chain which sags from his jeans. I wait to see the money before I hand him the weed, which he stashes away in a small wooden drawer that slots in the generic desk.

He asks if I have a contact number or a place he could visit for more. I don't want the phone in the hallway to have another excuse to ring, so tell him I will get in touch with him in a week's time on the number he had given me.

*

I knocked on room 9. Ali answers the door in seconds, and I am welcomed in. The bedsit is again dense in resin smoke and coffee with the TV blasting out crap fake nonsense. I dig into my pocket and pull out his return, thanking him as I place it in his palm. He thanked me for the quick pay back as he put the kettle on, asking me if I wanted to join him for a coffee and joint. I don't, but feel it is best to do so. After all, I have a good thing here. So, for the second time, I broke my rule of staying no longer than ten minutes as he passed me a pack of king size zig zags.

*

The next module in the music course booklet has a section on sequencers and samplers. I call Nick and ask how this section is to be completed. He advises that if I don't have access to such things, let him know so he can arrange with the art school a time best suited to use their music department. I advise him I have access to the equipment needed and will begin the module now. I then called Benny back in Salta, where he reminded me, we constructed a basic tune when I was last there, so I decided just to continue with that.

*

Benny had since added some ambient clicks and a small string section to a tune. All that were needed were vocals. We named the voiceless track 'Touch' which only took a couple of hours to produce. A 'Tricky' styled dub tune.

Mez comes from the kitchen with a pint glass of water. He then produces a small baggy with white powder in it. It is MDMA, or at least his $3^{rd}$ attempt at perfecting the art of manufacturing such a substance, and using his knowledge and combined university degrees, he thinks he has now perfected the quality.

He stirs the powder in the water, and I take a sip, handing it back to Mez, who takes a swig with caution. Benny drinks a good amount of it before it gets passed around one more time. The taste is sour, like licking a headache tablet. I smoked three roll ups before I felt alert and sociable. Feeling the groove of Excess by Tricky on the stereo, wrapping me up in warm and pleasurable drafts. Never has it sounded so clear and real. The company is vibrant too, and my jaw begins to grind and tense up. The cod shit we speak is deep for the moment but forgotten about in a short while, as the substance is absorbing and rushing through our bodies, bringing sharp, twisted, and unpredicted changes with no sense of harm or discomfort. I was hot and cold a few times but have no negative thoughts about anything. My vision blurred, but I am focused and aware. The effect didn't last too long, around thirty minutes, which was a shame. I congratulated Mez on his success.

*

I returned to the bedsit to find the frame near the lock of my door chipped away, and is exposing naked wood, bits of yellowing gloss sprinkled on the floor. I enter room 6 and I am hit with warmth, stale smoke and tinned curry. I empty my bag on the bed and slide my rolling board from underneath the stereo unit. I have my suspicion of who may have attempted the break in.

*

I scraped all the money I had and went to search for Ali. He answers his bedsit door looking caned and I can smell skunk. He welcomes me into his room and puts the kettle on.

Unfolding a piece of tinfoil, he exposes a small quantity of green and asks if I would be good enough to roll a joint out of it. We sit and drink coffee, and I stare at the TV that has a low volume with commercials for crap no one needs.

I don't want a holiday in the sun. Sex sells! The teen can't sing for shit, but she looks good on the screen. That's all that matters, right? Repetition is clear as the colourful flashes of hypnotic snaps catch the eye. The screen pulses simplicity for a dumbed down society and I wonder if Wimbledon is still on.

I comment on the quality of the weed and ask if he has a ten spot of resin I can buy. Stupid question. I know he does. He did the usual knife heating trick as he asked if I want a 1/4 on tick. I was unsure about the payback, but this does not concern him, however, as he wraps the brown block in cling film, which he lobs in my direction, hitting me on the side of my face.

*

Salta is wet when I take my first stomp on to the train station platform. I question my return as I have no further work to do on the music course that involves equipment or travel. The air is crisp as I exit the station; the breeze blowing towards the city. I heard someone shout for me and I swung around to see a skinny sharp-nosed familiarity. Steve and I have not seen one another for a couple of years now. His attitude towards a level and honest living is still non-existent and continues to spend other people's money on cheap cider and roll ups. His views on weed were strong and would give me grief whenever I smoked in his company. He looks at me for a second or two and asks if I have heard about Scott. Scott was apparently loving his glue more than ever but is now losing all control and grasp on reality. This is nothing new and I remind Steve that our glue sniffing friend has been that way since he grazed the shores of the town. Living in the same bedsit year upon year. Steve tells me with a hint of disgust as his lips curl down like sucking a dirty toe that Scott is buying cheap junk from across the bay near the west end. Steve is tapping his arm as he talks of how Scott has spent time digging for lines and spewing yellow fluids. I am surprised at this; I knew Scott was dumb, but not dumb enough to get hooked on smack, no matter how weak it was. I assumed he was scoring pantopon and muscle supplements mixed with other various toxins. Scott could easily get ripped off for 10-coin crisps, so Christ knows what poison he was pushing in his veins. Although I didn't want to, I agreed to go down to Scott's house with Steve, just to check he was OK, perhaps talk to him about his lifestyle choice.

*

Broken concrete and gravel stretch the small alley like a road, with no access at the other end. A 'No Parking' sign painted in large yellow letters obscured by crude amateur graffiti.

Scott doesn't answer his bell as we stand and wait at the main front communal door. You can smell the dirt and neglect humming out of the letter box. Steve uses a broken wooden crate to gain a little height so he could look in Scott's window. He slips off the rotten container and says he can see Scott's legs and nothing more but the bottom of the bedsit door. I ring three bells for different bedsits and hope the ring will have an answer. A lady around 40 years old opens the door with force, her light brown hair flowing around her face. She looks dopey about the whole experience. Thick yet transparent looking skin sagging on her chest and her legs buckling inwards, like balancing is more an art rather than an instinct. I ask for room 1 and she has no concern for us to come in and she just passes me and Steve to head back to the room she had come from. Silence. Steve gives the woodwork a stern kick and loosens the mechanics, just enough to fracture the door. The second attempt breaks it from its lock as we fall into the room where we inhale solvents and stale smoke. Unavoidable. Scott's breathing is shallow and steady. Blood has dried down his arm and has dripped on the rug, the needle dangling from his thin pale arm. Steve grabs his legs and begins dragging him out of the room and into the hallway. I put Scott in the recovery position and tell Steve to take care of himself before I leave. I hit the payphone and report an overdose to the emergency services, giving them the address before hanging up. What am I doing here?

*

I peek out the front room window by widening the slit in the heavy red material and see a police van, two cars, and three heavy suits. I put on my shoes and shirt and pocket my resin whilst thinking about answering the knocks. Benny comes into the living room and has the same conclusion that the coppers were indeed tapping us up.

He answers the door and is given a pleasant welcome and a soft-spoken manner towards him.

They come into the living room in a single file as I sit. They introduce themselves one by one, but I do not introduce myself, not until the fattest one prompts me rudely for one. Two more badly dressed coppers enter the house, one with a rugby ear and the other with the typical thin cop-looking features. The type you know is filth, even when the poor bastard is out doing his food shopping on his day off. He asks if Mez is at the premises as he is passing the search warrant around like a joint. We're asked to step outside with three of the five coppers, with their white trainers and fleece coats.

A thug in uniform enters with a sniffer dog and I look at Benny. His expression is worrying, of course, having sniffers and vans will never have a happy ending. They were there for Mez's experiments and equipment that is scattered around the house; no need for sniffers, as the crime is clear. The hairy wet nosed beast wanting a sniff of my pocket. It keeps creeping my way with interest, but the uniform keeps pulling it back every time the space widens between them. The copper is eventually told the mutt can go back in its cage. I am given the choice of a voluntary statement or the threat of arrest for one. Either way, they want my account.

Benny and I are driven to the butchers separately. It is a short ride from the house, and I am asked to take a seat in reception where Benny joins me a few moments later, only then for me to be asked to the front desk.

What does the copper not understand about me not living at Benny's address?

They call Benny from an open door, and it closes heavily behind him, and I say good luck.

I am told to follow the corridor where I am met by an officer in a polyester skirt and faded white blouse. She spreads her paperwork on her side of the square red table, a table small enough that our knees nearly touch. I feel she will be cold to touch and do not want to prove myself right, so I push my chair back an inch. The room is intentionally stuffy and dry. Questions come and go, with minimal yet substantial answers that appeal to the bland, oppressed civil servant with her cold knees and cheap pens. When asked about the car Mez drives, I say red. She asks how I know Mez and I tell her he is still a stranger and not acquainted with him. I tell her I have resin as she is writing for what feels like a lifetime but she has no concern for it. The scratching on the pad is distasteful. I leave the station two hours later and don't know what to do next. I figure Benny may still be engaged as he lives at the crime scene, so I just wander for a while. I take the scenic route back to the house after a pint, passing the train lines running along the right side, a green field on my left, and I feel enclosed. Benny is just ahead when I turn the corner, but I wait until I get to the door before I tap on it to be let in. I roll a mild joint and we discuss the situation. Benny had told the cops as little as possible but pressed for more because he lives at the address. Mez arrived back shortly after, on bail. His rimmed glasses shining in the light, enhancing the dark lines that droop near the tops of his cheeks. I hand him the joint and he kicks off his shoes. He was lifted around 6am driving from his parents' house, pulled over and cuffed as soon as he got out of his red car. The interviewing cop let Mez read our statements. He liked mine.

227

\*

The next morning was stale and still. Mez is speaking in Polish down the phone. He hangs up and tells me he is heading off to break the news to his parents. He has also spoken to a lawyer and is looking at four years' porridge with a court date still pending.

\*

She wore brown cord trousers and a red flannel shirt with the sleeves rolled up a few times. Chestnut hair lies scattered on her shoulders and flows down her back and between her shoulder blades. She called herself Sam when she introduced herself at the bar. I return the normality. She points over to where she is sitting with a friend and invites us to join her. Sam has the typical Salta twang and spoke with passion. The bar is becoming ever more crowded, and I wanted a joint. I felt lost. Why am I here?

\*

I woke up in a dusty room with boxes stacked along the walls and under the narrow window, only entertained by thin cloth to help disguise night from day. It is light out. Chestnut hair lies scattered on the pillowcase and brushes over the bare freckled shoulders. Her flannel shirt flung over the back of a chair. Her white trainers are next to mine.

Who is this girl? Her scent, dense in the air. At least ten years older than me.

I check my shoes and find money and tobacco, but no skins or lighter. I get up off the bed, which is lying diagonally on the halved carpeted damp smelling floor. There is a stir from the sheets as Sam rolls over to face me. Once fully dressed, we descend a small flight of stairs and come to a bigger landing where she taps on a room and enters; this room belongs to her drinking buddy and is in fact her house. I told Sam it was nice meeting her and she wrote her number down.

The walk back to town is pleasant with the sun trying hard to beat warmth over the usual cold streets.

*

The letter from the DSS was to be expected. I just didn't expect it this soon. A two-week employment and wellbeing' course. In which I am no stranger to as I have attended several of them in the past and assume this one is to be no different. Copious amounts of paperwork, usually signing various sheets with no understanding what we are signing. Shortly followed by team-building exercises and getting to know the other 'not economically viable' drips that are also forced to attend. You also decide whether to have either egg and cress or ham sandwiches for the next two weeks. Then it would normally be activities to 'pick spirits up.' or a discussion on why we 'feel the way we do.'

Mid-week will be job searches and job applications and so on and so on. This will continue until the following mid-week. The last day will have us lining up like criminals where you would sign your attendance sheet and have either a voucher for a clothes store or extra on your next dole pay.

*

The city of Salta is shining dimly, the wind still blistering in the air, however. The sun is just for show, it seems, not of any benefit to anyone; a 40-watt bulb dangling from the sky. Without fail. There she is. Sam. She is wearing the same cords and white trainers. She had invited me back to her new flat, which is basic and small, yet I still feel lost in it. She tells me it is cool for me to be there as little or as often as I want, and expected me to stay there whenever I visit the city. A city I do not know why I am visiting. I rolled a joint and looked through her record collection. Well, I say look through; I stopped at the second record. Boney M. After a coffee we went to call Sam's friend, who has a substantial and constant flow of skunk, and they agreed to meet later. We buy overpriced burgers and bread buns from a convenience store with nothing convenient about the cost. After we have some food, Sam watches TV as I sit at the round table in the corner rolling joints and look out the sixth floor living room window, displaying roof tops and dying day where streetlamps and headlights will soon compensate for natural light.

\*

Sam's friend is working on an old, beaten-up bus. His T-shirt bottom is damp from the rain, but his striped jumper keeps the remaining top half of his body dry, as well as the shelter from the curved metal element of the intrusive vehicle. He greets us and kisses Sam on the cheek. A black oiled, greasy hand holds itself out for me to shake, which I do not want to do. I shake it anyway. Bill's head is bald, and his gums have sunk and retracted back up into his soft mouth flesh. He invites us in, and we walk through a small square living room that smells of incense, paint, and skunk. We follow him into the kitchen. The sink runs under the window, which displays a rotten wooden fence. Sam gives Bill 40 notes where he goes to the cupboard under the sink and produces a bin liner sized bag full of various strains and amounts of cannabis. I wonder why our host has no concern that a stranger knows he has that much weed. We smoke for around an hour, and I am growing bored with conversations. Eventually, Sam takes the lead and suggests we leave. I shake the now clean hand of Bills', and he tells me if ever I want weed, to call him, even if I need it on tick. I tell him I will keep that in mind as he hands me his number.

\*

Room 6 is welcoming as ever, and I inhale the staleness, feeling the relief of being back. Letters on the fridge. Colin, the landlord, has left a note; I owe him money from last week. I contemplate calling him to rectify the issue but feel no real urgency to do so, instead just stash the money owed in the rent book and hope I will not need it for other things.

The Fun Lovin' Criminals' cassette sounds loose, so I take it from the deck with some care, as there is every chance it may have become tangled in the mechanism. I tighten it using the leaked red inked pen, turning the small plastic cog, and watching it retract to its cozy positioning. The trick is to fast forward and then rewind the tape completely to tighten it back up. The tape is now making a screeching noise. Like a deranged mouse. I wonder where one of my mugs has gone, then I remember Lisa still has it when I gave her some coffee. I wonder how she is doing and if Tony is still knocking about. Maybe he is doing a 'stretch' or still hiding his weed in stupid places. The buzzer screams at me from the wall. I ignore it. A longer, more persistent buzz is now ringing out. This time, the potential visitor is holding the button firmly in at their end. It stops and I pause the tape to establish if anyone is approaching my room. Silence from the hallway. I sit in the absence of noise and enjoy it. No one approached my door and there were no echoes coming from elsewhere. I rolled a joint and hit play on the tape deck.

*

I had spoken to Ali about the possibilities of buying from me. He had a few questions. I expected that. I told him I figured he could sell the skunk on, as he had connections and punters already. Then the talk of price came up. I agreed to 45 notes per 15 grams. This is a kick in the teeth, but I have no intention of keeping the weed or indeed trying to shift it myself. Of course I would keep some for myself anyway, finder's fee and all that. He asked where I was getting it from and what strain it was. He also wanted to know what quantity it was going to be, exactly. I could do nothing but shrug my shoulders and give a face to say, sorry, I don't know. Ali's goatee is becoming bushy, and his teeth are becoming smeared with brown stains, and I think about buying a new toothbrush. I assured him the buds were high quality and a good weight as well. We shook on the agreement, and I told him I will tap on him in due course. Though most likely for another block of resin.

*

The post office is under construction, with half the building now being blocked off with sheets of wood and plastic coverings. The high visible workers would flick past the plastic sheets in seconds, but the noise of the tools buzzed continuously. This inconvenience has caused longer lines than usual. This gives me time to think about what colour toothbrush to buy and where the guy in the queue had got his hat. It wouldn't suit me, but it is a nice fit for him. I finally roll up to the counter and sign the dole cheque. The lady grabs a few notes and counts out my amount. I go to the charity shop to buy some clothes and see if there are any more random pieces of vinyl, then I remember I left my beast of a toilet roll in the communal bathroom. No choice but to lift another one, if possible, as the chances of the beast still being there when I return to the shared bathroom were slimmer than a supermodel standing sideways. I bought a loose-fitting hoodie and some more jeans from the salvation army charity shop. I figured a hat would be beneficial too, but opted to buy that firsthand. I did have standards. I need car fresheners and a cheap jar of coffee, too. As for the toilet roll grab from McDonald's, I have a bag with me to stash it in this time.

*

I pitched up to the address on the letter for the 'employment and wellbeing' course a little earlier than intended. Chances are, those on time would end up just sitting around, waiting for the 'draggers' and the less inclined. Deafening silence in those rooms, no eye contact is made either. It is a good time to think about your life choices and convince yourself you are not like the tracksuit in the corner, the latecomer with a chip on his shoulder. Experience of such courses has taught me it is best not to attend under the influence, although this never deterred the few that would attend the course, including myself. I've got the feeling I will dip from this one and hope there is minimal consequence.

*

So, there I am, back in the grasp of Salta city. Bill's kitchen, to be exact. With his bald head and sunken gums in his soft mouth. The bin liner in the corner is packed with many strains, with stalks poking out of the bag. The aroma is familiar and warm. Sam is pouring three cups of coffee as Bill rolls a joint. I roll a cigarette as he talks of his plans with the death trap that sits ugly outside his house. Decaying from trim to seatbelt buckle. Once properly converted, he wants to take it on the road to 'live the dream.' I'm staring over at the bin liner packed with skunk. Oz upon Oz. Pound over pound of high-grade cannabis stuffed in there. I casually glance at my surroundings. Looking at what is behind the house and what direction the small paths behind it lead to.

The wooden framed back door is to be the entry point. I also wonder if he locks the bag away somewhere when he is out. I wonder also who his neighbours were. I tell him it seems a nice area where he tells me things I am glad to hear. People keep themselves to themselves and with a tendency not to engage much. I watch him pack a nice sized joint as I plan on how I was to get that bag out of there. Scoop and shift, I thought. I light my cigarette and put three sugars in my coffee. Sam takes my cigarette as she walks by and out of the kitchen. Cheeky, I thought. Playful too. I need to stay on track. Bill lights the joint and leans back. A cloud of greenish, dirty smoke hits the ceiling and looks like it is attempting an escape. Sam comes back in, and Bill passes her the joint. It is then she suggests the three of us meet later tonight. I agree with this and leave. I walk about halfway down the street before I notice a small, paved cut that runs across a small field, slicing a good chunk of the corner off. It also has the nearest and last phone box before hitting Bill's Street. I am now over thinking. Keep it simple I tell myself.

*

I changed into my new charity clothes I bought specifically for this ridiculous plan. I also snap the tag off the new baseball cap. Benny has since gone to the bar after we shared a bowl of sour rice. I take some plastic bags from the kitchen drawer and put them in my packed bag. I have car fresheners and the coffee jar I had bought at the top of the bag for easy access too. I leave Benny's in darkness. I haven't smoked a joint in a while and hope that being straight is to be of some benefit.

*

The cars chug passively as I fling the payphone door open. Expecting it to be heavier than it is. I take Bill's number out and slap two coins in the phone slot. I wait to hear it ring eight more times before hanging up to call the number again. After another thirteen rings, I am sure Bill is not home and has gone to the pre-arranged bar to meet Sam with the assumption I will be there too. I put the baseball cap on and head toward the corner.

The streets are lively, making my gut ache, which makes me feel like a stick at a pebble convention. I feel like a target. A man guilty, I ache badly, and I am doubting my plan entirely. I should have checked the train times back to Dalton West and timed it that way. No point in 'should of, could of'.

No lights shine from the house, but I knock on the door anyway just to assure myself that there will be no answer. I wait for what appears too long to be natural as sirens sway through the breeze. I look around for curtain twitchers. Some kids with daring attitudes are shouting from up the street. I walk slowly up the side of the house. The rotten fence is my only shade and the only way into the backyard. I get the baggy sleeve of the hoodie caught on a nail, but I have no time nor care in the garment, so just let it rip as I lower myself down onto the other side. I looked through the kitchen window and thought about needing light. Should of, could of. A steady boot in the right area gets the panel from its frame, exposing the warmth and odours from inside. I wait a few seconds before crawling through the gap in the door, feeling sharp pricks as the cold floor is attacking my knees. The black bin liner sits in the corner, and I take no time filling the two plastic bags from it. The buds fall around my feet, but there is no time to be tidy about the affair. Sweat is dripping off my brow and landing on my hand as I hook at the weed. One full bag and I am shaky. I can hear voices from the back alley and wait a second before scooping the sticky buds into the second bag. I squeeze the air from the plastic before cramming them both into the bottom of my bag. I then pop the cap of the coffee jar and let it spill over the contents. It is then I become overwhelmed with dread, fear, and guilt and it is intense, and I am grateful to bury some of the unsteadiness on my knees as I crawl back out of the gap. Point of no return. I listen for movement and jump the fence back on to public concrete. Stage one complete. Stage two, make it to the train station without seeing familiar names and faces, avoid at all costs.

The route I choose traces the outline of the city and scrapes three corner points before turning halfway down the fourth, where the entrance of the train station is. It is the longest route which brings with it issues, like the longer out, the more likely it is to bump into someone. It wouldn't matter who, but that you did. I dump the cap in a bin and take the hoodie off, flopping it over my bag. The dimming sky is treating me well as are the trees that are draped, concealing me as I turn to see the train station ahead. One more main road and a stretch of rail track and I'll soon be back home in room 6.

\*

235

Ali really wants to know where the bud has come from. I had contemplated spinning the man many tales but just end up telling him it was the last of a crop from somewhere near Benton Grange. I had heard of that place somewhere recently, and hoped he didn't know where it was.

We had agreed to a huge cut price for the whole thing, minus a small finder's fee for me. I didn't mind the small return, to be honest. I want rid of it and Ali has connections and clients who were already scoring off him. He could easily shift the crop. Easier than I could anyway.

The first few handfuls weigh 31 grams. Already that is 90 notes with 1 gram put aside. I bagged the quantities. 1 ounce per sandwich bag.

Ali talks about how there is not one case of a death because of cannabis. Nor anyone being killed because of it. I try to look interested but just want to bag the weed and make my excuse to bail as soon as possible.

The bagging goes on for some time until we have a small heap of them on the coffee table. I come out with just under 600 notes and around seven grams for my finder's fee. Ali invites me to stay for a joint, but I just want to wrap myself in the warmth and scents of my bedsit.

*

The charity shop worker seems more suspicious than thankful as I drop twelve gold coins into the charity box on the counter. Her lips moving and her head bobbing up and down as she is counting the drop of coins. I leave without a thank you and wonder if I am right to expect one. Bigger problems to worry about. I thought about my actions. Bill could only speculate who broke into his house and there was no tie to me. I had known him only for a short while. Introduced to him by Sam. A girl I have also only known for a short time. Meeting her one night in a bar on one of my many pointless visits to the concrete squared city. I have not told my whereabouts to anyone that didn't need to know. Bill knows my first name, and I know Sam. My ties beyond that are non-existent. Benny hasn't met Sam nor Bill. Benny, who I have known for many years, doesn't even know where I live. The only contact between me and him is the hallway telephone number, which is now ringing more than ever, and I assume Ali has put the feelers out and is now in high demand for his new score.

\*

I get woken up by the faintest of taps on my door. It is Lisa, the girl from upstairs. The playful chest whacker. She calls out to me as I get up from my bed and shout for her to wait a minute. I got dressed and opened the door to see her standing in a robe. Her hair is messy, and the eyeliner has dried on her cheeks. She is upset and does not wait to be invited in. I close the door as she tells me Tony, her boyfriend, is now in jail. A three-month sentence for fraud and theft. His absence, however, didn't prevent cronies and thugs he owes money to buzzing random intercoms to enter the grand house. I offer her a seat on the unmade bed and put a pan on the heat. Lisa tells me Tony is into some guys for 120 notes. It's likely the men know Tony is currently on holiday too, so maybe opting to threaten the female of the house instead. Her actions and her being upset were genuine and not a short con. Looking to dig cash out of some poor sucker. You can't blag a blagger. Even if I was a 'mark,' the money I have is dirty, anyway. I decided to pay his debt. This way, I know Lisa would be safe and karma may be kind to me if I ever need a favour. The guilt of my actions is decaying my soul. I ask Lisa if she can turn to face the window while I dig out some cash I stashed in my copy of Junky book on the old, thick, white glossed bookcase. I handed her 120 and told her to pay the debt or do whatever she sees fit. I assume now she holds the cash; it is up to her how she spends it. It is then Lisa leans back and unties her robe. Putting her legs up on the bed and placing her feet on my pillow. She is wearing a pair of pink shorts and a tight white vest. She looks good but I just give a polite smile and a nod. This felt appropriate. An unspoken gesture of appreciation. The pan of water is now at boiling point. I turn to the counter to make coffee and ask if she wants one as she ties her robe up. I hoped she wasn't too embarrassed or confused or whatever about the whole thing. The only thing I was concerned about, however, was her bare dirty feet that were on my pillow.

\*

The electricity meter only takes ten coins at a time. The full amount it can hold for the pin to point fully on the green section. I had broken my golden rule too, and bought a bumper nine pack of toilet paper, placing a roll in each of the three bathrooms. This is what guilt has done for me. Strange. The open window is doing nothing for the weed smoke as the thick clouds are gathering and swirling around the ceiling. 'Carry on' by Bran Van 3000 comes on the Sunday mix tape I had made one Sunday. Today, however, is Wednesday. I think. I dock the joint and opt for a resin one instead. After I roll it, I open a tin of vegetable curry and tip it into the pan. Where the smell will linger for days in the small space. A homely stench. I let the curry cool a little while I turn the tape over to the A-side. Hearing the phone echo and yell from the wall opposite. I let it ring.

\*

A dog walker had found me. I know, always a dog walker, right? And in Benton Grange, no less! Chucked in a ditch not too far from a small mud track there, with lazy scatterings of leaves and branches to help disguise me between fields and horses.

The knife wound in my right lung would suggest I am dead. As would the pale complexion and stillness. I was, however, still alive, though barely. The slobbering tongue and greasy nose of the excited dog had given me a sense of hope, as I could still feel something, both physically and emotionally. Even if that was to be drool from the pooch rolling down my cheek and resting on my lips. I also overcame a bright light occasionally, washing down upon me and attempting to have me open my eyes. I assumed it was the sun. Though I was not warm. Unlike the latex touch and soft tone of the paramedic, who arrived in a hurry after the dog walker's wife called the authorities.

So, now I am lying peacefully in a hospital bed in an induced coma. I am not sure who decided this and wondered if I would ever meet them.

So, apart from scent and hearing, I am still. And I gotta tell ya, it's trippy.

I decided soon after arriving at the hospital to note the chime of the city clock striking. However, I have since lost all concepts and length of time. I have also lost desire for many things. I don't remember how things taste or the last time I saw a pair of tits. Not only that, but I am experiencing earworm regularly. Short fragments of a tune just circling around and on repeat. On this occasion, Madonna's version of 'Love don't live here anymore.' It is a good tune. I must admit.

Most of the staff will share a moment to talk to me, but it's normally innocently gloomy. Like it's wet outside, raining all day, or that the nurse with the scent of strawberry jam forgets to pack her fruit this morning, as she was getting her children ready for school. Another sweet smelling, high heel wearing enigma also arrives daily. However, she is not a talker. She only squeezes, grips, injects and scribbles. No reassurance from her before she clicks away. But it is the only thing I look forward to. And, although I was slowly growing a tolerance to her supply of medication, it still brings with it a trickling warm sensation throughout. A fuzzy shell immersing me in all that is of comfort, a shield from the dirt of the world and it opens my mind to invite ideas, visions and stories, so vivid, so real. And I have been wondering if a coma patient can dream or is it that the brain is overworking, and looking for escape or release? So, after creating a world where gangsters are named after a bird or a private investigator that does not own a car or phone, or a scheme to rid the world of crime using questionable methods, sobriety hits. Like a slam to the ground from a great height.

Back to the big light and echoing TV. Like a shooting star stuck in a cobweb in a corner. A repeat of the retired couple, Geoff and Pamela. Geoff has since sold his tool business and Pamela was a lecturer at Bath University, but now with a hefty deposit and a budget of 900,000, they're looking for a 4-bedroom house in the Peak District where their children can visit. Susan, Geoff and Pamela's first child, is 23 and lives in Australia. Their youngest is Melody who is in her second year of an art history degree and will live in shared accommodation by early September. Geoff enjoys collecting vintage model cars so he will like a garage or outbuilding to which to stretch his collection where Pamela is looking for a spacious conservatory to write her crime novel in. They end up talking of the second home they viewed as the stern favorite, but after a glass of wine, they decide not to go ahead with an offer, even though it ticked most of the boxes. The double garage swung it for Geoff, but it appeared with the tone of Pamela, that it was her, who held the money bag in that little set up.

The high heels are clicking, and I am looking forward to what is on the other side of the door when she laces me with my meds. I am met, however, with the taste of copper. The doctor is shouting the decision of pulling the plug and it seems unfair for someone to seal a fate, the fate of a man who will never look eye to eye with the croaker and with a god like complex.

I am not scared, though. It is a strange sensation to want to show emotion, but I cannot flick a finger or eyelid, nor can I shout or mumble. I only have the smell of bleach and an ear out for the high heeled enigma's voice, but nothing, And I wonder what she looks like as the heels fade, along with the voices of the whitecoats.

I do have to let you know that cannabis is still not responsible for any of this. The guy living in room 6 before me was the target. Into that Pez fellow for a grand and a heavy score of horse. I was a case of misidentification. Of course, I will now not have the chance to tell the tale and laugh about it all.

I'm going to miss that bedsit, room 6. The warmth from the surrounding rooms, the lingering scent and the grand features. I also wished I could have a few moments upright and fully conscious, if only to advise people not to underestimate the sheer importance of toilet paper. And Madonna, get out my head will ya!